ZOMBIE WEDDING

ZOMBIE WEDDING

This is a work of fiction. All characters, organizations and events in this novel are products of the author's imagination and are not to be construed as real. Any resemblance to persons, living or dead, is entirely coincidental.

Copyright 2011 by Angry Sheep Publishing LLC
All rights reserved

Published by Angry Sheep Publishing LLC
Findlay, Ohio

ISBN-10: 1-938745-62-0
ISBN-13: 978-1-938745-62-1

Cover Design by For the Muse Design
Interior Design by JW Manus

SUZAN HARDEN

More Books by Suzan Harden
(Each series is in suggested reading order)

Bloodlines
Blood Magick
Zombie Love
Zombie Confidential
Zombie Wedding
Amish, Vamps & Thieves
Blood Sacrifice
Love, War & a Bulldog
Zombie Goddess
Ravaged
Sacrificed
Reality Bites
Ghouls in the Grocery Store
Resurrected
Bloodlines Shorts Anthology
Bloodlines: The First Boxed Set

Justice
Sword and Sorceress 28
("Justice")
Sword and Sorceress 30
("Diplomacy in the Dark")
Justice: The Beginning
A Question of Balance
A Modicum of Truth
A Matter of Death
A Touch of Mother
A Twist of Love
A Virtue of Child
A Hand of Father
A Measure of Knowledge
A Hint of Thief
A Cup of Conflict

Seasons of Magick
Spring
Summer
Autumn
Winter
The Seasons of Magick Anthology

The Justice Thalia Stories
Snowfall
Murder Most Fowl
The Sweetest Poison
A Granddaughter of Mine
Too Many Fish in the Sea

Tales of the Twelve
The Trickster Priestess and the Demon

Crossover Worlds
Invasion!

For updates, news, and giveaways, join Suzan's mailing list at suzanharden.blogspot.com/p/contact-me.html, or visit her website at www.suzanharden.com. You can also check her out on Facebook @SuzanHardenWriter.

*To Rhonda, who puts up with
my crazy shit and likes me anyway.*

Chapter 1

Tiffany Stephens leaned close and whispered, "Sam, get your mother out of my face, or I'm going to stake her."

My sympathy for my future sister-in-law didn't last long while we waited for Mom and Antoine to come back with a load of designer bridal gowns. I should have known the lunch invitation was a con job. And I knew Mom would start on my bridesmaid dress once Tiffany's wedding wear satisfied her Beverly Hills sensibility. Mom had already complained all the way to the boutique about buying off the rack with the wedding a week from Saturday.

I cast a surreptitious look at my brother's homicidal fiancée. With all the mascara and eyeliner, her squinted eyes were little more than black slashes on her nearly white face. A quick glance around the Rodeo Drive boutique reassured me that everyone else was out of hearing range. Normal hearing range anyway.

I leaned closer to her and whispered back, "Killing her would be the perfect Christmas gift for me."

She snorted at my teasing and pursed her purple-black lips. Her size two combat boot tapped an irritated rhythm. As one of the few human enforcers of the Augustine Vampire Coven, she could hold her own against any supernatural menace.

Standing up to my mother was another story. Not that Tiffany didn't do a superb job, but resistance didn't register in Mom's self-centered, materialistic universe. The bridal gown issue was a prime example.

The subject of our discussion charged back toward the dressing area where she had planted the two of us. Antoine, Mom's personal image consultant, floated in her wake, loaded to the gills with fluffy white material.

I wasn't precognitive—at least not yet—but I could see what was about to happen. Hell, the blind guy who panhandled outside of my apartment complex could have seen what was about to happen.

Mom shoved her purse in my arms. Mr. Cuddles, her toy poodle, poked his head out and growled. I wished the dog's hostility were because he detected my "change" two months ago. Unfortunately, his attitude toward me had more to do with his owner's and had existed from the moment Mom brought him home from the breeder. I set the purse on the floor, and Mr. Cuddles hopped out and trotted over to sit primly at Mom's feet.

She held up the first filmy concoction.

"No fuckin' way." Tiffany glared at her.

"Now, Tiffany, darling, since you don't have any family to assist you with planning your wedding, you really need me."

Smooth move, Mom. Remind the psychotic future daughter-in-law that her parents are pushing up daisies. I bit my tongue to keep from saying those thoughts aloud.

"I have my uncle, and I already told you I have a dress."

Even I could barely understand Tiffany through her gritted teeth.

Mom sniffed. "Really, dear, fishnet is inappropriate in a society wedding." Tossing the first gown aside, she snatched the next one in the pile.

Picking up the hanger, I straightened to find a perfectly coifed woman with a fake smile surgically grafted to her skin. The owner took the dress from my outstretched hand.

"Sorry," I mouthed.

Her eyes flicked from me to Mom and back, the pleading evident. Like I could stop Mom's rampage.

"No, no, this one won't do, either." The bundle of satin flew in my general direction.

Tiffany planted her fists on her non-existent hips, silver bangles on her wrists jingling. "I don't need—"

Mom just tutted and reached for the next dress in Antoine's arms. She held the blinding whiteness in front of the seething enforcer. "What do you think, Antoine?"

He shook his head. "I really would suggest off-white or pale rose with Ms. Stephens's coloring," Antoine simpered. "Nothing fitted considering her—" His cough barely registered as semi-discreet. "—delicate condition," he finished sotto voce.

Mom shot him a nasty look. I switched to gnawing on my lower lip and stared at the ceiling to keep from laughing. Tiffany's pre-marital pregnancy was a touchy subject—for everyone except Max since it proved my brother's manhood. But she was only a little over seven weeks along, so it wasn't like the baby would be showing on her petite frame at the wedding.

"I'll give him delicate," Tiffany muttered. I held my breath, but she didn't reach for the silver dagger tucked in her right boot.

A gusty sigh blew from Antoine's artificially puffed lips. "Not much we can do about the hair."

Red flared across Tiffany's pale cheeks. I released the pent-up breath when she didn't reach for the dart gun in her messenger bag either. A dose of the concentrated garlic and silver iodide solution may not be lethal to a human, but it stung like hell.

Antoine shook his head. "And that atrocious make-up she has on simply won't do—"

Tiffany leapt, black-nailed hands reaching for Antoine's throat.

Okay, I didn't foresee that one. Mr. Cuddles yipped and dove back into Mom's purse.

Honestly, I could have stopped Tiffany, but it was more fun to watch the nineteen-year-old goth try to strangle Mom's snobby image consultant. That is, if she could find his pencil neck amid all the taffeta.

"Samantha! Do something!" Mom's shriek had more to do with her mortification at the scene Tiffany was making than concern over harm to Antoine. Especially now that everyone in the boutique, not just the owner, watched Tiffany pound Antoine's head against the floor. Lucky for him, it was plush carpet instead of something harder.

I sighed and rolled my eyes. "Tiff?"

She was too far gone, screaming insults that definitely wouldn't win her brownie points with the Gay and Lesbian Alliance. I scooped her up under my left arm, but she still had a firm grasp on Antoine's emerald collarless silk shirt. I shook her, as if she were Mr. Cuddles and I'd caught him humping one of my stuffed animals. Unlike Mr. Cuddles, Tiffany ignored me and continued her assault.

I shook Tiffany again. Antoine's head bobbed, but she still wouldn't let go. On the third shake, it registered in her pea-brain that I had her hoisted on my hip. She dropped Antoine, whose skull hit the carpet with a dense thud.

"Put me the fuck down, bitch!" She began fighting me in earnest. Not that it had much effect in her awkward position or with my new gifts.

"Let me go, you freak! So help me, I'm going to whip your zo—"

I slapped my free hand over her mouth. Tiffany bit me. Hard. I discovered how difficult it was to keep a smile planted on my face while Goth Girl gnawed on my palm, but I managed.

"We're just going to step outside and have a little girl-to-girl chat. Be right back, Mom." I hauled the still struggling Tiffany out the boutique door and into the hot afternoon California sun. Mom said nothing behind me. I guess she wasn't too worried about Tiffany's "delicate condition."

Once outside of the boutique, I set Tiffany upright. She stomped back a couple of paces, her breathing heavy. She glared at me, fingers flexing, but she didn't reach for the silver dagger, the gun or the pencils in the pockets of her camouflage pants. She was the only enforcer I had met whose favorite weapon against rogue vampires was a yellow No. 2.

Eyeing her just as warily, I shook my right hand to get some feeling back into it. A quick glance showed that she had nearly severed off a large chunk of flesh. I may heal fast, but a wound like that still hurts like a sonuvabitch. After a few seconds, not even a bruise showed, but I had to fish in my shoulder bag for a tissue to wipe off the excess blood.

"You still haven't told your folks, have you?" Tiffany's expression wasn't friendly, but it no longer had that endearing maniacal quality.

"No, I haven't." I shoved the nasty-looking tissue back in a Ziploc I kept in my bag for these types of occasions, crossed my arms and glared back at her. I didn't like the reminder of the ticking clock over my head. "But you have no excuse for screaming the z-word in public. You know better."

She had the grace to look abashed and muttered, "Sorry." With a gusty exhalation, all the fight rushed out of her. She slumped against the boutique's brick wall. "You're right. I've never slipped up in front of Normals like that."

I believed her. Ignorance was bliss when it came to John and Jane Public. The less they knew about the supernatural world, the better off everyone was. And Tiffany had been living in the dual cultures far longer than my measly two months.

The tears welling up in her big, brown eyes disturbed me on more levels than I cared to admit. Weepy was not a word anyone would use to describe Tiffany. I stepped forward and laid a hand on her shoulder. "It's probably the hormones talking, but—"

"I know, I know." She wiped the tears away on the hem of her black t-shirt, leaving streaks of blue-black mascara across her pale cheeks. "I'll be more careful."

I let my hand fall from her shoulder, reassured that Tiffany had regained control of her temper. As I turned back for the door, her touch on my sleeve stopped me. My initial tension released at her uneasy expression.

"Sam, it's not my business, but—" She paused as if searching for the right words. This had to be a first. I mean, Tiffany? Using tact?

She glanced around to make sure no one was near, but she still lowered her voice. "Maybe you should tell your parents." Her hand dropped. "Before they find out accidentally."

"Ri-i-ight." I glanced around myself, but few shoppers were on the sidewalk this time of day with the unusual spring heat. "The only thing Mom and Dad are going to love more than Max knocking you up is finding out I'm a zombie."

Chapter 2

Later that night, my erstwhile boyfriend, Duncan St. James, took a sip of his wine and leaned back against the red vinyl seat. "Tiffany is correct. You should inform your parents before they discover the information on their own. Assuming you plan to tell them and not obtain a new identity and relocate."

"You're just taking her side because she's your niece." I glared at him while I shoveled the last forkful of lasagna into my mouth. I was hungrier than normal after Mom's failed wedding dress expedition. The rich flavor of oregano and tomato swirled over my taste buds, and I sighed with delight.

One of the few joys of my new undead existence was that I could still eat normal food. So what if it was an obscene amount? Unfortunately, it meant watching the restaurant budget unless someone else was paying. Like tonight.

"Tiffany is a niece sixteen generations removed, and I was not taking her side because of our blood relationship. I am merely stating the obvious facts, which you have chosen to ignore." Like the centuries made a difference when he had raised Goth Girl since she was a baby.

"I'm already joining the damn coven." I reached for the bread basket. *Yes.* One slice of garlic bread was left. "Why is everyone pressuring me now?"

Duncan set his glass down. "Because it would make planning security more efficient."

I glared at him. "So I'm just a check mark on your to-do list? The fairies know I'm part of Augustine Coven. They haven't done anything."

Except it didn't mean they wouldn't either. As the only remaining sentient zombie, I was a pretty unique individual. So damn unique that the fairies wanted to drop me in the middle of Three Mile Island when they found out about me. Of course, their attitude might have more to do with the teeny-tiny robots that kept me functional. They viewed my body full of nanites as the equivalent of a dirty nuke in their backyard. And according to the supernatural rumor mill, the fairy queens had put a price on my head.

Which meant I needed supernatural help. Which meant joining the Western U.S. Vampire Coven. Which meant I had to follow their sucky rules.

Ha! Sometimes I crack myself up.

"You are assuming a direct attack, Samantha. The sidhe rarely work that way."

I mopped the last of the sauce with a hunk of crusty Italian bread. "Caesar gave me until the day after Max and Tiffany's wedding. I still have a week."

Duncan's eyes narrowed. "If you do not believe your parents can be trusted, then the matter is moot."

"Dammit, I hate when you get all logical." Max wasn't an issue since he'd known about the supernatural community for years and had kept his mouth shut, but the risk of exposure was too great for the supernaturals to take the chance of Mom gossiping at the country club without "assurances." My other choice was ending up in the vampires' equivalent of the Witness Protection Program.

Duncan gestured for our waiter. "I am assuming you want dessert."

"That's a stupid question." I jabbed the sauce-soaked bread in his direction before stuffing it into my mouth. "And you're changing the subject," I mumbled around the soggy crust.

"It was more a statement of fact than a question." He signaled our waiter, Jimmy. "And yes, I am. I do not wish to argue tonight."

Two minutes later, Jimmy plunked two plates of the house specialty, chocolate mousse pie, in front of us while giving Duncan a come-hither look. The Little Sicily staff had fought over who would serve us since I started bringing Duncan here. I wanted to chalk it up to Duncan's generous tipping, but it really had more to do with his vampire charisma.

Though truth be told, Jimmy would have flirted with anything with a penis. And Duncan was definitely all male.

Duncan's mojo kept the staff and other patrons from noticing I ate both my dinner and the one he ordered while he drank a bottle and a half of wine by his lonesome. What else were we supposed to do when he's on a liquid diet and I ate more in one meal than the Rams' entire offensive line?

Jimmy filled our coffee cups and gave Duncan a seductive smile before returning to the kitchen. I ate half my pie and washed it down with the rest of my wine before I continued.

"This isn't an argument. And it's not that I don't think Goth Girl has a point—" Duncan grimaced at my nickname for Tiffany, but I ignored him. "—but do you really think my parents could handle the fact that I'm the z-word?"

"Your father loves you, Samantha." He practically purred my name, which sent warm wet fuzzies through my pelvic region until I realized he said it in conjunction with Dad.

Ewwwwww.

"Stop it, Duncan. I'm serious. Mom's having enough trouble with the whole pregnant teen thing."

He smiled as wide as he dared in public with his extra-sharp canines. "I take it neither you nor Tiffany have bothered to enlighten your mother that Tiffany's twentieth birthday is next Friday."

I grinned back. "What? And spoil all the fun? Besides, Max could have told her and didn't bother." I sighed and took a sip of coffee while I contemplated my dilemma. "Finding out her daughter and half the wedding guests are the living dead would give her a heart attack. No problem then, right?"

Duncan's eyes narrowed. "I am not dead."

I sighed again. Technically, he was right. Vampirism was caused by a virus and considered a chronic human illness with no cure by the rest of the supernatural community. I, on the other hand, was very much dead according to my local witch doctor. Well, she's really a witch who happens to be a licensed M.D., but it was so much fun to piss Bebe off by calling her my witch doctor.

"I'm sorry I called you dead, but you know what I mean," I said.

Duncan raised one of those damn aristocratic eyebrows of his. "I believe the current term is 'win-win situation'. You would fulfill your obligation to the coven and eliminate your mother in one stroke."

I rolled my eyes. That British accent of his could convince me of almost anything. "Don't tempt me. Anyway, if Mom knew Tiffany could run rings around most SEALs, she'd blow an aneurysm, but I'm saving that little tidbit for a special occasion. Maybe Mother's Day." I took another sip of coffee and decided to ignore my situation for now. "So what's the plan for tonight?"

"*Dawn of the Dead* is playing at the revival theater." He reached across the table and began stroking my wrist. Tremors spiraled through my body.

I smiled sweetly. Two could play that game. "How about the new *Underworld* movie instead?"

Duncan's eyes turned neon green, which would be a good sign if we were about to have sex. "That is not amusing. Those films are an insult." Displeasure tinged his voice. He bent his head, shoulder-length raven hair falling over his face to hide his internal struggle. Glowing eyeballs don't exactly reassure the rest of the restaurant's clientele no matter how much mojo a vampire has.

Jerking my hand out of his now uncomfortable grip, I leaned across my booth seat to check under the table. Damn. From the appearance of his jeans, maybe it *was* the sex thing and not the pissed-off thing. I popped back up. "If I'd known you had a thing for Kate Beckinsale, I would have put on my black wig and skintight leather ages ago."

He didn't look up. "You do not have a leather catsuit."

"But I do have the black wig." My breath matched his short, rapid pants. I shouldn't be teasing him, especially since I was the one who instigated the latest break-from-sex rule.

Air blew from his flared nostrils and ruffled the dark strands spilling across his face. "This would be so much easier if we were wed."

He might as well have thrown a freezing bucket of ice water in my face. I tossed my napkin on the table. "Now why'd you go and ruin the evening by bringing up *that* subject?"

Our age difference emphasized the gap in our views of relationships between men and women. Duncan had insisted that we get married to protect my honor just because we did the mattress mambo. More than once. In several different places. In several different positions.

It wasn't like I could get knocked up since I was already dead.

Chalking up his antiquated POV to his sixteenth century upbringing, I also hated to point out to the big lug that I had lost my "honor" at senior prom. I had insisted that we date for a while to make sure we had something in common besides mind-blowing orgasms. Right now, I really wondered what we did have in common.

Duncan's head rose. His eyes were their normal, everyday green, but his brows twisted in an angry frown. "Why do *you* treat matrimony as if it is one of George Carlin's seven words?"

"Because it should have been the eighth."

"It was your idea to—" His face scrunched in pompous distaste. "—date."

I leaned closer to him. "FYI, buster, this is our fourth date."

He crossed his arms again. "And?"

"Normally, I put out on the fourth date, but you blew it."

"I put out on the first."

Duncan and I both looked up. Jimmy stood next to the table, check in hand. He shot me a skanky look before giving Duncan a not-so-demure smile.

"Thank you, Jimmy. That will be all for this evening." Duncan reached for his wallet and handed a couple of Ben Franklins to Jimmy, who stalked off in a snit. You'd think the kid would be ecstatic over that kind of tip. Little Sicily was one of those places that had only one dollar sign next to it in restaurant guides.

Then I saw the phone number Jimmy had scribbled on the receipt.

I glared at Duncan. "Did you have to put the whammy on Jimmy just to make me jealous?"

I did not *put a whammy on Jimmy!*

I crossed my arms. I *so* wasn't stooping to his telepathic level. "Uh-huh. If it weren't coming from a guy who's worn hose longer than I have, I'd take it a little more seriously."

Duncan was out of the booth faster than even my undead vision could follow. He grabbed my hand and practically dragged me out of my seat.

"Slow down," I whispered. "Someone's going to notice us."

His pace eased a fraction.

"We haven't decided which movie to see."

He ignored my token protest and continued his beeline for the exit, hauling me in his wake.

"Where are we going?" I ignored the jealous looks from Jimmy and the rest of the waitstaff.

"Home." Duncan didn't bother looking at me.

"Why?"

This time he stopped and turned toward me. His eyes glowed neon. The sexy neon. He leaned close and whispered, "To show you my codpiece."

His warm breath tickled my ear, sending another kind of warmth surging through my nerves.

Without another word, we headed straight for his SUV. I fumbled the keys out of my pocket and climbed in. "You know, you're not helping your manly cause when you can't drive your own freakin' vehicle." In the two months I'd known Duncan, I still hadn't found out why he couldn't or wouldn't drive anything with a combustion engine.

He didn't have a problem riding in them since he was already in the passenger seat. The shoulder strap across his black long-sleeved tee only emphasized his broad chest. His long fingers stroked my thigh, reaching higher and higher as I flipped the ignition. And that was the only answer I got out of him until we reached his townhouse.

Chapter 3

"Cleopatra Selene Antonius is dead."

The basketball sailed through David Head's outstretched hands, his first rebound miss in three years. He turned and stared at Francois "Frankie" LeBeau. The werewolf snagged the orange ball and loped down the custom-built court in Head's New Orleans mansion. The rhythmic thump of leather matched the slap of rubber soles on the wood, the only sounds in the wake of Frankie's announcement. The were's dunk belied his five foot two frame. Human frame, that is.

The harsh sound of the buzzer filled the practice room, triggering a grin from the smaller man. David wasn't sure what surprised him most, the bomb Frankie had dropped or the fact the little bastard used it to win their scrimmage. No, the latter shouldn't have surprised him at all. Then the realization of what Antonius' death meant exploded in his overloaded skull.

Frankie retrieved the ball and dribbled back to where David stood. The pounding echoed through the cavernous room. "Man, you're drooling all over the floor."

David clamped his jaw shut before he seized the were's arms and shook him. The orphaned ball bounced three times before rolling toward the free throw line. "You're sure about this? How reliable is your source?"

Frankie's eyes narrowed, and he shrugged off the grip. David sucked in a deep breath, a desperate attempt to get hold of his excitement. Even though he towered over the were by nearly two feet, there was no doubt who was the stronger, and meaner, of the two men.

"My cousin works security for the San Antonio Packmaster. He saw the whole damn thing when he escorted his boss to some big-ass meeting Selene held in Los Angeles a couple of months ago." Frankie grinned, a ruthless look that would have sent anyone with common sense running. David was the first to admit he didn't have much common sense. Otherwise, he wouldn't be lusting after the hottest vampire he'd ever met.

His heart pounded as Frankie continued. "Duncan St. James shot his maker right through her fucking heart with a crossbow in front of everyone. She melted faster than Margaret Hamilton."

"Ding, dong, the bitch is dead," David whispered. He slumped to the floor, disbelief coursing through him. He never thought he'd live to see this day. Cleopatra Selene Antonius, the Augustine Coven's queen, no longer stood between him and the one person he desired most in the world.

Frankie's words sunk through his dazed brain and he glared up at the were. "Two months ago? Why are you just telling me now?"

Frankie shrugged. "Just found out last night." Another grin. "And you now owe me five big ones."

David shook his head at his friend's tactics. "Asshole." Frankie's maneuver to win the bet didn't matter though. Nothing mattered except getting to Los Angeles as fast as possible.

"Thought you might say that." The were grinned even wider at David's unconsciously spoken words. He thumbed toward the doorway. "Already got reservations on the eight o'clock direct flight to LAX. Miz Claire's packin' our bags as we speak."

"Davy, what the hell are you planning?"

He turned. Yvonne stood in the doorway to the court. From his sister's glare and fists on her hips, she'd heard his exchange with Frankie.

"Nothing that concerns you. Stay out of it."

She stalked across the hand-sanded planks. He didn't know what pissed him off more—that she deliberately stomped her stilettos into his pride and joy or her I-have-my-powers-and-you-don't attitude. Her client must have left. He didn't get why she bothered with the additional income. Even if Jean-Pierre Rousseau didn't pay her an exorbitant amount, he could more than take care of his own sister.

Fear etched lines around her eyes. "Don't you even be thinkin' about courting no vampire, boy." She wagged a manicured fingernail at him. "Even if you're smart enough to use protection, he could still get carried away and bite you. Then where'd you be?" she said, tossing her cornrows so the clacking beads emphasized her point. "No juju can save you once you're infected."

"Maybe the risk is worth it." He gave her a devilish grin. "Besides, you're the one who introduced us."

Anger lit her hazel eyes. "Don't you even go there, David Jebediah Head. I had to call in favors to make sure you were protected when you were playing in Los Angeles." Other than Frankie, she was the only person who could get away with talking back to him.

"Yeah, playing for both teams." The were's low voice was followed by a snicker.

David ignored him. Maybe the L.A. coach and owner hadn't been ecstatic when one of the tabloids outed him, but they loved the ticket sales and his ability to fill the arena with fans. His breath seized at the memory. First, Brandon had walked out after the harassment by the paparazzi. Then, the nutcase Bible-thumping stalker had picked up where the media left off. St. James gave him something to focus on, someone to hope for . . .

But L.A. had been two years, several million dollars, a free agency, and one broken heart ago.

He glared at Yvonne. "And what kind of favors do you trade with

Jean-Pierre? You telling me you don't want to get down and dirty with a certain vampire master?"

Instead of laying into him as he half-expected, she merely shook her head, a sad look on her face. "Davy, honey, it isn't good to want something you can't have."

"Who says I can't have St. James when I haven't said shit to him about how I feel?" The ache inside could only be relieved by pursuing the cause. He didn't need any of Yvonne's lame-ass love potions either. Not when he laid his case before St. James. Now, if the man didn't respond to the direct approach, *then* he wasn't above a little hoo-doo to help pave the way.

Frankie crouched next to him. "So what do you want to do, boss-man?"

"L.A.," David whispered. He climbed to his feet, barely conscious of his movements. Desire, thick and hot, rose in his mouth. "I need to get to L.A."

Yvonne stepped in his path. "Wait until next week, Davy. Then you can accompany me with Jean-Pierre—"

"I'm not waiting for some lame ass political bullshit junket. Why don't you come out with us since you have to be there anyway? Have some fun for once."

Yvonne shook her head again, staring at the polished floor. "This isn't a good idea, Davy."

David ignored her as a glimmer of suspicion flared through him. Was her reluctance because she was jealous? No, asking the same damn question wasn't worth dealing with her shit. Instead, he eyed the were. "You got first class?"

Frankie raised a hand to the sweat-soaked t-shirt covering his chest in mock horror. "Is there any other way to fly?"

The shrill electronic version of Elton John's "The Bitch is Back" jerked me awake. In the darkness, it took a minute to remember I was at Duncan's townhouse.

Duncan groaned next to me. "You cannot find another song for your ringtone?"

I elbowed him in the ribs. "That's no way to talk about your fellow countryman." Besides, that particular ringtone applied to only one individual. A person I had no interest in talking to this freakin' early in the morning, but I knew if I didn't answer, Mom would just turn around and call my home number, which I had forwarded to Duncan's place.

He rolled over and buried his head under his pillow. The comforter quickly followed over top the goose down cushion.

Resigning myself to the inevitable, I grabbed my cell off the nightstand and punched the "Talk" button. "Good morning, Mom."

"Good morning? Samantha! It's two in the afternoon!"

"Thanks for the time check, Mom. To what do I owe the pleasure of your melodious voice this afternoon?" I flopped back against my own pillow in anticipation of her latest tirade.

"That girl insists the reception *must* be catered by someone named Epstein." Mom sniffed, her distaste with Tiffany's selection obvious. "I've never heard of these people and none of my friends have either."

"Mom, Jacob Epstein is a family friend of the Stephens. I hardly think he'll deliberately ruin Max and Tiffany's reception. And it's great that he can do it on such short notice." I resisted the urge to add the Epsteins were witches and could quietly keep the supernatural guests in blood and whatever the hell else they might consume.

"Well, I'm not paying for it. It's bad enough I have to take care of the entire wedding." My mother, the drama queen, sighed. A long suffering sound that only a Beverly Hills snoberati could produce.

"Mom, Max and Tiffany did not ask you to plan the wedding."

I tried to keep my voice calm and even, but her repeated tirades about the ceremony were wearing thin. And I wasn't even the bride.

"No," she snapped. "*She* wanted to have the ceremony in City Hall. Downtown Los Angeles is no place to have a wedding." Another long-suffering sigh. "But what can you expect from a girl who has no money and has to trick a man into marrying her?"

Duncan shot up from under the covers, eyes glowing neon and fangs bared. With his super vampire ears, he'd heard every nasty word out of Mom's mouth. This was a guy who'd staked other vampires through the heart and beheaded werewolves to protect his niece. If I wasn't careful, he'd do something equally ugly to my mother.

Then again, maybe that wasn't such a bad idea.

Against my better judgment, I waved him down. "Mom, Max is a big boy. He knows how to use a condom."

"Samantha, don't be so vulgar!" Another gusty exhalation sounded through the receiver. "Besides, that girl probably poked a hole in it."

Of course. My dear older brother could do no wrong in her eyes. I snorted. "They probably used the one Max has been carrying around in his wallet since he was fifteen. They have an expiration date, you know."

Laughter erupted next to me.

"Who's with you, Samantha?"

I sat up, grabbed my pillow and shoved it over Duncan's face to smother the loud guffaws issuing from his mouth. "No one, Mom. Just watching Comedy Central." Our supernatural strength was pretty evenly matched. When Duncan couldn't pry the pillow off his face, he resorted to tickling me. I dissolved into a shrieking giggle fit.

"This isn't funny! Samantha? Samantha! Are you listening to me?"

Stop it, Duncan! When he didn't, I resorted to the next weapon in my new arsenal. I dipped into my welling irritation and let loose a psy-bolt. Duncan tumbled backwards off his king-size waterbed, dragging the covers with him, and landed with a loud thump on the hardwood floor.

Bebe was still trying to figure out where that little half-telepathic, half-telekinetic talent came from. Supposedly, only witches had a similar skill. And if I wasn't careful, I ended up with one hellacious headache. My nanites were supposedly patterned after the vampire virus, but without the nasty side effects like an aversion to UV rays. Obviously, something had gone awry in the lab.

"Sorry, Mom. I was watching an old Tim Allen routine." I wiped the tears from my eyes. Duncan's head popped over the edge, and we matched glares. "Was there anything else you needed?" I said into the cell.

With one last dirty look, a very naked and very gorgeous Duncan stood up and stalked into the bathroom. Naked except for the gold locket that had been his sister Margaret's. I'd never seen him without it around his neck. I had thought that maybe after the death of Margaret's murderer, the same bitch who'd Turned Duncan, he'd let go of the past, but no such luck.

After the door slammed shut, the hum of the double shower caught my attention. I loved Duncan's shower with its wide marble ledges and flexible show massager. Moisture flooded between my thighs. Maybe it was time to test the shower in a new capacity.

"You're still coming over tonight, aren't you, Samantha?" Mom's voice jarred me out of my fantasy. Crap, I'd forgotten about that damn family dinner. Mom continued without waiting for my reply. "That girl is bringing her uncle, so you need to be here on time."

Why the hell was everyone expecting *me* to be the buffer between the families? I had gotten the same plea from Max, Tiffany and even Duncan. How could I possibly keep the peace when I was the last person any of them listened to?

Against my better judgment, I said, "I'll be there at seven sharp. See you tonight, Mom." I clicked off before she could launch another round of Tiffany bashing. Plumping my pillow behind me, I leaned back against the headboard. If I went into the bathroom right now, Duncan and I would never make it to Mom and Dad's Beverly Hills McMansion. Sitting up and looking around the bedroom, I tried to remember where I left my jeans when my cell beside me started singing again, this time to Huey Lewis's "Workin' for a Livin.'"

Dammit. I was supposed to have the weekend off from *The National Scoop* for once.

I punched the "Talk" button once again. "What's up, Ralph?" A series of hacks and wheezes greeted me. I rolled my eyes and waited for my boss's coughing fit to finish. "You know, Ralph, that carton a day habit of yours is going to kill you."

Ralph snorted. "Right. Like I need health advice from the dead chick."

Ouch. Well, at least I could trust no one else was in his office since Ralph O'Malley, editor-in-chief extraordinaire, was on the Augustine Coven payroll and had his own little secret.

He didn't wait for my fabulous comeback. "We got a tip there's a semi-private party that purple freak's throwing tonight." He had a low opinion of Duke Miller, the grand master of danceable funk. "Your boy, Head, is supposed to be there." As a die-hard L.A. Sabretooths fan, his opinion of David Head was slightly higher. Two years ago, Ralph hadn't been happy when I showed him the photos I took of Head playing tonsil-hockey, among other things, with a member of a certain boy band. But bless his heart, Ralph did his job and ran the story. It'd been my first cover.

"Ralph," I whined. "You promised."

"The only other person I got is Agnes. Do you really want me to send her to scoop you on a David Head story?"

He was right on two counts. There was no way Agnes Durley could con her way into an exclusive party. The woman wore a tin foil hat to protect herself from the FBI reading her thoughts for chrissakes. Not that the aluminum could really stop the rest of us who had a little telepathic talent. Also, Ralph knew my weakness too well. The chance to nail a photo of Head's latest paramour wasn't an assign-ment I could pass up.

"Ralph, you know I've got a dinner at Mom and Dad's tonight. And His Freakiness's parties don't start until two in the morning at the earliest." I kept the protest in my voice as reedy as possible.

"You're a freakin' creature of the night," he shot back.

"You can't hold next week's edition of the *Scoop* past four a.m." I had to keep my warning delicately balanced.

"Fine, fine," he muttered. "One thousand bonus on top of the usual rate if you can get the pics here by three-thirty."

"Five thousand."

"Twenty-five hundred, and that's it, Sam." He gave me the ad-dress for the after-hours shindig.

"Deal. I'll see you in thirteen hours, Boss."

Ralph responded with a grunt and a slam of the phone.

I smiled and said, "I love you, too, Ralph." I couldn't take it per-sonally. Ralph was crotchety with everyone. The job also meant I needed my higher-res mini-cam as well as a change of clothes for tonight.

Duncan? I need to run home before we head over to my parents. I've got an assignment for tonight.

For a minute, I didn't think he was going to answer me. Then wet feet slapped against the marble and the bathroom door opened. I swallowed hard at the vision of six feet, four inches of dripping male nakedness.

God, save me from temptation.

His eyebrow swept upward as he gave me a suspicious once over. "And you could not plan how to use tonight's torture of some un-suspecting celebrity to extract yourself from your mother's dinner party?" He shook his head and tsked. "Samantha, I am highly dis-appointed."

"It's a secret concert that doesn't start until after the bars close." I crossed my arms, suddenly realizing I was still naked as well. The best defense was a good offense, otherwise we seriously would not leave his bedroom. Maybe last night wasn't such a good time to break the sexual fast. "And I'm highly offended you would even suggest I would renege on my promise to go with you," I said, matching his tone.

He crossed the floor in two quick strides, his grace reminding me of a leopard. "I am sorry, darling." He bent and I let him pry one of my hands loose to kiss the palm.

Shivers ricocheted down my spine. I couldn't stop the breathy gasp that escaped from my lips. Duncan's mouth slid to my wrist, the light press of his fangs sending an electric wave in counterpoint to his wet locks tickling my hyper-sensitive skin. He didn't dare actually bite me though. The last person who tried that stunt had exploded in a cloud of metallic dust.

Reluctantly, I disengaged his attention with a quick peck on his mouth and a hand on his chest to prevent any follow-through. Hunger flared in his eyes, but he managed to pull himself upright.

Along with a very large portion of his anatomy.

"Let me get dressed and I will come with you," he murmured.

I shook my head, knowing all too well what would happen if I did. "No garage and no UV film at my place makes my sweetie a crispy critter."

"Move in with me."

My just-found pink satin panties dropped from my suddenly nerveless fingers. He didn't just say what I thought he just said. I looked up at his very serious green eyes. "Why the hell are you bringing this up now?"

"I had planned to bring it up when you woke, but your mother interrupted." He rocked on his heels, his expression a mix of hope and impatience.

I blinked and swallowed hard. Was that what last night's seduction had been all about? It was difficult to think clearly with Duncan's erection bobbing a few inches from my face. Sucking in a deep breath, I pretended to ignore the tantalizing body part and retrieved my panties from the floor.

"You are not even going to do me the courtesy of a reply?" It sounded like the impatience was winning.

I snagged my panties over my feet, pulling them up as I rose. We both knew I was stalling, but God, I so didn't want to get into this discussion right now. I couldn't deal with Max's impending wedding and deciding whether to come clean with Mom and Dad. Duncan's repeated attempts at commitment only added to the suffocating weight on my head.

Grabbing his hands in mine, I gazed up into his eyes. Honesty was my best bet to get out of this. "You threw me for a loop, you big lug. We don't have the time for a real discussion, and I sure as hell don't want to go to Mom's fighting with you."

He jerked his hands out of mine, anger cooling his expression. "I see. I am trying to compromise here, Samantha, and you throw my offer into my face."

I sucked in another deep breath. The effort to check my own temper burned an acid hole in my cast-iron zombie stomach. "All I'm saying is that I can't deal with your offer and the fiasco of tonight's family dinner at the same time."

My vision started swimming from the tears collecting in my eyes. Why was he dumping the commitment thing on my head now? I died a little over two months ago, and I was still adjusting to that little bon mot. Not to mention my new role as Jimmy Carter at Camp David. Actually, the former president had an easier time brokering peace between the Egyptians and Israelis. I was stuck between—

God, I couldn't even come up with a comparison remotely as bad. Top that off with possibly having to walk away from what little I could call a life in my undead existence.

The wave of anxiety shocked me as the floodgates opened, and I collapsed in a heap back on the rumpled bed. Strong arms wrapped around me and rocked my body in time to my sobs. The words "just can't" slipped out into between each gulp of air. Dammit, James Bond didn't cry while the clock was ticking, so why couldn't I hold it together?

For a few minutes, we sat on the edge of the bed, waiting for my pathetic weeping to stop.

Duncan brushed damp strands away from my cheek. "I am sorry, darling," he whispered in my ear. "I truly did not realize you were under this much pressure."

"No," I said, swiping away the wetness with the backs of my hands. "I've got a couple of major decisions to make in nine days, my brother's getting married in eight, and everyone expects me to play fucking mediator tonight." I sucked in a deep breath to steady my voice before I eyed him. "Cut me a little slack here."

Suspicion flared in his eyes. They closed and a deep, heartfelt exhalation escaped from him. I couldn't bear the pained expression on his face and turned to stare at my newly-painted green toenails.

When I polished them yesterday, a zombie with green toenails had sounded hysterical. Now, the grass-toned toes seemed oddly prophetic. I may be dead for real before this month was over. Could a zombie die a second time from a stress-induced heart attack?

"Not only have you not told your parents about your new status, you have not told them about our relationship, have you?" he said, giving voice to his realization.

I shook my head. Misery seeped through every pore in my body. I wasn't sure if he felt my movement or had opened his eyes, but he kept talking anyway.

"Samantha," he said, keeping his voice gentle. "Have your parents met any of your courters?"

I shook my head again. They had met Jake, but I sure as hell wasn't bringing up my ex-fiancé right now.

"Oh." When I was sure he wasn't going to say anything else, he added, "There is no reason they need to find out tonight."

I flung my arms around him and kissed him soundly on the lips.

"Oh, thank you, thank you, thank you for understanding, Duncan." I squeezed him hard in my joy. Thank God, he could handle my rib-crushing hug.

When I broke the embrace, he leaned back, concern in his gaze as he stroked my cheek. Tendrils of love and caring wove through my brain, the sensation of being cocooned a little overwhelming. *You are going to have to tell them the truth soon, Samantha, or you will be required to cut ties with them. You agreed to our laws in return for Caesar's influence.*

I snuggled against his shoulder, taking what little comfort I could before facing the Gates of Hell. *I know, honey. I know.*

Chapter 4

Contrary to my four-hundred-year-old boyfriend's opinion of my flakiness, I thought long and hard about the pros and cons of dealing with the parental units on the drive back to my place.

I parked at my apartment complex, switched off the ignition and let my head hit the steering wheel. That's what it came down to, wasn't it? Either I trust my parents with my little undead secret, or I give up my career. My family. My life.

Okay, maybe not my life. That was already gone.

Fuck it all to hell! I kicked the car door. If not for the reinforced steel of my brand-new, customized Accord, I would have ripped the door off its hinges in my pique. As it was, I cracked the interior panel. I sighed and made a mental note to call the "special" body shop tomorrow. The nice thing about being part of the supernatural world was the access to an array of after-hours services.

In less than half an hour, I had showered, swiped on a little mascara and blush, slicked my hair back in a ponytail, and slid on an LBD that would work for both my parents' dinner and an after-hours party. I also took ten minutes to ingest a loaf of wheat bread and a pound of colby longhorn. It wouldn't do to have my stomach growling before Mom's dinner. Duncan and I would still have to stop somewhere for my third evening meal on the way to Duke's party. I thanked God on a regular basis that Taco Bell's drive-thru was open until three a.m.

I wove through the beginnings of Los Angeles's rush hour traffic on the drive back to the townhouse. By the time I arrived, Max's brand-new Volvo sat in Duncan's driveway.

My big brother still hadn't forgiven me for the loss of his Camry a couple of months ago. It wasn't my fault my creator's thugs had totaled Max's baby in their attempt to kill me. Which goes to show how much the bad guys sucked at their job because I was still human when they rolled the car with me in it. I'd survived though the Camry hadn't.

When I walked into the kitchen, Max and Tiffany sat at the kitchen table, looking anywhere but at each other. Duncan, on the other hand, stood at the counter and sucked blood straight from the bottle.

O-k-a-a-y. Not a good sign. Duncan always nuked his meals in mugs. This was the first time I'd ever felt waves of nervousness roll off my guy.

I crossed my arms. "This ain't a funeral, folks."

"Could be," Tiffany muttered.

"Don't worry, kid. If anything goes wrong tonight, Mom will be sure to blame it on me."

"Sam—" Max started.

Tiffany stood, the unconscious brush of her hand across her thigh a weapons check. "She's right, honey. Let's get this over with." Wow. Goth Girl on my side?

Either that, or she planned to finish off Mom if the subject of the wedding dress came up.

I strolled over to Duncan while he sucked down his last drop of blood and gave him a quick peck on the cheek.

"Let me brush my teeth and I'll be ready," he said. The brushing was for my benefit. I was still a little queasy when it came to his dietary needs, so I distracted myself by admiring the view of his butt in his tailored trousers as he strode from the kitchen.

"Ewwwww! I'm scarred for life." Tiffany covered her eyes with both hands.

I must have shot her a confused look because Max said, "You were transmitting again, Sam."

"Oops," I murmured. "Sorry about that." Getting a handle on my brand-new telepathy had been a major struggle over the last two months. I slipped every once in a while, but it was worth it last week when I accidentally made half the male staff at the *Scoop* question their sexual orientation.

I checked the waste can as I strolled over to the fridge. The unusual number of empty bottles tinted with red residue sent a shiver of unease through my nerves. Was there something wrong with Duncan? Every time I turned around I learned something new about vampire physiology, but the only time I had seen Duncan drink this much was after Sierra Mallory stabbed him through the chest with a silver elf-forged sword. He was damn lucky the heiress couldn't aim worth shit and missed his heart. I grabbed a soda, but before I could ask Tiffany about Duncan's consumption, he stalked back into the kitchen.

Tossing me his keys, he muttered, "I am ready." No one said anything as we trooped through the back door into the garage. Once Duncan and I were safely in the SUV, I flipped the control for the garage door, and the last evening sunlight spilled in.

I eyed Duncan. I couldn't help it. Every time we left his place before sundown I was a nervous wreck, scared shitless that I'd screwed up and left a window in his Suburban cracked open or a door ajar. Anything that let in that tiny sliver of fatal sunlight.

Thank God for UV film.

Duncan shot me a reassuring smile, and I backed out of the garage once Max and Tiffany were clear of the driveway. The endless drive to Beverly Hills was even more unendurable thanks to full-blown rush hour. The only terrific thing about the whole ordeal? Pulling through Mom and Dad's front gate fifteen after seven, a full four minutes after sundown and fashionably late.

I parked behind Max, but Duncan made no move to get out. His face twisted like he'd been sucking lemons instead of blood as he stared at the white monstrosity my parents called home.

I grinned at him. "Don't worry. They don't know you had anything to do with trashing the place."

He snorted, not taking his eyes from the house. "I was not the one who shot your mother's favorite Mikasa vase. Nor was I the one who shattered the bedroom door."

"Yeah, well, I'm not the one who smeared cookies 'n' cream ice cream down Mom's very expensive wallpaper. Do you have any freakin' clue how hard it was to get a match to repair that?"

He turned to me, an evil look in his eyes. "We could ditch. As you have repeatedly pointed out, your parents would expect such an action from you." For Duncan to suggest such an action, as well as use American slang, showed how nervous he was.

I patted his knee, one of the few spots I could touch that wouldn't result in immediate hanky-panky. "Do you really want Tiffany to have her baby in prison? Because you know Dad and Max won't be fast enough to stop her when she goes for Mom's jugular."

He exhaled, a drawn out, tortured sound if I'd ever heard one, before he said, "I would rather experience the Spanish Inquisition." He opened the door but stopped and shot me a very pointed look. "Again."

"Hey, you two! Get your asses moving!" Tiffany stood at the bottom step to the front door, hands on hips and looking perturbed.

"Show time," I muttered under my breath. I prayed the house and everyone in it would be intact at the end of the Dinner From Hell.

Yvonne shifted her awareness, using Sight to examine Davy's aura as he tipped the bellboy. The excitement over his hair-brained scheme rippled bloody crimson over the normally cheerful salmon pink. Underneath that, a silvery gray crisscross pattern overlaid the shards of black diamond, just as it had for the last sixteen years.

Davy shut the door and turned. His flashy smile faded to a scowl when he noticed her watching him. "You got a problem?"

She shook her head. "Tired." A weak smile followed to enforce her excuse. "It's my bedtime in our zone. You know I've never been good with jetlag." An involuntary yawn slurred the last word.

Brotherly concern replaced the scowl. "You want some supper first?"

Another shake of her head sent beads clicking. "I'm going to get some sleep." She headed for her room in the hotel's presidential suit before he could convince her to go out with him. Shutting the door behind her, she released the pent-up breath she'd been holding. Was it her imagination or was the binding on Davy duller than she remembered?

Wrapping her arms to ward off the chill of the A/C, she sat on the edge of the king-sized bed. It had to have been her imagination. The New Orleans coven had said the bindings would last his lifetime. Her eyes squeezed shut, a desperate attempt to block the ugly memory of what Davy had done all those years ago. It wasn't how she wanted to remember their mother.

She swiped the couple of tears that had escaped and reached for the phone. Her hand shook as she punched Jean-Pierre's number. Talking to him always reassured her.

It took only one ring. "*Chére?*"

"Hi." She cleared her throat. "You said you wanted me to call when we got to Los Angeles."

A throaty chuckle sent a shiver of unrequited desire through her. How pathetic was she to have a crush on her boss. Her drunken confession to him years ago should have squelched the feelings. Except he'd shared his own feelings that night.

Not that either of them could ever act on those desires.

"I wish you'd waited and flown with me."

"I—" Sweet Goddess, how did she explain this? "Someone needed to keep an eye on Davy and Frankie."

The silence lasted so long, she began to believe the connection had dropped. Then Jean-Pierre's soft French accent said, "What's wrong, Yvonne?"

The giggle caught her unaware, the situation so ludicrous. "Remember the security Augustine Coven provided for Davy a couple of years ago? He has a crush on their chief enforcer."

Hearty guffaws filled the earpiece. "St. James?"

"Ridiculous, I know." She joined in Jean-Pierre's laughter. Davy's childish infatuation warranted the humor, though she would never hurt her baby brother by throwing it in his face. "That's the reason he wanted to come out a few days early."

"I doubt if the boy's impatience will be rewarded." Jean-Pierre made a rueful noise. "Can you keep him from causing a major diplomatic incident, or shall I fly out early?"

Relief spread through her. Leave it to the coven master to show how ridiculous her fears were. "No, I can handle him."

"Save a dance for me, *chére*. I haven't been to a good wedding in decades."

"Of course. And thank you."

As she replaced the handset to its base, a tremor of unease rippled up her spine, replacing Jean-Pierre's suave confidence in her. After gathering her magick supplies, she sat cross-legged on the plush carpet. She needed advice, advice Jean-Pierre for all his charm and age couldn't provide. So why did she worry that for once she might not be able to save her baby brother from his own stupidity?

Mr. Cuddles' greeting barks turned into a high-pitched whine the moment Duncan stepped into the foyer. The toy poodle launched himself out of Mom's arms and scurried out of sight. I prayed it would be the only weird incident of the night.

We made it past introductions and were seated in the living room with pre-dinner drinks before Mom made her first snide comment.

"You're awfully young to be raising a teenager, aren't you, Mr. St. James?" Mom gave him a withering smile before sipping her martini. She shifted in her chair and crossed her ankles, attempting to look every inch the society matron, an act she'd been practicing long before she'd left Wheeling, West Virginia. Well, technically, she ran away since she was a minor when she boarded that bus for California.

I caught Max's attention from where he sat next to Tiffany on the couch. *Less than ten minutes. You owe me fifty bucks.*

He grimaced and rolled his eyes. The doofus had really thought Mom would go easy on Duncan and Tiffany if he and I were sitting there to run interference. Like my interference ever made a difference to her.

"Please call me Duncan." He flashed Mom a charming smile, one I had to admit worked pretty damn well on me. He shrugged. "A man does what he must to help family."

Mom wasn't about to be deterred in her digging. "To give up your life in England like that and come all the way to America to raise your niece? And you couldn't have been more than a child yourself."

Oh crap. She'd noticed how young he looked. I opened my mouth, but a reassuring mental touch nudged the new subject from my head.

Duncan chuckled. "I was already living in the United States, and I assure you I was of legal age when I was made Tiffany's guardian. Ellie and Rick would not have left their precious daughter to anyone in whom they did not have full confidence."

Taking a gulp of my gin and tonic to cover, I had to give Duncan credit. He didn't fidget next to me on the loveseat while under Mom's barrage. Old-world charm exuded from him.

Mom sipped her martini, taking a moment to calculate the next shot before continuing her interrogation. "Yes, but the work and the cost to raise a child these days? It had to have been overwhelming for you."

Her coyness didn't fool anyone. Tiffany's jaw dropped, but Max reached for her hand and squeezed it. Hard, I suspected, from the way her fingertips turned white. She closed her mouth and gave him a glare that promised he would pay for his actions later. Dad stared at his scotch on the rocks, but the tips of his ears turned red. I knew from bitter experience he wouldn't interfere when Mom pulled this kind of shit.

Duncan eased forward on the loveseat and set his own scotch on the coffee table. He stared at my mother with such an intense look, I thought for a second he was trying to put the vampire whammy on her.

"You have made it very clear to Tiffany you believe she got pregnant on purpose in an effort to have your son support her," he said. "Not that it is any of your business, but Rick and Ellie left a substantial trust fund for their daughter. *My* first assumption was that Max was trying to take advantage of Tiffany." He glanced at Max before returning his gaze to Mom. "But I believe your son when he says he loves Tiffany. I am not enthusiastic about the situation anymore than you are, but I will accept it because I care about my niece's happiness. As I know you will accept it because you love your son."

Mom's mouth fell open, then it shut with an audible click of her teeth. Even Dad looked up from the depths of his tumbler in surprise. Few people had the guts to stand up to her, and Duncan did it with a finesse I sorely lacked.

"I see." Mom's frosty voice held a wary edge. Maybe she'd finally met her match.

Thank God the maid interrupted the silent, shocked tableau by announcing dinner.

David paced the length of the presidential suite's sitting room while Frankie yakked with an old buddy. With legs as long as his, it amounted to a whole five steps. "Well?" he asked when Frankie hung up the phone.

"If you don't chill, I'm gonna break your kneecaps, man." The were's voice was icy calm.

And deceptive. David had heard Frankie threaten to shatter the fingers of someone who'd cheated him at pool once with the same tone. And the were had proceeded to do exactly that when the man refused to return Frankie's money.

David dropped to the couch and held his hands up. "I'm cool. I just want to know what you found."

Frankie tossed him the pad with Duncan's number and address scribbled on the top sheet. "I got his business info, but the place is closed for the night. No go on the home."

David shrugged, not surprised. Few vampires advertised where they lived, even to the supernatural community. God, he hated the delay in his search.

Frankie leaned back in his chair and raked his fingers through his greasy locks. A gigantic yawn racked him. "Let's take a tip from Yvonne and get some shut eye. Then we'll hit Duke's party and throw back a few before heading over to Reno's."

David shot to his feet. "I want to go to Reno's now." The bar catered to L.A.'s supernaturals, the best place to start tracking down Duncan. His mouth watered at the thought of the tall, dark-haired vampire.

Frankie shook his head. "My friend won't be there until close to dawn. Besides, if you want to keep your image as basketball's bad boy, you need to make an appearance at Duke's. We'll sling back a few drinks, get you to relax, then hit Reno's."

Fuck. Frankie knew his buttons too damn well. Staring at his reflection in the wall mirror hanging above the were, David ran a hand over his close-cropped lime curls. He had tried to explain the color of Duncan's eyes to his stylist, and this was the best the bitch could do. Nerves itched to be out on the street. He'd gotten tired of playing by everybody's rules a long time ago, but Frankie wasn't making rules, just common sense. He needed to take his approach with Duncan slow, or he'd blow any chance he had with the vampire. Maybe Duke's party would take the edge off his jitters.

He nodded his acquiescence to Frankie, headed to the suite's bar and grabbed a bottle. He didn't bother looking at the label. He needed something, anything, to calm his nerves.

"Wake me when it's time," he said as he headed for his bedroom, not bothering to look over his shoulder. Frankie grunted an acknowledgment behind him.

David kicked the door shut and took a long swallow of alcohol, letting the fiery liquid burn away his impatience. He set the bottle on the nightstand before stripping off his sweats and t-shirt. Throwing himself on the bed, he reached for his dick and imagined Duncan St. James stroking the shaft.

Chapter 5

Through salad and the main entrée, everyone managed to keep the topic on wedding preparations. Mom drilled Duncan about the Epsteins. He assured her Jacob and his family had catered the wedding for Tiffany's parents and had done a wonderful job.

I nibbled on my asparagus stalk, not liking the speculative gleam in Mom's eye. Since Duncan's revelation concerning Tiffany's financial status, her expression left no doubt that she was calculating Duncan's net worth as well.

"What do you do for a living, Duncan? Tiffany wasn't exactly clear." Mom probably thought her smile charmed everyone, but it gave me the willies. That smile also meant she would make sure Duncan would know the appropriate pecking order in the family. Now I understood Caesar's explanation of the attraction of gladiatorial games in his day.

"I am a private security consultant." He didn't elaborate, but Mom wouldn't leave well enough alone.

Damn. If she'd stop staring at him for two seconds, he could slide the huge slab of prime beef from his plate onto mine.

She leaned her chin on her hand. "I'm sure that must pay well."

"As you remarked earlier, well enough I could raise a child." His cool, polite voice held a hint of steel.

I wanted to cheer my man on to victory. No one stood up to her except me. And she always made sure I was punished for my transgressions. Someway, somehow.

"So who do you provide security for?" The smile she gave him would have scared the shit out of a great white shark.

"I am not at liberty to discuss my clients, Elizabeth." The tight smile Duncan gave her in return was the only visible indication that irritation with Mom crawled under his skin. Unfortunately, his nerves started inching along my spine, despite my attempts at shutting out his emotions using all the little witch tricks Bebe had shown me. Nothing worked, which didn't help my peace of mind.

Max wiped his mouth and said, "So, Dad, how do you like your new car?"

Mom batted aside big brother's attempt at redirection. "Some celebrities? Maybe one of your clients has thrown Samantha out—"

"Hey, why don't I show Duncan the new landscaping you put in the back, Dad?" I jumped out of my chair like someone had jammed a cattle prod to the cushion.

Dad nodded, for once playing along with my attempts to minimize the destruction in Mom's wake. "Elizabeth, why don't you check on dessert while I show Max and Tiffany our latest addition?" He rose, waving the other two to follow him. "Safety ratings are important, but you kids need to think about room. I remember everything we had to haul around when Max and Samantha were little . . ."

Dad's voice faded as he disappeared around the corner, Max and Tiffany scrambling after him. I made a beeline for the back door, Duncan tight on my heels. I dared a peek over my shoulder. Mom sat with her mouth hanging open at everyone's abrupt departure.

Once we were outside, Duncan twined his fingers through mine. Neither of us said anything as we wandered past the pool and wove around the heavy foliage. Apparently, Southeast Asian jungle was the new in-thing thanks to Angelina Jolie's latest series of adoptions. Duncan's touch comforted me now I was outside of Mom's sphere of evil. I sighed. If we could make a break for his vehicle . . .

He chuckled. *She is not that terrible.*

I glanced up at his pale face shining in the moonlight. *Do you realize she was calculating your net worth and gender preference in order to decide if it was financially feasible to ditch my father?*

He winced before he brushed my cheek with his fingertips. *I am sorry, darling. I had hoped you had not* heard *that thought from her.*

My heart sank into the prime rib and asparagus fermenting in my stomach. I had been making my usual wisecrack. I hadn't caught Mom's gold digging scheme in my efforts to keep Duncan's irritation and my nervousness from blowing my shields wide open. Still, it cut to hear Mom's true nature laid out before me.

His soft, soothing strokes shifted from my face to the nape of my neck in his attempt to distract me. I felt rather than heard his rumble of amusement. *Fear not, Samantha. I evaded the plots and wiles of many women interested only in my fortune for years in Queen Bess's court. Trust me to handle your mother as well.* He tugged me closer until I was nestled against his chest.

A disturbing thought crossed my mind, and I raised my head to meet his eyes. *Then why do you insist on marrying me?*

He grinned, a full one that displayed his extra-sharp canines under the silvery light. *Because I know you only want me for my body.*

"Hey!" I shoved against his chest hard enough to break his embrace. "Just for that you conceited assumph—"

Too busy being pissed off, I missed his step. Vampire speed and strength had me wrapped in his arms. He kissed away my protests with a slow languid exploration that left me breathless. Wanting. So aroused, I considered ripping my panties off and jumping him.

When we came up for air, I licked my lips trying to remember why I was angry with him.

Are you reinstating your no-sex rule?

Oh yeah, that's why.

"I'll give you a no-sex rule, you jerk." I leapt on him, landing us both in the middle of some weird fern thing. Grabbing his head in both hands, I gave him a wet, tonsil-exploring kiss. His hands roamed in their own exploration, sending my nerves dancing. Teeth nipped my neck, not enough to break the skin but enough to drive me crazy. His very erect cock pushed and throbbed against my thigh, trying to find its way past all the material we were wearing.

Okay, material he wore. My dress was hiked up to my waist, and talented fingers worked their way past my thong.

"SAMANTHA!"

Mom's shriek brought us both sitting upright in a flash, trying to tug everything back in its place. Dad, Max and Tiffany stood behind her, their smirks a counterpoint to Mom's expression of absolute disgust and horror.

"Five minutes, you two." Tiffany rolled her eyes. "We cannot leave you alone for five minutes."

Chapter 6

"I want an explanation, Samantha Marie Howell! And I want it right now!" If anything, Mom's shriek was higher-pitched and more appalled than in the garden. She slapped her palm on the bar counter to emphasize her point.

"It's Ridgeway now, Mom." I was surprised at how calmly my voice came out. Duncan, sitting next to me on the loveseat, squeezed my hand.

"I don't give a shit if you call yourself Sunbeam Moondoodle. Your birth name is Howell and I will damn well use it!" Nice to know she still hadn't forgiven me for legally changing my name once I graduated from high school. But what reporter wants to be accused of riding on the coattails of her Pulitzer Prize-winning older brother?

"Now, Elizabeth, give the girl a chance to tell her side." Dad gave me a reassuring look from his seat on the opposite couch. Max had already handed him another scotch. "Samantha obviously felt the need to hide an important relationship from us, and we should give her a safe place to talk."

Max and I shared a quick look as he mixed Mom another martini. Mom must still be dragging Dad to her shrink, not because she wanted to improve their marriage, but because it was the "in" thing to do.

"Relationship! Is that what you call her humping *our* guest like she was—"

"Mr. Cuddles?" I offered.

An answering bark echoed from somewhere in the house.

For the second time tonight, Mom's mouth gaped open, but nothing came out. She was, however, turning an interesting shade of purple. Max handed her the martini, and she downed it in one gulp.

Dad jumped into the silence. "So how long have you known my daughter, Duncan?"

"Two months, Ted."

"I see." Dad took a sip of his scotch before he continued his Ward Cleaver act. "And how long have you been dating?"

I bit my lip to keep from laughing since Duncan had nearly four centuries on Dad.

Serves you right for not introducing your father to any of your gentleman callers. While silently chiding me, Duncan answered Dad without missing a beat. "We have only been courting for four weeks."

I pinched Duncan's thigh. *Hey, it's been almost seven weeks.*

He refused to look at me as he answered. *Intercourse and courting are* not *the same thing.*

Mom thrust her glass in Max's face for a refill. "You should have gone with your first instinct if it took you a month to decide to ask Samantha out."

A soft, cottony warmth swallowed the anger and pain threatening to explode my skull into a million shards. I wanted to scream at Mom for all the snide comments. I wanted to get mad at Duncan for using his mojo on me.

She is not worth it, darling.

In his mental voice was all the affection I'd ever desired. I didn't have to beg for it or debase myself to earn it. And the realization hit me that he wasn't using his mind control at all. Sitting on the couch surrounded by Duncan's love, my vision blurred.

I swallowed the tears and their accompanying lump for the ultimate surprise of the evening.

Dad rose from his chair, setting down his tumbler with a sharp click of ice. Dark pink suffused his face, but his blue eyes were glacial. "That will be more than enough, Elizabeth. If you can't be civil to your own daughter, there's no reason for you to be in this room."

"You're taking her side?" If possible, Mom's voice rose even higher. She stalked over to Dad and jabbed a manicured nail in his chest. "She rejects us, rejects our name. Embarrassing us at every opportunity—"

My tongue went dry, then I realized my mouth was hanging open. This was an event for the Guinness Book, the first occurrence of Dad openly defying Mom.

Dad covered her hand with his and pushed it down. "The only person embarrassing herself right now is you, Elizabeth. And I'm not losing the chance to know my grandchildren because you drove the kids away!"

Grandchildren? Holy crap, did Dad think I was pregnant too? Mom and Max's face wore shocked expressions that probably matched the one that stretched mine. Tiffany snickered.

Dad turned to Duncan and me, his hands spread. "Not that I'm putting any pressure on you two."

"Thanks, Dad." For once, sarcasm didn't fill my voice. Did this mean he approved of Duncan? My throat grew tight with the wishful thought.

Dad cleared his throat. "Are you pregnant?"

"Dad!" I didn't know whether to be shocked or amused.

"You do not have to worry about such a thing," Duncan said as Dad retrieved his scotch and resumed his seat. Pink flushed Duncan's pale neck and face.

I opted for amused.

"Really?" Dad's voice was nearly as dry as Mom's martinis as he rattled the ice in his tumbler. "Because I rather got the impression in the backyard that you two were already having sex."

I swallowed my laughter at Duncan's embarrassed expression. He actually hemmed a little before answering, "Things weren't as they appeared."

His irritation crackled through my brain. *This is not funny, Samantha, and you are not helping.*

I can't promise anything if Dad asks what your intentions are.

"Then what exactly are your intentions toward my daughter, Duncan?"

I slid off the loveseat and hit the expensive Berber amid loud guffaws.

"Samantha, get off the floor!" Mom found her voice as she marched to the bar, glass out for another refill.

"I had wanted to ask your permission to wed her shortly after I met Samantha, but she refuses to allow me to do so."

Dad nodded, a sage expression on his face. "She can be rather stubborn."

"You've known Samantha for only a month, and you want to marry her! Are you fucking insane?" Mom shrieked, stomping back over to the couch.

"Mom!" Max yelled.

"Elizabeth!" Dad hollered at the same time.

I stopped laughing. Dad and Max presenting a united front between me and Mom's anger? Tonight's wonders were never ending.

I glanced at Duncan as I resumed my perch on the loveseat. His eyes narrowed, and he slowly rose to his full height until he towered over Mom. "Elizabeth, with all due respect, you will not insult Samantha." He folded his arms over that fabulous chest of his, all raw intimidation. And he didn't bother with any vampire whammy either.

Mom melted under his withering glare. Her eyes widened until white surrounded her icy blue irises, and weird, little burble sounds issued from her mouth. Finally, her gaze dropped to the floor. "Well, of course, um, I suppose we need to talk about the rehearsal dinner."

Mom's classic way of dealing with a losing argument—change the subject.

Which, frankly, was fine by me.

Two uncomfortable hours later, I sat in the nearest McDonald's, scarfing down my second Big Mac. Duncan came back from the counter with three more plus a large carton of fries, two chocolate shakes, and a large Coke. He swapped trays before sliding into the seat next to me.

Sitting across from us in the booth, Max rolled his eyes. "I don't know what's worse, you inhaling everything in sight or Tiffany puking everything she eats."

Duncan glanced over his shoulder toward the short hallway leading to the restrooms. "Should one of us check on her? She has been in the ladies' room an abnormally long time."

"No!" Max and I said simultaneously.

"Trust me, honey," I said, patting Duncan's thigh. "Interrupting Tiffany in the throws of morning sickness will just leave you with something sharp shoved through your eyeball." In my case, it had been a metal nail file at Max's house last week.

Duncan took our warning in stride. He busied himself with clearing the trash from my first round of food while I started on the second.

Max leaned an elbow on the table and rested his chin on his hand. "I just wish she'd get morning sickness in the morning instead of ten at night. You're not supposed to have sleepless nights until *after* the baby is born."

Tiffany stumbled back to the booth, drawn and even paler than normal. She sank down next to Max. "I wish I hadn't just wasted a perfectly good prime rib dinner."

"So do I," I mumbled around a mouthful of hamburg and pickles. "Consuela gave me an odd look when I asked for seconds. If I knew you were going to puke it all up, I'd have stolen yours."

Tiffany must have felt super crappy because she didn't even flip me the bird.

Max wrapped an arm around her hunched shoulders. "Why don't I get you home, sweetheart? A little Seven-Up and some saltines will settle your stomach."

"Sounds good *urp*—" Tiffany slapped a hand over her mouth and raced for the restroom.

There was a loud *plunk* as Max's head hit the table.

"Do you need assistance taking her home?" For a sixteenth century guy who supposedly hadn't been educated in the finer points of women, Duncan could be awfully supportive. It kind of made me wish we could have babies.

Max rolled his head to peer up at him with bleary eyes. "No, but thanks for the offer. I covered the back seat in plastic garbage bags and keep extra bags and clothes in the trunk. Normally, we're not out after nine, but Mom kept rambling on and on about the damned rehearsal—"

He shot up at the pissed look Duncan gave him and waved his hands frantically. "Not that I don't want to marry Tiffany! I love her, and I want our baby." He blew out a breath. "I just wish we could do it without Mom involved."

Duncan relaxed and gave Max a curt nod. "Apology accepted. After dinner with your mother, I now understand Samantha's severe aversion to marriage."

Tiffany plopped back down next to Max and leaned her head on his shoulder. She looked terrible except there was no color beyond white to describe her face. "I think we're safe to make a dash for home, sweetie. I've lost every meal I've had since I started eating solids."

I slurped the last drops of milkshake, tossing the cup in the trashcan while I followed everyone out to the parking lot. A minute later, Duncan and I exchanged looks. I could hear Tiffany dry heaving as the Volvo raced by us, Max waving a half-hearted good-bye. Which meant Duncan could hear the poor kid, too. For once, I felt sorry for both Max and Tiffany. It was going to be a long night for the two of them.

I climbed into the SUV, a difficult procedure in the sheath I wore. "You sure you want to go to Duke Miller's party?" I peeked at Duncan as he buckled his seatbelt. Someone could have dropped a unicorn in the middle of the Beverly Center, and I would have been less surprised than when he volunteered to go on this assignment with me.

"Will it not be less suspicious if you arrive with an escort?" An adorable frown creased his features.

I grinned. "You obviously haven't heard about any of Duke's parties."

"Yes, I have, which is why I am accompanying you." His seductive smile made me wet my panties. "I will be the only man you couple with today."

Starting up the SUV, I pulled into traffic, narrowly missing a Lexis when Duncan slid a finger up my inner thigh and nestled it underneath my thong. Three orgasms and two near-misses later, I still hadn't told him to remove his hand.

Chapter 7

David glanced at his watch again. Two-thirty. Frustration pounded in time with the music blasting through the sound system. Bodies pumped and thrust to the tempo, except for one couple tucked in the alcove formed by some amps and a potted palm. Yep, those two were having their own personal party by the way the girl's dress failed to cover her naked ass. Watching them didn't ignite the usual itch.

For the first time, he understood why Yvonne looked so fucking bored at these parties. She'd been awake when he checked on her, but she refused to leave the hotel room, stating with her annoying surety that the loa weren't inclined in his favor tonight.

The loa didn't fucking understand a man's needs.

"Someplace you have to be, sugar?" The redhead clinging to his arm pursed her lips into what he was sure was supposed to be a sexy pout. "And here I thought we were having a good time." She sidled around him and rubbed her barely covered breasts against his stomach. "It could be even better," she practically purred, reaching for his dick.

He grabbed her hand before it made contact. Any other time, he'd have taken both her and her blond girlfriend upstairs in a heartbeat. Maybe his reputation as a party animal would go to shit, but he just wasn't in the mood for pussy tonight.

"Sorry—" He tried to drag her name out of his memory but couldn't care enough to give it much effort. "—Red, I've got places to be." He raised the scarlet-clawed hand to his lips. "Give me your number, and I'll look you up the next time the Blues are in town."

She smiled and pulled a lipstick out of her purse. Bending in front of him so he could get a thorough look at her D cups, she lifted his shirt and wrote a number in a bold scrawl across his abs. Red also swirled her tongue around his bellybutton while she was at it. Probably would have moved further south too, if he hadn't pulled her upright and given her his promise in the form of a kiss that went way past French. He sent her on her way with a solid smack on her behind.

The antsy feeling demanded his full attention as he wove a path through the writhing dancers. He didn't have all of Yvonne's talents, but he'd learned long ago to trust the anticipation racing along his nerves. He owed the national rebound record to it. And he needed to get out of here.

Now.

Frankie leaned against the wall, whispering in some starlet's ear, his paws staking possessive claim on the girl's hips when David clapped his shoulder.

The irritated expression on the were's face turned to disappointment. "Aw, come on, man! Give me a break. Just a few more minutes."

Little Miss Starlet flung a hank of dyed blonde hair over her shoulder and glared at Frankie. "Excuse me? A few minutes?"

"Now." Damn. It wasn't like Frankie didn't get enough on every other road trip.

"Sorry, babe. Boss calls the shots." Frankie pinched her tit hard enough to elicit a squeal. He fell in step as David pushed his way through the crowd.

"What's the hurry?" Frankie asked.

"Feeling." A sliver of relief shot through him that Frankie didn't question his motive this time, but for the were to say absolutely nothing . . .

He looked back only to find Frankie frozen in place two paces behind him. Turning to follow Frankie's stare, he found the emerald eyes that had haunted him the last two years.

I'd gotten used to vampire reticence when entering crowds. For them, it was probably like a starving human walking into a bakery, surrounded by mouth-watering aromas. Or I thought I had until we got past the foyer to Duke Miller's club-in-a-mansion and Duncan jerked to a stop.

What I didn't expect was David Head, standing a yard away and looking like his mama had just bitch-slapped him.

"Hello, David." Duncan held out a hand, but his move was almost . . . hesitant.

The normally egomaniac basketball player trembled, actually trembled, as he reached for Duncan's outstretched palm. "How ya doin', man?" His voice was a little more stable. Not by much though. The strong scent of roses filled my nose.

Head was in love, but who . . .

My eyes traveled from the b-ball player to Duncan. No way.

Somehow I'd gone from the Dinner From Hell to the Twilight Zone. What was I missing here? No hint came from Duncan, his shields tighter than I'd ever felt.

A sharp musk hit my nostrils, and I followed it to the were standing at Head's right arm. His nose wrinkled as he evaluated my scent in turn, the normal reaction I get from a were because I smell like a steak knife rather than steak. Then his eyes narrowed, his look downright ugly.

From his and Head's body language, they weren't bedmates. So why was Head at a party with a were? Was he Head's bodyguard?

"I am well, thank you. And your sister?" Duncan tried to extract his hand from Head's grip, but the Blues' new star player clung to him like a life preserver.

"Yvonne's fine. She's here in town, too." Head now carried that dewy wide-eyed look. You know the one. The kind his ex-boyfriend's preteen fans used to carry before I outed the two of them.

Duncan finally managed to pull free, in a semi-non-insulting way. A pleasant, and way-too-fake, smile spread across his features. "Please give our coven's regards to her and to Jean-Pierre." He turned to tug me further into Duke's mansion, but Head laid a platter-sized hand on his shoulder.

I felt like I was watching one of those PSAs of a slow-motion auto accident. Except I was the crash test dummy in the passenger seat. My assignment was exploding into as many shards as the proverbial windshield when my face smashed through it.

"Maybe you'd like to meet up with us for dinner tomorrow night?"

Head's puppy dog expression looked so pathetic and hopeful I almost felt sorry for him. The broccoli scent of his desperation joined the heady roses and hung in the air around us.

Duncan shook his head. "My apologies, but my fiancée and I have a family obligation."

I nearly choked on my spit, but before I could clear my throat, Head registered my presence. His eyes widened slightly, but not just in recognition. More like someone sizing up the competition.

A smile to match Duncan's filled Head's prominent features. "I didn't know you were engaged. Congratulations."

A vinegary aroma filled my nostrils, and behind it was the spicy tang of ginger. The double revelation sent my reporter's instincts racing, but I'm not sure which surprised me more, that Head was jealous of me or that he had witch blood in his background.

"We'll be in town for a while. Maybe some other night?" A pleading tone filled his voice.

I wasn't about to spend the evening playing nice to someone who had a crush on my guy. Even if my guy was a lying fink. Why hadn't Duncan said something about knowing David Head when I mentioned my assignment?

Screw the bonus. I had bigger vampires to fry. "I'm sorry, Mr. Head." I gave him a smile that I was sure was far more sincere than the ones he and Duncan wore. "But my brother's getting married a week from Saturday, and with both of us in the wedding, we just don't have the time, but thank you so much for the offer."

This time, I pulled Duncan away from the two men. When I glanced over my shoulder, both of them were staring at me. But their expressions carried two different forms of intense scrutiny.

Why didn't you tell me you knew David Head? I didn't bother quashing my irritation.

If I had known he would be here, I would not have come. Orange and red colored Duncan's mental voice.

While I was relieved he was talking to me, I still couldn't get past his surface thoughts. I twisted to face him. *He was my assignment tonight!*

Duncan twitched under my arm. *I am sorry, Samantha. I assumed your target was Duke Miller. You did not mention David.*

I did too!

No, you did not. Before I could protest, he flashed me his recollection of our conversation. Damn, I hated it when he was right, but I couldn't see past the immediate memory to find out his connection with Head.

Which meant Duncan was definitely hiding something.

I made a face at him. *Yeah, well. You know what they say about people who assume.*

Humor returned to his eyes. *You were the paparazzo that exposed David's occasional predilection for young men.*

I couldn't meet his eyes anymore. For some strange reason, equal parts of worry and embarrassment raced through my nerves that he'd put two and two together regarding my past experience with Head. Without having a clue, I'd crossed a witch two years ago.

Did things I'd done as a human count against me now? I sucked in a deep breath and released it. After seeing some of Bebe's spell-slinging, I should be thankful that I hadn't had an "accident" before now in retaliation for outing Head.

I looked back up at Duncan. Needing an anchor in reality, I dropped the telepathic connection. "How did you two meet?"

A wry smile twisted Duncan's lips. "A gentleman objecting to David's personal preferences threatened him. Since David's sister works for Jean-Pierre, he asked Caesar to resolve the situation."

Oh, crap. Puzzle pieces lined up in my brain and dropped into place. The rumors about Head's stalker were true. When I'd pitched the follow-up on Head to Ralph, he'd nixed the idea.

No, he hadn't just nixed the idea. He'd drop-kicked it into lunar orbit. At the time, I'd thought he'd been furious the Sabretooths were considering a trade of their top rebounder thanks to my story.

In reality, Ralph had accidentally brought unwanted attention to a supernatural.

I had outed a bisexual pro ball player who happened to be a supe.

And the stalking may have been about more than just Head's switch-hitting.

Oh God, Caesar must have been pissed.

Which meant I'd gotten someone killed.

Nausea overwhelmed the Big Macs I'd eaten earlier.

"It was not your fault, Samantha." Duncan's whispered words did little to comfort my churning stomach.

I blinked back tears. "Yes, it was. If I hadn't done the story, you wouldn't have had to protect Head. Y-y-you wouldn't have had to-to . . ."

He shook his head, and a wave of yellowish exasperation washed against my shields. "Now you are the one making assumptions. We did not kill David's assailant."

My veins froze. There were worse things than death. Right now, I wished I didn't know that, and I really wished I could have stopped my next words. "W-what did you—"

A disappointed look filled his face. *He was a mentally ill young man. I erased his knowledge of David Head, and Bebe had him admitted in a facility where he could get the care he needed.*

My gaze dropped from his again as heat flooded my cheeks. Of course, they had. Guilt joined the swirling emotional mud. No wonder he'd shut me out. I'd hurt Duncan's feelings by even suggesting he hadn't done the honorable thing.

My shields quivered under the dual pressure of my own feelings and the charged atmosphere of Duke's guests. Unable to handle the overload, I pivoted on my heel and made a beeline for the front door. A whisper of movement and a hint of sandalwood told me Duncan followed me.

A beefy arm stopped me at the door. "The boss wants to talk to you."

My blurry vision followed the black-clad arm to its owner. Stern brown eyes met mine.

"If you'll just wait here for a moment ma'am," he added.

"What's the problem? I'm leaving."

"That is the problem, Ms. Ridgeway." The internationally recognizable voice came from behind me. A voice so rich and smooth it could make a woman shed her clothes just to hear more of it.

Gathering the shreds of my dignity, I turned to find Duke Miller standing in the foyer. Tonight, instead of his signature purple, the diminutive entertainer dressed in pale gray slacks with a matching fedora. A bright yellow silk shirt fell unbuttoned to his waist. To accessorize his appearance, his background singers, Ruby and Sapphire, clung to each arm. Since I couldn't tell the twins apart, I didn't know which one wore the black mini-dress and which one wore the white.

An impish grin filled his delicate features. "First, you chase one of my guests away, and then you don't even bother taking any pictures. Your readers, and my fans, will be sorely disappointed."

That's when the tantalizing scent of rich honey reached me. I cursed my abilities and fate in general.

Miller and his girls were fairy.

And I didn't mean that in the politically incorrect sense that some of our rival magazines had suggested. It definitely explained his musical genius. But it was one revelation too many tonight. Add into the mix the rumors the fairy queens had put a contract on my head, and the urge to flee sucked my breath away.

"I'm sorry for crashing your party. We were just leaving." I took a step back toward the door.

Ringed fingers flicked a dismissal of my apology. "I wouldn't have had Ruby leak the information if I didn't know it would attract your attention."

I stiffened at Duke's admission. And I'd lay good money the real reason Duncan insisted on coming with me was he knew Duke's status. Oh, someone was *so* going to pay!

My arms crossed over my chest. "What do you want?"

Duke's gaze moved in a slow up, down, up examination, not really sexual though the man exuded sensuality. "I was merely curious." His lips formed a pout. "I must say that I don't share the Courts concerns."

I glared at him. "Concerns about what? I'm not violating IC law by coming here, and you just admitted to luring me on false pretenses."

The International Council was the Supernaturals' equivalent of the U.N. Duncan and Caesar had made me memorize the IC code. All 28,440 pages. Thank God, I had retained my terrific memory after my death, the earlier lapse with Duncan notwithstanding.

Duke's eyes widened slightly. "No, you certainly didn't." He sidestepped his own complicity. Another amused grin appeared. "And the Queens' concern ever an army of tabloid journalists invading sidhe territory is ludicrous." He nodded at Duncan. "Good night, Chief Enforcer."

"Good night, Your Grace." Duncan returned the polite nod before grabbing my elbow and steering me out the door.

We were in his Suburban and half-way back to his place before either of us spoke. Of course, I was the one who finally broke the silence.

"What is Duke Miller?"

"He is Sidhe."

I smacked a palm against the steering wheel. "Tell me something I don't fucking know! Like what is he to the fairies that he'd host a party for the sole purpose of attracting my attention?" I stole a glance at Duncan. Headlights played across his pale face, but he didn't turn in my direction.

"He is Millanthropas de Dannan. A duke of the Seelie Court."

A whistle escaped through my front teeth. "A real duke, huh? But why lure me? Aren't the Seelie supposed to be the good fairies?"

"Good and evil are nebulous terms, Samantha. Vampires are the spawn of Satan, according to certain authorities." No mistaking the mild sarcasm in his voice.

"You seem pretty damn evil to me right now. Next time you and Caesar want to use me as bait, ask first." The snarl in my voice sounded like a were's to my own ears. L.A.'s alpha were would rip apart anyone who'd pull this kind of shit on him. I was sorely tempted to follow his example.

Silence. Duncan didn't even bother to deny the accusation. My chest ached. He and his boss, my boss too since I had accepted vampire influence, had deliberately dangled me in front of a fairy noble, knowing damn well how most of the fairies felt about my existence. The pain fed the fury itching to cut loose.

"Was Ralph in on setting me up?"

"No."

Good. That was one less person on my shit list.

Why? Nothing. Nada. His shields were tighter than Fort Knox. I knew he could hear me knocking, but he refused to open the mental door, not even a crack.

I clutched the steering wheel to keep my fingers from trembling and cleared my throat. "Why, then?"

He shrugged, but at least he answered. "Given the Sidhe Courts concern that Caesar will create more . . ."

I shot him a glance before returning my attention to traffic. "Go ahead. You can say it. Zombies."

"Samantha, you are no more a—"

"I'm technically dead, and I'm walking, aren't I?" I snapped.

"Technically, you are driving." He laid a cool hand on my thigh.

I wanted to slap his touch away. I wanted to break every bone in his fingers. I wanted him to say, "I'm sorry. I didn't mean to betray you."

Instead, he said, "And as Tiffany has repeatedly pointed out, you have not started eating brains yet."

My stomach chose that moment to gurgle. Loudly.

Duncan's amusement tickled my psyche, but that just pissed me off more. It had been almost five hours since the McDonald's stop. As Bebe had predicted, my appetite had tapered off where I wasn't eating five-course meals every two hours, but I still ate an obscene amount. It wasn't like the extra calories showed up on my thighs, but I still hated it. All of my so-called disposable income fed my undead appetite, and that was by working two jobs.

If I quit working for Caesar, I'd have more problems than paying my grocery bill. I wouldn't stand a chance on my own against the entire might of the fairy world.

I didn't know what to do with all that anger, so I did what any semi-prudent hungry zombie would do. I pulled into the closest Taco Bell drive-thru.

"How could he!" David pitched another bottle at the suite's wall. The shattered glass and spray of alcohol did nothing to alleviate his fury, any more than the other twenty bottles. He was running out of ammo. "It's only been two fucking months!" He snatched a vase and hurled it at the ruined wallpaper.

With a wave of her fingers, Yvonne threw up a shield to protect her and Frankie from the crystal shards as the vase exploded. "Davy, calm down." Even muffled by the condensed air, her voice rose.

Her tone penetrated the fire filling his vision. The last time he'd heard her sound that scared, they'd been kids. The same night he'd brought their mother home. He turned to find Frankie standing between him and Yvonne, like David had stood between Yvonne and their stepfather years ago. He had never wanted to be the cause of that same expression on her face.

Hot wetness replaced the flames. He swiped a hand across his face and through his lime curls, trying to hide the tears that escaped. "Damn, I'm sorry. Yvonne—"

She took a hesitant step past Frankie, but the were grabbed her arm. The fact that Frankie thought he needed to protect her from her own brother lashed across David's soul, the pain worse than the ache that racked him when Duncan introduced that bitch as his fiancée.

No. David shoved the pain aside before he sucked in a deep breath and released it. "It's okay, man. I'm not going to do anything stupid." If anything, he needed to be smart about getting what he wanted.

Yvonne rushed into his arms, her hug hard against his ribs. "Don't you ever scare me like that again."

"I'm sorry," he whispered into her hair. "I didn't mean to scare you."

"It's okay, Davy." She patted him on the back. The same comfort she had given on those dark nights when their mother and stepfather's drunken shouting matches got physical. "It's okay. Let's go home and forget about all this."

He pulled back so he could look her in the eye. "Come on. We came all the way out here. Let's stay a few days. Have some fun."

She shook her head, a bemused smile on her face. "Our ideas of fun are two different things."

"Let me make this up to you. We'll do Disney or Universal. Maybe hop the shuttle up to Napa." He shot her an impish grin, the one he used to con his way into and out of a whole lot of messes.

Sure enough, it still worked on his big sister because after two seconds, she laughed and shook her head again. "I swear, David Jebediah, the things I let you talk me into."

He pushed her gently toward the door to her bedroom. "Go get some sleep. We'll plan out the rest of our vacation tomorrow."

Yvonne raised a suspicious eyebrow. "You promise you're staying in for the rest of the night?"

Crossing his heart, he nodded solemnly. "Hope to die."

She stared at him for a long time before smothering a yawn. "Good night then." She crossed the suite and the door *snicked* shut behind her.

The prickly feeling on the back of his neck made him turn and face Frankie. An ugly frown pinched the were's sharp features.

"What are you planning?" Frankie asked.

"Nothing." David stalked over to the phone.

Before he could punch the numbers, Frankie's hand covered his wrist. "I think you've had enough tonight, boss."

"I haven't had a goddamn thing to eat since we got to L.A. Now get your paw off me." Not that his words carried any real threat to the were, but Frankie let go of him anyway. "You want anything?"

Frankie nodded and folded his arms across his chest.

Once David placed both of their orders, he plopped down on the couch and propped up his feet before he snatched the remote on the side table and started flipping channels. The weight of Frankie's stare finally snapped his last nerve. He twisted around to face the other man. "What?"

Frankie shook his head, his expression definitely not mirroring Yvonne's earlier amusement. "I know you, man, and you're not my baby brother. What are you really planning?"

Irritation washed over David. He knew he wasn't that fucking easy to read. Otherwise, he wouldn't have so many national title trophies on his shelves back home. "How can I be planning something?"

"I recognized the woman with St. James, too. Samantha Ridgeway, right?"

David turned back to the T.V. and thumbed the button. The tall, hot chick from the Weather Channel, the one who needed to ditch that damn orange lipstick, popped up on the screen. "So?"

"There's some things you may not know about her." From the soft *whoomp*, Frankie had dropped into the overstuffed chair next to him.

"I know enough." Brandon hadn't been the same when his band-mates kicked him out rather than lose their record deal shortly after the piece appeared. David had offered to help him put together his own label, but the stress of the ugly press had been too much on his boyfriend's fragile ego. Thanks to the bitch, he'd lost the best rela-tionship he'd ever had.

The relationship that kept him from doing something stupid like getting his throat ripped out by pursuing the wrong supernatural.

"According to the rumor mill, she's the reason St. James killed Selene Antonius."

David shot upright on the couch. "What? Why didn't you tell me that earlier?"

Concern brightened Frankie's eyes. "I didn't take it or the other thing I heard seriously. Until I got a good whiff of her tonight, that is."

The urge to wring the information out of the were seeped into his brain. "What'd you smell besides garbage?" he sneered.

Frankie leaned closer. "That's just it. She smelled like stainless steel. According to my cousin, the story is Antonius turned her into a zombie using some kind of mini robots."

David stared at Frankie for a full ten seconds before he slapped the couch cushions. Laughter rumbled from his belly. "Good one. Good one, man. You had me going."

"I'm not joking."

The snarl in Frankie's voice quelled some of David's humor. He shook his head and propped his elbows on his knees. "I'm not making fun of you, but there's no way Ridgeway could be a zombie."

"Oh, yeah. Since when are you an expert?"

The memory of his one experience with the undead sobered him completely. "I may not be in Yvonne's league when it comes to magick, but I can tell you this." He held up his index finger. "A little too well preserved for one thing." He thought about his conversation with Duncan and Ridgeway and held up his middle finger. "And a little too bossy for the other."

Frankie dropped the subject when a sharp knock brought him to his feet.

As the were dealt with the room service, David considered this new information. If Frankie's cousin was right about Ridgeway, this might work out even better than his original plan for St. James. He was no longer a kid messing with resurrection spells out of grief. This time he'd do it right.

Nothing would be more delicious than fucking over the New Orleans coven. Except stealing a man from the woman who'd ruined his ex-boyfriend's life.

Yep, the old folks were right about how to serve revenge, and he would remain frosty until he eliminated the competition and got Duncan St. James in his bed.

Chapter 8

I would have preferred cutting off my toes, just to see if they grew back like the cheerleader on *Heroes*, rather than deal with Ralph in the wee hours of Saturday morning. But I couldn't sleep without fessing up to the man to whom I owed my career. I had *never* missed a fucking deadline until now. And I was too angry at Duncan to even want to join him in bed. After leaving him at his place, I drove to the *Scoop* offices and strode into the bullpen at three-forty-five.

"Where the hell have you been, Ridgeway? I've held the line for your damn pictures." Ralph's bark resembled that of the English bulldog at his heels. Emerson gave a low growl to back up his brother. The O'Malleys gave true credence to Caesar Augustine's penchant for taking in strays.

"Don't have 'em. We need to talk." I could be just as blunt.

"Goddammit, I need pictures, not—"

"Family business, Ralph. Now."

Ralph's tirade turned to stone-cold sobriety at my mention of Family. Yeah, he recognized the capital "F". "Family" as in supernatural business. "My office." He turned to Bill Morton, the newly appointed assistant editor. The job that should have been mine if I hadn't died. "Use the second cover lead and have printing start the run."

Amid Bill's ass-kissing reassurances, I followed Ralph and Emerson through the frosted glass and wood door. He had the only private office at *The National Scoop*, other than the publisher's executive suites upstairs.

Despite the no-smoking ordinance, Ralph lit up before his ass hit the cracked chair leather. He sucked in a lungful of smoke before he said, "What happened, Sam?"

I dropped into one of the visitor's chairs and swallowed my fury as I met Ralph's concerned gaze. He so rarely used my first name, but I needed to know the truth. Duncan hadn't let me read him after the showdown at Duke's place, which bothered me. A lot. Probably more than his initial betrayal.

But even James Bond would try to get the truth before he whacked the bad guy. I'd follow his example though I wouldn't have to rely on threats. "Ralph, I want permission to read your mind."

His mouth dropped open, and the cigarette hit a pile of papers amid a shower of sparks. After tossing the butt in the overflowing ashtray, he swatted the embers smudging someone's story.

Emerson whined before trotting over to rest his huge head on my knee. I scratched his ears, the same as I'd always done before I found out he was a werebulldog. Just as Ralph was trapped in human form due to a genetic quirk, Emerson would forever be a man imprisoned in the shape of an ugly, slobbering dog. I wasn't sure which of us had it worse at the moment.

When Ralph's eyes finally met mine again, I said, "Just surface thoughts, Ralph, so I will know if you're lying."

"Sam." For the first time I ever witnessed, fear tighten his craggy features. The thick smell of ashes filled the air, an odor that had nothing to do with Ralph's two-pack-a-day habit.

"You know I wouldn't ask unless something was seriously wrong." My vision swam slightly, as much from my own emotions threatening to break through as Ralph's scent. "I respect you too much, you old fart."

Ralph's ashy fear melted into the acid sharpness of worry. I hated being able to smell/taste other people's emotions, a by-product of Mallory's little science experiment, but never more so than now.

He gave a curt nod before he said, "Ask."

I dropped my outer psychic shields, and the mustard wave of Ralph's thoughts rushed into the space. "Did you know Duke Miller was a fairy?"

He shook his head, but frustration replaced the worry. "Damn, girl, you know that rumor's been floating around—"

Despite the bizarre chaos of my night, a laugh worked its way out of my throat as I held up a hand. "No, I mean a, um, sidhe."

Ralph grinned as the clean cotton of truth swept through him. "No shit. Really? Explains a lot." He reached for another cigarette.

"So you didn't know the fairy courts have been gunning for me?"

Emerson raised his head and barked. I couldn't read his thoughts and emotions the way I could Ralph's, but he was obvious in his own way.

Ralph clicked his lighter and took a puff before answering. "All the Families know. That's why I'm so freakin' happy you're dating St. James." His eyes narrowed as my unspoken suspicion hit him. "I didn't set you up, Sam."

Blessedly, his thoughts remained Downy fresh, but with the tinge of laundry left out on the line during a lightning storm.

"But you knew David Head was a witch."

Mildew replaced clean cotton. Another whine reverberated from Emerson's throat and he ducked under the desk.

"Dammit, Ralph, why didn't you tell me?"

In all the time I'd known him, I'd never seen regret in his eyes. Until now. It took a couple of seconds, but Ralph changed his mind about lying to me because the mildew cleared from my perception. The sad part, he was probably scared I'd force my way into his brain, which contrary to the stories Normal folks believed was a gross, painful process, for us as well as them.

"I couldn't Sam, you know the rules. You were human then." He sucked in a lungful of smoke before he blew it toward the ceiling. "You weren't Family either."

Family again. A supernatural or a normal human who was related to a supernatural either through blood or marriage and could be trusted with that knowledge. Occasionally, the term was used for a Normal who worked for a supernatural.

The thought only dredged up the morass of my own problems, and I could no longer meet Ralph's eyes. Could I trust my parents with my new status?

Max? Yeah, him I could trust, though he did try to shoot me the day after I died. He knew about supernaturals long before he knocked up a certain vampire's niece. Anne Levy, the homeless girl I thought was one of his street sources, had turned out to be one of Duncan's enforcers.

My head swung up so I could glare at Ralph. "Wait a minute! Max knew Anne was a vampire long before he ever met Tiffany. How come he got a free pass, and I didn't?"

Ralph's gaze pinned me through the smoky haze hanging over his desk. "Sam, do you really think Augustine would've cut me slack for breaking the rules just because he did for her?"

Damn, I hated admitting Ralph was right. Caesar took Anne into his coven after a rogue had bitten her. The vampire master practically regarded her as his daughter. It still didn't answer my original question.

"So why'd you send me after Head tonight if I'd gotten you into trouble the last time?"

Ralph sighed, a loud gusty exhalation that stirred the microscopic layer of ash that lay over everything on his desk, and crushed the butt. "The supernatural celebrities understand the business the same as Norms, Sam. As long as I don't publish anything that'll reveal their supernatural status, they're fair game. And frankly, they like the publicity as much as anyone else." His fingers twitched in the desire for another smoke. Instead, he ran a hand over the scraggly remains of his hair. "The problem wasn't the original story. The guy stalking Head after you, uh we, outed him as bi may have been nuttier than a Baby Ruth, but he knew way too much about supernaturals. Augustine and Rousseau couldn't take any chances."

I could understand the need for secrecy from Joe Average, but something wasn't quite right here. Just as Caesar was the master of the Western U.S. Vampire Coven, Jean-Pierre Rousseau controlled the vamps in the southeastern states.

"Why would Caesar and Jean-Pierre care when Head's a witch?" I frowned, twisting the complicated jurisdictions and political connections around in my brain. "A witch living in Los Angeles would come under Silver Bear's purview." For a tiny little Jewish woman, the Silver Bear Coven's high priestess was just as formidable as the vampires.

"Not when his sister is Rousseau's eclectic."

Ouch. This situation was getting more screwed up by the minute. I should've just walked out of Ralph's office, but now all of my reporter's instincts had kicked into high gear.

He chuckled before he broke down and reached for another cigarette. "I recognize that look. Go ahead and ask. I'll tell you what I can."

My right eyebrow rose of its own accord. "What you can or what you know?"

Another chuckle before he took a drag of the fresh smoke. "Okay, okay. What I know."

"Is Head eclectic too?"

Ralph nodded and leaned back, his chair creaking ominously. "Some incident when they were teens got 'em kicked out of the New Orleans witches' coven. Don't know the details but I heard it had something to do with their mom and stepdad's deaths. The Laveaus hushed everything up." He shrugged. "Most of the witch covens don't want the embarrassment splashed around, and perpetrators are usually ecstatic to get exiled from witch society rather than the death sentence."

Interesting. I would have pegged Head as the chooser, not the choosee, of exile. I'd have to ask Bebe for dirt when I got the chance, but she'd already given me the scoop on the reasons why a witch would voluntarily become an eclectic. The rest of the witches didn't like one of their own working for the competition instead of pretending to be a Normal, so if a witch wanted to work for one of the other supernatural groups, he or she cut ties with their coven.

Except something didn't make sense. I eyed Ralph. "Why pro basketball instead of working for Jean-Pierre too? He'd make a hell of a lot more money."

Shifting forward, he tapped the cigarette against the ashtray and took another puff as he leaned back in his chair. The clean cotton of his thoughts didn't override the stench of smoke filling his office. "From what I've heard, Head doesn't have a whole lot of talent in the magick department. There's always been some question of who was the real culprit in the incident that got the kids exiled. Head claimed responsibility so his powers were bound by the coven."

My grin matched Ralph's. "Really? I can't imagine why." Head's penchant for boasting had been cause for jubilation in the Sabretooth locker room when he'd used his free agency to join the New Orleans Blues.

Ralph blew a smoke ring toward the overhead fluorescents, and his mood turned serious. "Ridgeway, I expect something a little more substantial for next week's edition."

So much for our little heart-to-heart. My editor was back.

"And I want to get this puppy put to bed before Saturday morning," he added with a smile. "I've got a wedding to go to Saturday night, and I'd like to get *some* sleep." Max had worked for Ralph under a pseudonym in high school and college, so of course the old fart had been invited.

I rose from the guest chair and reached for the doorknob. "You and me both, Boss."

Emerson crawled out from under the desk and gave my hand a good-bye lick, but Ralph's not-so-discreet cough made me pause at the door. I looked over my shoulder.

"If this is going to be your last issue, I'd like it to be pretty damn spectacular."

Damn, him. He wouldn't ask me straight out, and I hated that he knew me so well he'd already assumed which decision I'd make. I nodded and stalked out of his office before the welling tears could fall.

Chapter 9

I avoided Duncan over the next four nights. The bastard had stabbed me in the back. It would have been less painful if he'd actually used a knife. A dull, rusty butter knife. How could anyone say he wanted to marry me, then turn around and use me as fairy bait? Why didn't he tell me Duke Miller was literally a duke of the Seelie Court. I ignored his repeated voice-mails. The bastard couldn't even say he was sorry in his messages.

Wedding preparations and hours spent staking out local celebrities helped keep me out of my apartment. At least until Brittany and K-Fed provided me with the perfect cover story late Wednesday morning. Ralph was on cloud nine, and as I unlocked my front door, I thought I had plenty of time to finish planning tomorrow night's bachelorette party.

"Samantha."

I jumped back, swinging my camera bag. Duncan caught it before it connected with his head. If I'd known it was him, I would have swung harder. No, I would have weights in the bottom, or used some fancy martial arts move like Jet Li.

The bastard had stayed upwind, so I missed my opportunity.

We stood there for several seconds, staring at each other under the security light.

He blew out a breath. "I understand you are still angry with me—"

"Get off my front step." I jerked my bag out of his grip.

"I would like to talk—"

"I don't want to hear it." I really wished I could walk through my front door, and he wouldn't be able to follow me. But the story of vampires unable to cross a threshold without an invitation was bullshit.

Just like Duncan saying he loved me.

I looked at him, really looked. There was no hint of remorse, only that stony visage of Mr. Chief Enforcer. "If you'd—" I clenched my jaw shut. There was no use rehashing the same old issue, and I wasn't going to beg him to apologize.

"If I would what?" He reached for my face, and I slapped his hand away.

"If you won't leave, I will." I stomped out to my car. When the Honda's door slammed shut, the broken panel rattled. Between deadlines and the wedding, I hadn't had a chance to take it to the shop.

I glanced back at my apartment in the rearview mirror as I pulled away. He stood there, not chasing after me with vampire speed. Not doing . . . anything. The bastard just stood there and watched me drive into the night.

The problem was I had nowhere to go. I didn't want to deal with Tiffany's morning sickness at Max's. Mom and Dad's was a joke. Ralph would tell me to suck it up and get over myself. As far as I was concerned, Caesar was as much to blame as Duncan, so his and Bebe's place was out of the question. Anyone else I knew in the supernatural community would call Duncan the minute I showed up on their doorstep. So I drove in an aimless pattern through the dark streets.

Maybe my driving wasn't as aimless as I thought when I recognized which neighborhood I cruised a couple of hours later. My driving must have been on autopilot because the car pulled into the driveway of an all-too-familiar little bungalow.

Jake Wong pulled open the front door, even though I didn't remember knocking. Water dripped from his short blue-black hair, and his dark brown eyes widened in surprise. He tightened his grip on the towel wrapped around his waist. Every muscle on his delectable body was as honed as it had been when we'd been a couple. For a minute, it was like two years had disappeared.

"Sam? You okay?"

I burst into tears.

Jake's bungalow was as warm and cozy as I remembered, the décor an odd mix of Eastern and Western styles, but it worked. He handed me a steaming cup of oolong tea. I had never been able to convert him to coffee. What was it about me and tea-drinking guys?

He sat down across the kitchen table with his own cup. He'd taken a minute to throw on jeans and a t-shirt before making the tea. Part of me regretted the change in his attire.

"Why do I get the feeling this isn't a booty call?" he said, sliding a fresh box of tissues to me.

Dammit, James Bond did booty calls, but he didn't bawl his eyes out on an ex's front door step. I wiped my nose and gave Jake a weak smile. "I'm sorry. I-I just didn't know where else to go."

He laid his hand over mine. "You know I'll always be here for you." His expression turned serious. "Is this about Max's wedding?"

My mouth dropped open. It took a couple of attempts to make it work. "God, no! How'd you even—"

"I saw the notice in the paper a couple of weeks ago." He let the silence grow for a minute before he said quietly, "What's his name?"

"Who?"

"The guy who broke your heart."

My anger resurfaced, and I could no longer meet his steady gaze. Instead, I stared at steam rising off my tea. "Who says it's about a guy?" When he didn't answer, I stole a peek.

A sly smile had spread across his lips. He let go of my hand, and leaned back in his chair. "So . . . you want me to beat him up for you?"

Despite all his training as a martial artist and a stunt man, Jake was severely outmatched, but the idea that he'd defend my honor eased my tension.

"No." I shook my head. "If anyone's going to smack the shit out of him, it'll be me."

"So what's his name?"

Part of me wasn't sure how much I should reveal without crossing the supernatural line. The other part was uncomfortable talking about the current boyfriend with the ex. So, did I still consider Duncan my current?

"I'm sorry. I shouldn't have come here." I started to rise, but Jake laid his hand on mine again, his touch comforting, and far warmer than a certain British jerk's.

"He asked you to marry him, didn't he?"

I didn't answer him. I couldn't. Not when I'd turned down Jake's proposal two years ago.

"Sam," he said softly. "It took me a while, but I finally figured out you ran because what we had scared you."

Frozen in place, I stared at him. I couldn't move as he tossed the harsh truth at my feet. "I'm so sorry. I—" Swallowing the renewal of tears, I looked away. "I never wanted to hurt you."

"I know that now, Sam," he whispered. "But don't throw this thing with . . ." He waited, letting the silence stretch and crack.

"Duncan," I finally said.

"Duncan," he repeated. "Don't throw things away with Duncan because you're scared."

"I'm not scared," I muttered.

"So why are you at your *ex*-fiancé's house right after another man proposed to you?"

"You're right. I shouldn't have come because you're an asshole,

Jake Wong." I swiped at the tears that had managed to escape and stood.

"Uh-huh." He grinned, the brightness reminding me of things best left forgotten. There was just too damn much water under our bridge.

He rose from the chair and pulled me in a tight hug. "Go home, Sam. Give this Duncan a chance to make up for whatever he did to piss you off." His fingers tilted my chin up, forcing my eyes to meet his warm gaze. "Before we both do something we'll regret."

I couldn't deny the temptation. Jake was familiar. Comfortable. Safe. And I'd screwed him over completely. I knew if I told Jake things were over with Duncan and asked him for a second chance, he'd give it to me in an instant. But it wasn't fair to him. I'd ripped holes in both of our souls because of my fear two years ago.

And how would he handle the whole zombie thing?

No, I couldn't do that to Jake. But I wasn't sure if I could trust Duncan to replace the emptiness in my heart.

Chapter 10

Duncan was gone when I got home. The only trace of him was the faint scent of sandalwood on my front step. I needed to think, but instead I threw myself into the last minute preparations for Tiffany's party. I was probably avoiding again, but I found inspiration always came when I focused on something else.

So, shortly after sunset on Thursday night, a limo full of rowdy women headed into the desert night with me, bound for Las Vegas.

Okay, rowdy except for Mai, who made a point of locking the partition in the "up" position while she drove. I wished Miko had come, but Mai's baby sister had bowed out, claiming one of the senior daytime security needed to be in Los Angeles in case supernatural wedding guests arrived early. Tiffany had been bummed Miko was the only bridesmaid not coming, but when I said I'd talk to her, Goth Girl threatened to shove her nail file somewhere even more uncomfortable than my eyeball.

Personally, I suspected Caesar or Duncan ordered Mai to come in Miko's place. She was the only Augustine enforcer more dour than Duncan.

And he must not have mentioned our fight to anyone because no one even broached the subject of why we weren't talking. Instead, a current of excitement enveloped the bridesmaids, and Mai had raised the partition out of annoyance. Or maybe it was the champagne corks ricocheting through the limo.

Even the bride-to-be exhibited good spirits, probably because

Mom declined to come when I told her our destination. And here, I thought it'd be Anne, the Amish vampire bridesmaid, who'd protest the mostly naked entertainment. God, for once, I loved being the maid of honor.

"I'm telling you," Tiffany said as she sloshed more sparkling grape juice in her flute, "the last two nights of sleep have been pure bliss!"

"I told you the morning sickness wouldn't last forever." Dr. Bebe Zachary, our resident witch, took a sip of her champagne.

"Really?" Tiffany flashed her a smile that promised trouble. "When was the last time you puked every night for a month straight?"

"Tiffany." Passing headlights shifted along Phillippa Mann's face, making her skin glow more than usual. Not that Normals could see it. "No picking fights tonight."

I wasn't sure if Tiffany accepted Phil's chiding because she helped Duncan raise my future sister-in-law or because she was a freaking demigoddess. Either way, Tiffany leaned back against the plush leather bench.

Ever the peacemaker of the group, Anne Levy held up her goblet of blood. "Here's to Tiffany and Max. May their union be blessed."

"Well, it's already fruitful," I said, tinking my own champagne glass against the others, and everyone, including Tiffany, burst out laughing.

"So? Where're we going?" Tiffany bounced up and down in her seat.

I grinned. I hadn't been able to keep it a secret from the other gals, thanks to my ineptitude with my mental shields. But I was rather proud that I'd managed to keep it from Tiffany.

The bride's smile fell. "Tell me or I use my nail file on the other eyeball."

"Geez, is this how you treat Santa Claus too?"

Anne snickered. "You don't want to know what she did to him."

I could feel the blood drain from my face. "Please tell me we're talking about a department store variety and it didn't involve a felony."

Phil laughed. "We wish."

Bebe shot confused looks between Phil and Anne. "What'd she do? Run over one of the reindeer with the SUV?" Like me, she was a relative newcomer to the Augustine Coven, even though she and Caesar had been an item for a little over two years.

Anne tucked a lock of hair behind her ear and sighed. "That would've been so much easier to deal with."

We all were laughing hysterically for the rest of the trip as Phil and Anne told stories of all things Tiffany.

Frankie shifted on the balls of his feet. "Are you sure you want to do this?"

David ignored the nervous were and concentrated on the lock. A muttered spell, a soft click, a push. He smiled to himself. Good to know he hadn't lost his touch.

"Why couldn't you pick a funeral home?" Frankie's voice hissed in David's ear.

"Because fresher is better. Now shut up. I need to focus." He'd never had the chance to master blurring or invisibility spells, which left a good, old-fashioned power surge. The security camera promptly spat a flurry of sparks. He slipped through the door stenciled with "Clark County Morgue," Frankie so tight on his heels the were practically climbed up his ass.

"Damn, I hate the smell of these places."

For the first time, David felt sorry for Frankie. No matter how much anti-septic and disinfectant cleaner they used, decay permeated the air of a morgue. While the stench bothered him, he could only imagine what his friend's hyper-sensitive nose picked up.

"Ridgeway's still going to have a witch and a vamp with her," Frankie continued. "Not to mention at least two human enforcers, and no one knows what the hell Mann is!"

The continued stream of complaints grated on David's nerves. "Why do you think I'm getting back-up?"

Between the two of them, it hadn't been hard to track Ridgeway in the course of preparing for her brother's wedding. It was the social event of the season for the L.A. supernatural community. And there had only been two logical places for the ladies to go once he found out Ridgeway planned the bachelorette party for tonight in Vegas. A couple of franklins confirmed which show time she had bought tickets for.

"We could have hired someone to take care of her *after* we left Los Angeles." Frankie stood next to the door, peering out through the glass and mesh window. "That way St. James won't think it's you."

David settled cross-legged on the scrubbed linoleum before he flicked a scarf from his backpack and spread it before him. He eyed the were. "Why would he anyway? He doesn't know how I—" He swallowed the rest of the statement. Taking out the other necessary items, he arranged them carefully on the scarf. "Besides you're the one who's always saying it's best to take care of these things yourself."

"*Now* you decide to take my advice?"

"Keep your voice down before someone hears us." He poured the tiny bottle of Baccardi in the shot glass. Nerves jangled so he inhaled a deep breath and shook his arms to drive out the memories of the last time he'd performed this ritual. It sucked that this was his only magickal talent besides picking locks and blowing up electronics.

The Laveaus thought they were so fucking clever. *Lifetime my ass.* The binding spell was slipping, but he'd been careful to keep the illusion going, even around Yvonne. No sense courting trouble with the coven before he was ready.

Knowing he was running out of time, he clipped the cigar. A flick of a match and a couple of short puffs ensured the end glowed. A welcoming curl of smoke floated toward the stark ceiling.

David began the summoning spell. He only hoped Papa Ghede was in the mood to listen.

"C'mon, Mai! You've got to come with us. I got you a ticket, too." I reached over the front seat and waved said ticket under her nose. Okay, technically it was Miko's, but her big sister didn't need to know that.

Mai's expression was tighter than her glossy black French braid. "I'm on duty." She had dropped us off at the Karnak long enough to stow our luggage at Caesar's penthouse and say a quick hello to her grandfather, the vampire who ran Las Vegas in Caesar's name. Damn, it's hard not to love a billionaire boss. Now, she wove through Strip traffic toward the Rio.

Tiffany's head poked over the front seat to join mine. "No one said you had to drink. C'mon, it'll be fun!" At Mai's silence, she switched to a baby voice. "You know someone will be vewy, vewy angry wif you if someting happens to his pwecious baby awound all those big, bad, *naked* mortals."

Mai snorted and reached up with one hand to shove the ticket out of her face.

Tiffany looked at me and return to her normal voice. "You know the only reason she's not cursing us out right now is because you're screwing her boss."

"And your uncle."

"Eeewwww." Tiffany ducked back into the rear compartment.

"Mai, you can honestly say you were doing your duty by keeping your boss's niece from sticking her hands down strange men's pants." I grinned. "And you know I'll tell him."

Almond-shaped eyes flicked up to stare at me in the rearview mirror. "Your attempts at blackmail are pathetic, Samantha." Her attention returned to the surrounding pedestrians, who were starting to spill from the sidewalk into the street.

"So's your reason for not coming with us." I stuck out my tongue.

"It is not."

"Is so."

She sighed. "You're all drunk."

"Are not!" Tiffany's voice rang from the back.

"Neither am I," Anne added.

Mai shook her head. "Someone should keep an eye on the lot of you."

A cheer went up from the back compartment.

I clapped Mai on the shoulder. "You're not going to regret it."

She sighed again. "I always regret coming to this damn city."

A deep chuckle echoed inside and around the stainless steel refrigeration units. Frankie LeBeau had seen and done enough freaky shit in his life that the invisible entity drinking the rum and puffing on the illegal Cuban didn't bother him.

But the muffled sounds of someone, of several someones, moving around inside the units made him want to wet his jeans. As much as he loved David like a littermate, what that boy could do wasn't fucking natural.

Unseen hands released all the latches at once. David's sing-song bass voice died until there was total silence. The stench of grave dirt and rot rose, threatening to overwhelm his canine senses. Then the sounds of scrabbling, fingernails on steel, cloth and skin sliding along the trays rippled through the air. Limbs covered in mottled flesh emerged from the units, followed by heads. Finally, the corpses crawled out of their little cubby holes.

Frankie tried not to look at the blue-gray skin and vacant stares on their faces. Most of the dead were in decent shape. Except for the three obvious victims of this afternoon's pile-up on I-15. Even his mind had trouble wrapping itself around the fact meat shouldn't be moving once it'd gone cold.

Someone screamed behind him. He whirled to find a petite blonde in navy scrubs. Her clipboard clattered on the floor, and shrieks of panic continued from her wide-open mouth. Cursing his inattention, he reached for her, only to see his partially shifted hand rake the pale flesh of her arm.

The pain seemed to knock away her fear. She pivoted out of the cold storage room and raced for the alarm. In two bounds, he'd caught her. He had to give the bitch credit; her thumbs thrust straight for his eyes. But her attempted blinding wasn't enough to stop the snap of elongated jaws that tore out her throat.

Shit! Damn! Mother-fu-

The remaining air in her lungs bubbled out through the blood filling the cavity once containing muscle and cartilage. With a sick, wet thump, the body crashed to the floor. Red pooled around the head, soaking the blond hair before spreading across the linoleum.

He reached up for his snout, only to feel skin on skin, his form already shifting back to human. He'd been so careful not to lose control over the past ten years. Jean-Pierre would not be pleased, but the vampire master's anger would be inconsequential if John Lannigan's wolves caught up with him. The Los Angeles Packmaster would order him shredded in a heartbeat for killing a Normal.

Frankie paused in wiping the blood from his jaw. The woman's body continued to twitch and jerk. This wasn't right. The death spasms should have stopped by now. He took a step back, then another.

And bumped into something clammy and unyielding. He jumped to the side. The corpse had been a fifty-something male. Dead hands reached for him.

"No!" David's command echoed in the empty hallway. Shuffling behind him came the other six zombies. The corpse let its arms fall to its side.

Frankie's relaxation lasted less than a second. A warm hand grabbed his. A shout rammed out of vocal cords as he leapt away from the woman he'd just killed.

"Ah shit, man! Did you have to kill her?" Disgust filled David's voice.

Frankie couldn't look away from her blank eyes, the film already creeping across the big, blue irises, to answer David. She reached for him again.

"Stop." David's order halted her movement, but it seemed like her attention was fully on Frankie.

"Frankie?"

He licked his parched lips, nerves on a hair-trigger, wanting to shift so he could run far, far away from this place. Swallowing hard, he struggled to remain on two feet and not sprout fur.

"Frankie?" David said again, this time laying a platter-sized hand on his shoulder. A warm, blood-pumping, living hand.

"I-I'm sorry. It was an accident. She attacked me and-and—" He gulped. She stared at him with those unseeing eyes, instead of lying on the floor like a proper dead person. "I'm sorry. Instinct kicked in—"

"'Sokay, man. We need to get them loaded into the van and head out. Are you going to keep it together?" David shook him slightly.

Frankie nodded before inclining his head toward the assistant coroner, according to her red-stained security badge. "Do we have to bring her?" Dammit! It was an accident. He didn't mean—

"Yeah," came David's soft reply. "We can't let her run loose. She was too close—" He took a deep breath. Even without him saying it, Frankie heard the unspoken accusation. "She'll be looking for revenge without me to control her," David continued. "The spell will be over at dawn, and she'll just be dead again."

Frankie nodded then fell in step behind David and his little troop of zombies. He wasn't going to hell like his mama had said.

He was already in it.

Chapter 11

Tiffany's shriek nearly pierced my undead eardrum. The cowboy thrust his package in her face, and she shoved the five-dollar bill into his fake suede G-string. Bebe waved a fistful of cash at the dancer, and he gyrated over to her.

Stone-faced Mai actually cracked a smile as a "police officer" showered her with attention. Then again, maybe it was the handcuffs dangling from his hip. Or it could have been the gold embroidered badge that barely covered his assets.

Even Anne had loosened up. Instead of peeking through fingers as she had during the first half of the show, she bounced her black flats in time to the music. But every time one of the performers approached her, she edged back in her seat, shaking her head.

The only one looking absolutely bored was Phil. I didn't know what James Bond would do in this situation. For one thing, he wouldn't be caught dead at a male strip show.

I dropped cash on the waiter's tray and plucked up the two strawberry daiquiris. Nudging one in front of her, I caught her eye. *You okay?* There was no other way she could've heard me with all the women screaming around us.

I'm sorry. She gave me a wistful smile. *You worked so hard putting this evening together. It's just—* Sadness filled her blue eyes. *When you get to my age, you've seen it all. Literally.*

Somehow I didn't think she was only referring to male genitalia. *Max isn't taking her away from you, you know.*

Phil shook her head, the gray rain taste of her thoughts threatening to drown my own alcoholic-assisted good mood.

And it took a *lot* of freaking alcohol these days to even get a slight buzz.

I . . . She sucked down half the pink drink. *I know it's stupid, but she's the closest thing I've ever had to a daughter.*

Who'd have thought Phillippa Mann had pre-wedding mommy blues? I laid a hand over hers and squeezed in sympathy while the last notes of the current number died amid thunderous applause. Dancers strutted across the stage and behind the curtains. Tiffany and Bebe's cowboy blew them kisses before jogging after his fellow performers.

Anticipation lay thick in the air though the pause between numbers couldn't have been more than a couple of seconds. The stage lights dimmed to an eerie blue, and the opening beats of "Thriller" filled the air. Women screamed in excitement as the dancers shambled on stage. Each one's monster make-up and costume were a weird blend of sexy and bizarre.

"Oh, gross!"

I followed Tiffany's line of sight to the last man on the left. Instead of the ripped and buff men entertaining us all night, this guy had a spare tire Homer Simpson would envy. Compared to everyone else on stage, his expression was slack, not flirtatious.

"I thought Vegas didn't allow . . ."

My gaze dropped, and my realization met Phil's at the door. The man hadn't bothered with his G-string. I cocked my head as I examined the goods. Why on earth had he used body make-up on his privates instead of wearing the G-string? In a stiff lockstep out of time with the music and the rest of the dancers, he aimed for our table.

Goddess! That man's really dead!

The same time Bebe sent her warning, Mr. Naked plowed through the table closest to the left side of the stage. The ladies he knocked over shouted insults. One took a swing at him.

I didn't see if she connected. Something frigid grabbed my neck and jerked me backward. I landed hard on my ass and looked up. Decay and rot filled my sinuses as I stared into unseeing, filmy eyes. I didn't have any room to duck the fist headed straight for my nose. Flinching to one side, bone cracked when the blow landed on my left cheek. It felt like my eyeball exploded along with the nerves. Sucking on the pain, I aimed a vicious kick at the asshole's groin.

Only to have my red stiletto stuck in the way-too-giving flesh.

Before I could pull free, my shoe disappeared along with my opponent. Something crashed into the bar from the loud shattering of glass. Another hand, this one warm and definitely alive, yanked me upright and tottering on one heel.

Phil peered into my good eye. "You okay?"

"Yeah. Nothing thirty minutes won't fix," I muttered.

The music died as the DJ realized there was something wrong. Two of the dancers closest to Mr. Naked grabbed his arms. With a shake, he sent them flying into other customers. Angry shouts around us turned into screams of raw panic. The crowd around Mr. Naked had parted at the sight of Mai's semi-automatic and were stampeding toward the main doors. She squeezed off a couple of shots.

Mr. Naked didn't even grunt. Sheer physics made him pause, but he resumed lumbering toward us when he regained his balance.

"Sam!"

Tiffany's warning didn't come fast enough. I caught a hint of musk and death before I was jerked off my feet again, much easier this time thanks to the missing four-inch heel. Hovering over me was a blonde in navy scrubs. At least, I thought she was blonde. It was hard to tell with the semi-dried blood matting her hair. Semi-dried blood that probably came from the huge gap where her throat used to be. What concerned me more than the horrendous wound was the scalpel she held in her right fist.

Fear and anger built. Deep down, I knew I wouldn't get a second shot and cut loose with a hard-core psy-bolt, one that'd leave me with a migraine for the next three days. Light bulbs popped behind my eyeballs and something stabbed the center of my brain.

Flashing spots cleared in time for the results. The woman flew backward and landed in the middle of a group of vacated chairs. Plastic crunched under her dead weight. One down.

Except the shattered chairs kept crunching. Acid gathered at the back of my throat. Like something out of a slasher movie, she rose, kicking aside crumpled bits of furniture. My telekinetic blow didn't faze her.

A flash of lightning blinded my good eye, almost as instantaneous as the crack of thunder that destroyed what was left of my poor eardrums. The smell of barbequed meat hit me. When I could see again, Psycho Doc was nothing more than a crispy critter. A grim smile lit Phil's face. So glad to know she'd found some enjoyment in the evening.

Mai had given up on the gun and had pulled out a couple of Japanese-style short swords. If we survived tonight, I'd have to ask her how she hid all that hardware underneath her black business suit. Whirling around Mr. Naked in a complicated dance, she chopped bits and pieces off him, but he still kept coming.

A quick glance at the rest of the group showed we were all in various degrees of trouble. Tiffany had smashed the kneecaps of one of the creeps and proceeded to beat him over the head with a chair. Using her vampire talons and fangs, Anne tore her opponent limb from limb. So much for her Amish pacifism. Meanwhile, Bebe took her cue from Phil and threw fireball after fireball at another zombie.

My heart stopped. That's what they were. *Real* zombies.

Phil jumped between me and another lumbering corpse. "These things are fixated on Sam!"

"No shit-ugh!" Tiffany's final blow crushed the man's skull. He twitched, but there were enough broken body parts he couldn't get up.

The corpse Phil faced off looked like it might have been a man in his late twenties when he was alive, but way skinny, even without part of its cheekbone and jaw missing. My own broken cheekbone throbbed in sympathetic pain. We were too close to Tiffany for Phil to risk another lightning bolt. Instead, she threw a punch at the zombie's stomach. Her fist went clear through his mid-section, spraying bits of vertebrae across the floor and splashing assorted goo all over her gold lamé dress.

Paralysis from lack of a spinal cord obviously wasn't a problem for him. Dead fingers wrapped themselves around Phil's throat.

I couldn't help her. Another nightmare smashed a fist into my already broken cheekbone, sending a tsunami of pain through my skull before I landed on a table ten feet away. Attempting to roll with the hit saved what was left of my face. The zombie Phil had thrown into the bar cracked the table in two with a double-fisted blow.

The daiquiris threatened to erupt from my stomach. What I'd missed earlier was the fact that the woman's entire ribcage had caved in. No blood oozed from the millions of shards of glass embedded in her naked body.

Or from the entrails dragging along the floor.

And my shoe's heel was still embedded in her crotch.

I backed away, only to have her buddy join her in stalking me toward the stage.

"Get behind us, lady!"

Two hard bodies pulled me up onto the platform and inserted themselves between me and the zombies, so I wasn't sure which man had spoken. I did have a very nice view of the backsides of Mr. Cowboy and Mr. Policeman, but they were about to die for their chivalry.

There was a loud crack as Phil broke one of the zombie's arms.

"Tiff-*cough*-Tiffany! Quit-*choke*-messing with that-*cough, cough*-corpse and call for backup!"

Phil's order seemed to get the attention of the remaining zombies. Their undead stares turned toward Tiffany, who dived under our old table to retrieve her purse. Once she was clear, Phil electrocuted the dead boy still trying to throttle her.

While my dancers and I backed away from the shambling zombies, Bebe took a running jump onto the other side of the stage. How she did it in the red leather mini-skirt and heels, I'll never know. Behind her, smoke trailed from the corpse she had charcoaled. "Sam! Get their attention back on you!" She skidded to a stop next to me and swiped my damaged cheek with both hands, sending fire across my overloaded nerves. "And get the Norms off the stage!"

My rough shove sent the boys sliding across the polished wood on their perfect pecs. I'd apologize for the friction burns if I survived tonight. Clapping my hands, I yelled, "Tiffany! Phone!"

Her throw from a kneeling position under a table would have done any professional quarterback proud. The little cell arched over the heads of the zombies. However, my attempted catch would have ended my career as a wide receiver. The bit of plastic and metal slipped through my nerveless fingers to shatter on the stage.

It did get the three remaining zombies' attention. Mr. Naked joined my two assailants. Apparently, he had too much fat for Mai to cut off because, other than his now missing hands, the rest of his limbs were working.

Bebe appeared at my elbow. "Back up two steps."

Fear made me a bitch. "You'd better have a fucking good plan."

"I do." Under her breath, she added, "If it works."

I did as the doctor ordered and glanced down. Under the blue stage lights, the stuff smeared in a circle around us looked black. A hard gulp rattled my throat when I realized I saw my own blood. It was a heck of a lot of blood, too.

The zombies crawled on stage, their movements stiff and awkward but still menacing.

"When I tell you, jump left out of the circle," Bebe whispered.

Perspiration soaked my little black silk number as the zombies lumbered closer and closer. Since I'd died, I'd ruined more clothes with more bodily fluids than humanly imaginable. Focusing on my wardrobe kept me from pissing my panties when Mr. Naked reached for my neck.

"Now!"

At Bebe's shout, I launched my body to the side. Raw agony blacked out my vision for an instant. I blinked tears out of my eyes. Or maybe it was blood. The zombies had lumbered into the circle Bebe had drawn. As one, they turned their blank faces toward me.

With both of us clear, the doctor slapped a hand on the blood circle, muttering alien words under her breath. At least, they seemed alien to my pain-filled head. A hemisphere of golden light sprang into existence.

And the zombies collapsed in a heap. No movement. Not even a twitch.

The same couldn't be said for the other five zombies. Even the three fried corpses were trying to crawl, except ash and chunks of meat fell at a rate that almost made them comical instead of threatening. Mai gave Anne one of her swords, and the two of them proceeded to hack the remaining bodies to bits.

Tiffany crawled out from under her table just as the smoke wafting from the crispies triggered the sprinklers. "Anybody else got their cell phone?"

Chapter 12

The back of the limo lightened despite the UV film as dawn poked her head over the mountains behind us. I'd never been so glad to see the "Welcome to California" sign in my life.

I leaned my head against the cool glass of the limo's window. The smashed cheekbones had healed over the last few hours, but I still had a ringing migraine thanks to the telekinetic stunt I'd pulled at the Rio.

Mai's umpteenth-great-grandfather Kensai Osaka and his boyfriend Jamal had originally planned on hitching a ride back to Los Angeles with us for the wedding. What the boys hadn't planned to do was clean up mutilated corpses at a strip club.

It may have been business as usual for the rest of the supernaturals, but I was at a total loss. No one I knew ever had zombies show up at her future sister-in-law's bachelorette party.

I eyed the physician seated across from me. "Are you sure, Bebe?" I couldn't stop asking for the umpteenth time.

"Yes, I'm sure!" Her ever-calm demeanor cracked, but it felt so good to share the headache. "I've always been taught that real zombies are impossible."

Next to the doctor, Kensai stroked his chin. "Something animated those corpses, Bebe. Perhaps the victims gave permission to sacrifice their lives to be reanimated. If so, it wouldn't be true black magick."

Bebe closed her eyes and let her head drop back against the

leather seat, but her clenched fists revealed her exasperation. "Goddess, how many times do I have to tell you people magick is neither black or white."

I wanted to say Caesar's Vegas lieutenant had a point, but I also didn't want a fireball shoved up my ass.

Jamal reached through the partition and patted her shoulder. "Take it easy, girl. No one's questioning your expertise. We just need answers."

"Perhaps, Grandfather, we're looking at this problem from the wrong angle." Mai met my eyes for an instant in the rearview mirror before returning her attention to the freeway.

Something about her look sent a shiver up my spine, which ended with a spike of pain in my frontal lobe. Unfortunately, there wasn't anything in Bebe's bag that would work on me. Damn nanites.

"What do you mean?" Kensai twisted on the side seat to look at her, almond eyes wide. The entire fourteen generations removed thing still unnerved me, especially when he looked more like her baby brother home fresh from college.

"We're agreed that the . . ." She paused, searching for a politically correct term.

I sighed. "You can say it, Mai. Zombies."

She nodded. "Very well. The zombies were fixated on Sam. Perhaps if we can discover the reason for their attraction to her, we can backtrack the magick to their animator." She cleared her throat. "There is another possibility though."

I swallowed the desire to smack our driver's head. "Spit it out, Mai. No one back here is in the mood for twenty questions."

She flicked another glance in the rearview mirror before she said, "Perhaps you're responsible for their animation."

"Hey! They were trying to kill me!" Pain spiked again when anger-based adrenaline flooded my bloodstream. Or maybe it was the fact Mai had voiced the same ugly thought that popped into my brain while I shoveled body parts into buckets.

"You've already exhibited talents other than vampiric ones," Bebe pointed out.

"Yeah, and it was no secret Selene and Mallory experimented on weres and witches as well as vamps when they were designing the nanites." Heat edged my voice.

"Perhaps you are evolving beyond your original programming," Mai said.

I waited for Tiffany to make some snarky Trekkie comment while everyone digested Mai's suggestion. And waited. And waited.

Tiffany sat next to Phil, tucked in the corner of the rear bench seat, arms wrapped around her knees, nearly motionless except for the slight expansion of her chest muscles when she drew a breath. From the look in her eyes as she stared out the window, she wasn't anywhere in the state of California.

Before we left Vegas, Bebe had "borrowed" a sonogram machine to check both Tiffany and the fetus. I knew she wouldn't have risked either patient by clearing our return drive, but Tiffany's withdrawn behavior was freaking me out.

"Tiffany?" I whispered.

Gray, gooey fear washed through my migraine-shredded shields when she met my gaze. "All I could think last night was they were going to kill my baby, Sam."

"But that's just it." We all turn to look at Anne. "Those things didn't hurt anyone unless the person was between them and Sam."

"But—" Bebe started.

"No." Anne edged forward on the leather. "Think about it. The first one? Who came out with the dancers? He knocked those ladies over because they were between him and Sam, but he didn't deliberately hurt them. Yes—" she held up a finger when Phil opened her mouth "—he backhanded the lady with the beehive. But she jumped in front of him and hit him first. Same with those two, um—" Pink tinted her cheeks as she obviously remembered the half-naked dancers.

For the first time in hours, animation returned to Tiffany's face. "She's right. The rest of the zombies came through the audience. I don't remember any commotion behind us before that one with the crushed ribs decked Sam."

"Maybe because you were too busy playing with the scenery," Phil teased.

"No," Bebe said, waving an index finger at Phil. "They're onto something. They ignored Tiffany until you told her to call for help."

I could almost see the hamsters spinning the wheels of her mind into overdrive.

"There's a common thread here. All of the corpses were fresh, too. Less than twenty-four hours dead. And they all came from the county morgue."

Kensai grunted. "Don't remind me. You will all be getting Clark County morgue scrubs for your next one hundred birthdays to pay them back for the damage we did." He had a team take the chopped and fried bits, along with the three more intact corpses, back to the morgue once his people had figured out who was missing some bodies. The Vegas vampires then used their whammy to fudge memories and clear the building. As far as L.V.F.D. was concerned, a chemical flash fire had damaged the cold storage room. The only fatality was the assistant coroner, who'd been on duty at the time.

Something about the whole situation still smelled rotten, and it wasn't the zombie stench all six of us ladies had scrubbed off before we climbed back in the limo. Okay, a couple of somethings.

"Giving Mai the benefit of the doubt here," I began, "if I *accidentally* animated those bodies, why would I send them after myself?"

"Suicide?" Tiffany offered.

I stuck out my tongue at her.

"You have been under a great deal of stress lately," Phil said. Soft, blue eyes watched me. "Maybe their animation was accidental. Maybe it was an unconscious attempt to avoid the wedding and the decision of whether to leave Los Angeles."

Jamal grinned, fangs too white against his dark skin. "I've got my fingers crossed you'll leave."

Kensai took pity on what I was sure was a very puzzled look on my face. "The contingency plan is already in place."

"What contingency plan?" I didn't want to know the answer.

"You and Duncan moving here." Jamal's expression turned serious. "Is there anything I can do to sweeten the pot? I miss Los Angeles, and I hear you've got a thing for dark chocolate." He waggled his eyebrows.

"Jamal."

The Moor shut up at Kensai's admonition, but the urge to scream filled my aching head. Was this the real reason Duncan asked me to move in with him? Just another manipulation in his bag of tricks?

I couldn't deal. Not now. Instead I focused on my other concern about the attack. "What about the coroner? Bebe, you've said blood magick is one of the strongest forms."

She nodded. Her fine black eyebrows knitted in worry.

"Would it make a difference what species' blood is used?"

She shook her head. "No, and I used yours to set the circle. It worked just fine. I don't get where you're going with this, Sam."

I waved a hand. "Nowhere, I guess. I thought maybe supernatural blood might be more powerful than Normal blood. I could have sworn I smelled were on the assistant coroner back at the club."

Again, Bebe shook her head. "If the coroner was a werewolf, which she wasn't, it wouldn't make any difference as far as blood magick is performed."

This would be so much easier if I could think through this damn headache. I leaned forward, rubbing my temples. "We still don't know how she died."

"You mean, other than the gaping hole where her trachea used to be?" Phil's wry smile did nothing to alleviate the anxiety aggravating the ache in my brain.

I blew out a deep breath, trying to shove the awful vision of the poor woman out of my mind's eye. "What I mean is, did she get in the way of the zombies like Anne pointed out? Or was she sacrificed to animate the other corpses?"

"I didn't detect any blood magick—" Bebe muttered through gritted teeth. She squeezed her eyes shut and pressed the heels of her hands against the lids. "Okay," she said before dropping her hands to her lap and fixing me with a pointed stare. "Assuming your theory has merit, yes, it is possible that she was a sacrifice. But—" She held up an index finger when I opened my mouth. "A blood spell practitioner would need all of her blood for something of that magnitude. That usually means a draining cut to the throat, not to mention how it taints the magickal energy . . ." She frowned as she worked through the idea. "I didn't see her before Phil had to fry her. Tell me more about her injury."

Phil and I repeated all the gory details we could remember from the insanity.

"That sounds more like werewolf or vamp damage," Jamal offered when we were finished. "Sam, you said you thought you detected were musk. Did anybody else? Because all I smelled at the club was dead human and fear."

Phil, Anne and Kensai shook their heads.

We all fell silent as the limo rolled another couple of miles from the site of Tiffany's disastrous bachelorette party.

"It could be a vampire," Anne said. "Maybe some of Selene's people who escaped. She'd been trying to wipe out Duncan's family for centuries, and it's no secret Duncan killed Selene to save Sam. In that kind of, um, crowd it would be hard to distinguish individual vampire scents."

Gotta love a mass of horny women. I kept the thought to myself though because the limo grew even quieter at the implication that Caesar's twin sister was still wreaking havoc even after her death.

"No," I finally said. "This was aimed at me personally."

"Uh, Sam?" Tiffany raised an eyebrow. "Selene's attack on you a couple of months ago was pretty fucking personal."

I shook my head. "Not the same. I was her experiment that escaped as far as she was concerned. Okay, I happened to be sleeping with her ex-boyfriend, too." I didn't like thinking about the bitch, or her Normal partner, Tyrone Mallory. Maybe no dead person ever likes thinking about the assholes who killed her. Especially if they brought her back from the dead to be their immortal prototype to display to potential human customers. All the glam of vampires with none of the nastier side effects, like a severe aversion to ultra-violet and a liquid diet.

Except the pain of the transformation made my current migraine feel like a Hawaiian vacation. I still woke up from nightmares of what they did to me, cold sweat drenching my nightshirt. One of the reasons I started the break from sex with Duncan was to work on sleeping alone again. I couldn't depend on him forever to deal with the post-nightmare shakes.

"Besides—" I shrugged, trying to regain my emotional equilibrium. "—she's dead. If anyone would hate me now, it'd be the fairies." I jerked upright. "Wait a minute! What about fairy creatures? Are there any that could tear out a person's throat like that?"

Phil grinned. "Maybe a ticked-off reindeer?"

Tiffany flipped the bird at her former guardian.

David tapped the steering wheel in time to Kanye West on the digital player as they wove through the Los Angeles rush hour traffic back to their hotel. Frankie still wasn't talking to him, but the rising sun promised a brand new chance in his quest. He'd approached the situation with Ridgeway from the wrong angle. Frankie had been right. Brute force in a public arena hadn't worked. All right, it failed dismally. If she was really a zombie, he needed an alternate idea.

Grabbing the spiral notebook off the dash, he glanced at her schedule. Wedding rehearsal at her parents' place tonight, followed immediately by the rehearsal dinner at Anthony's. He grinned. Getting into Anthony's wouldn't be a problem. Getting back into the kitchen would take some serious sweet talk and greasing of palms.

Yeah, on any court, a player needed a Plan B.

"We should go to your old place," Frankie muttered.

David turned to stare at the were. A horn blasted next to his ear, and he jerked the steering wheel, whipping the rental back into the correct lane. "Damn, man! You don't talk for hours, and *that's* the first thing you say!"

"I shouldn't be around Normals." Something shook in the unflappable were's voice.

"That woman was an accident, Frankie. No one's going to find out about her. They've already burned all the evidence." The Las Vegas radio stations had talked of nothing but the early morning fire at the morgue, which was why he'd switched to the digital player long before they'd hit the state line. Supernatural standard procedure demanded the destruction of evidence, but he had to admire the Augustine Coven's efficiency in cleaning up the fiasco at the Rio.

"You don't know that!"

"Well, I sure as hell don't want to go back to—" He swallowed hard. It'd been almost two years since Brandon walked out his front door. He shouldn't care—

"Then why don't you just sell the fucking place and be done with it?" Frankie bit back.

David tightened his grip on the wheel. He'd been asking himself the same question for a very long time, but something in him couldn't quite let go of hope. Maybe part of him saw himself moving back to L.A. once he retired.

Maybe because he saw himself living there with someone else. He'd already had the light blocking drapes installed to cover the massive windows overlooking the pool months ago, along with UV film on all glass.

"You're right," he said quietly. "No sense staying at the hotel when I've got a perfectly good house in Los Angeles."

For the first time since the accident at the morgue, Frankie's tight frame relaxed. "Only thing you've said that's made sense all week."

Neither man said another word the rest of the drive into the city.

Chapter 13

Yvonne scanned the hotel lobby crowd with her Sight. No supernaturals. Good. Slipping down a quiet corridor, she spotted the old-fashioned pay phones. Any calls from their suite would show up on the bill, and she couldn't risk Davy or Frankie borrowing her cell phone and checking the call log.

She hated going behind her brother's back, but his obsession with the vampire was getting out of hand. He refused to say where he and Frankie had gone last night. And the mix of ginger and mold surrounding him when they'd come back this morning had been too thick to ignore. He was practicing again. The coven's binding hadn't held.

Her hand shook when she lifted the receiver. It took three tries to insert the coins, but she punched in the old number without hesitation. If Davy wouldn't listen to her, only one other person could talk him out of this madness.

"Hello?"

Her breath caught in her throat. She forced it out. Davy's sanity, maybe even his life rode on this slim chance. "Brandon?"

"Yvonne?"

"Yes." She gulped. "I need your help." Tears threatened. Davy would be so furious if he knew, but he'd listen to Brandon.

"Anything for you."

"We're in Los Angeles."

For the few seconds of silence, she wondered if Brandon would hang up on her. "He never stays here. Did he decide to sell?"

"No, *chére.*" Nails dug into her palm. "He wants to stay at the house. I—"

"I'll get my things packed."

"Brandon, no. I want you to be there when we arrive."

"I—I can't, Yvonne. I love him, but—" The silence weighed between them. Finally, Brandon sighed. "Thanks for letting me stay here. I close on my new place next week. A hotel will do until then."

"Brandon—"

"I'm sorry, Yvonne." A click, then static filled her ear.

She leaned her head against the cool stainless steel of the divider. Now what was she going to do?

"A bad dress rehearsal is always a good sign." That statement earned me glares from the entire bridal party, not just Mom. I shrugged. "That's what Matthew Broderick told me."

Tiffany slapped a makeshift bouquet of soggy toilet paper flowers in my gut. "Ferris Bueller is not running my wedding," she bit out through clenched teeth. She stomped out of the banquet room at Anthony's to begin the run-through for the fifth time.

Unfortunately, the toilet paper wasn't the only thing soggy. The entire wedding party was a little damp. A freak thunderstorm had started as Tiffany walked down the staked-out aisle in Mom and Dad's backyard. A power surge from the storm blew the backyard lighting system, a necessary item for nighttime nuptials. And they weren't the first problems we had today.

Neither the tent, the runner or any of the chairs and tables had arrived at Mom and Dad's at noon as promised. The rental company claimed they had no record of the reservation. Then the florist called to say a malfunction with their refrigeration units had destroyed their entire flower supply, including the arrangements she'd already put together for the wedding. She promised she'd have something for us by tomorrow, but the substitute flowers weren't acceptable to Mom. Dad pulled the phone out of her hand when she threatened to shove a cactus up the florist's ass.

Mai and Miko had whipped together beautiful origami bouquets made from toilet paper of all things, just so the bridesmaids had something to practice with.

But Mom's tension hadn't started with the florist. Phil had intervened on Tiffany's behalf in the wedding dress search earlier in the week, pissing Mom off to no end. None of us knew what the two of them had picked out, but Tiffany was happy, which satisfied Max. While Mom bitched about Wal-Mart specials, I prayed the unseen matching bridesmaid dresses weren't totally hideous.

When Caesar suggested we adjourn to Anthony's a little early to practice there, we all sighed in relief. Except no one kept track of Reverend Mitchell, a buddy of Dad's from the country club, who'd agreed to perform the ceremony. He'd taken a wrong turn and arrived a half hour behind the rest of us.

The situation hadn't improved after he finally showed up. Anne, of all people, had tripped walking down our practice aisle and fallen flat on her face. Greg Evans, Max's best friend and best man, forgot Tiffany's ring. And Phil had rammed a door into Alex Stanton's nose, breaking it. We played it off as just a nose bleed so the Normals wouldn't suspect anything when the usher/vampire healed within minutes.

Given Phil and the sexy blond enforcer's history, I don't think that "accident" had anything to do with our stream of bad luck. Luckily, everyone kept their mouths shut until Mom stomped back into the banquet room to restart the canned music.

"This is too much for coincidence," Bebe said as we followed Tiffany out of the banquet room. She looked over her shoulder. "Anne?"

"With the storm, there's ozone everywhere," the vampire grumbled. "How would I know if there's a spell? You'd see it before I'd smell it."

"Sam's right. A bad rehearsal is a sign of good luck," Miko said.

"Only in the theater," Bebe muttered.

"All of you need to shut the fuck up," Tiffany growled.

"Tiffany." Duncan's eyes glowed neon green in the dark hallway. Lucky for us, it was just us girls and he wasn't in full vamp-out mode.

His gaze shifted from the pissy bride to me. The two of us hadn't been alone since I had arrived at Mom and Dad's, deliberately late, I admit.

I wasn't sure how much of his irritation was the same as everyone's general bad mood or because I walked away from him Wednesday night and continued avoiding him. Despite Jake's advice, I was scared to find out Duncan's real feelings. Maybe I'd pushed him too far by refusing to talk to him for the last week. Maybe I'd screwed up by not giving him the chance to explain. Maybe I'd lost the man I loved.

Maybe I was still furious because he'd already made plans to move us to Las Vegas if I didn't tell Mom and Dad the truth.

More than anything, I hated other people telling me how to live my life. I'd hated Mom trying to shove me into her Beverly Hills princess mold. I'd hated Dad's not-so-subtle pressure to go to law school. I'd hated being compared to my Pulitzer-winning brother while I was on the freaking high school paper.

Honestly, if I never saw my parents again, it wouldn't cause a sleepless night. As opposed to the severe insomnia I'd suffered the last week because I couldn't snuggle up to Duncan and talk out my worries. He would have stroked my hair, whispered reassurances in my ear, made me feel normal again.

Ah, damn. Jake was right. I did love Duncan, and my chicken-shit commitment issues had reared their ugly heads.

And honestly, I'd miss Dad. Maybe Mom, too.

The music started again, and first Bebe, then Anne, and finally

Miko glided through the door. I counted off the beats and had taken my first step when Duncan seized my arm, whirled me around and planted a kiss on my mouth.

A very thorough and passionate kiss.

I had the vague sensation of something cold and wet pressing against my stomach in contrast to the liquid heat deep inside me.

He broke our contact. Green eyes gleamed in the dim light. "We *will* talk after the rehearsal."

"Sam."

Mom's hissing and waving at the doorway barely penetrated the fog in my head. Luckily, she was too intent on me to notice Duncan's eyes. I floated down the aisle, smashed toilet paper flowers glued to the front of my dress, and took my place by Reverend Mitchell. Turning, I watched Duncan escort Tiffany into the room. The look he gave me could have melted steel. I loved him. I wanted to trust him.

I didn't know if I could.

The entire wedding party got through one whole run-through without any more screw-ups, and Reverend Mitchell declared it a raving success. Everyone either headed for the bathrooms or the bar while Anthony's staff started wheeling in the buffet. Except for me. I snatched a handful of hors d'oeuvres from a passing tray and crammed them into my mouth. The taste of the stuffed mushrooms was a little off, almost like taking a drink of Coke after eating an Andes mint. I tried to figure out the unusual flavor when Duncan appeared at my elbow, millimeters away but not touching.

"May I speak with you outside, Samantha?" The heated look in his eyes belied the formal tone of his voice.

I nodded, not daring to answer with my packed mouth. Grabbing a handful of pigs-in-blankets, I followed Duncan through the main dining room of the restaurant and out the front doors.

The parking lot pavement shone under the security halogens, and everything had that fresh rain smell. Everything, except Duncan. Sandalwood rolled off him, giving the night an exotic scent. Once we were well away from the valets, he turned and asked, "Are you all right?"

I blinked. Out of everything I expected him to say when I had rehearsed tonight's encounter over and over in my head, a stiff inquiry to my wellbeing was not it. Swallowing the last of the funky tasting mushrooms, I said, "I'm fine." At a total loss as to where this conversation was going after that fabulous kiss he'd laid on me, I added, "How are you?" before popping the a couple of the mini hot dogs in my mouth.

He shoved a hand through his dark locks, a sure sign he was already exasperated with me. "Bebe and Tiffany said you were injured last night. Bebe suspected a fractured skull on top of everything else, but she said you refused to let her check."

Tattletales.

I finished chewing, the dogs a hard ball as they went down, and crossed my arms, only to be reminded of the soaked paper flowers pasted to my mid-section. Peeling toilet paper off my cotton floral print dress kept my eyes and hands occupied while I answered. "Tiffany should have been her priority. Beating a zombie's skull in was a little too much exertion for a pregnant chick."

The thick foliage surrounding the restaurant muffled the street traffic. Otherwise, we were both silent for a long time, except for the faint squish and plop of the toilet paper hitting the concrete.

"I understand you are upset with me—" He held up a hand when I looked up and opened my mouth. "Let me finish."

Crossing my arms over my chest again, I closed my mouth. I'd give him his chance. He'd better make it pretty damn good, though that kiss had gone miles in muting my anger.

"Caesar is concerned about last night's attack. We agree with the ladies' assessment that it was aimed specifically at you."

My heart dropped at his words. "Caesar is," not "I am." Hugging my arms tighter, I closed my eyes, so he wouldn't see how his words cut my soul.

Duncan continued his relentless dissection of my heart. "Caesar recommended, and I concur, that for your safety, you move in with him and Bebe for the time being. With the estate's twenty-four-hour guard, it is unlikely another attack will occur. If it does, you will have a more than adequate defense."

This wasn't my boyfriend concerned about my safety. This was the chief enforcer of the Augustine Coven analyzing a potential threat to a member. The difference sliced the still beating organ out of my chest and served it up, hot and steaming. And with all this zombie crap, he didn't even want me staying with him. I swallowed the huge lump of tears forming in my chest. Or maybe it was the dogs coming back up.

After clearing my throat a couple of times, I managed to croak out a "No."

"This is not a game, Samantha." His eyes brightened under the halogens. "Someone tried to kill you."

"And who waved me in front of the fucking fairies like a red flag." My voice was flat, my angry tears solidifying into a ball of ice in my gut.

"Bebe does not believe either of the Sidhe Courts committed last night's attack."

"Oh, really? Dr. There's-No-Such-Thing-As-Real-Zombies is absolutely su-u-ure the fairies aren't involved? That makes me feel so much better." I wasn't about to point out Duke Miller had set a trap for me and didn't bother to trip it because he deemed me inconsequential. Truth was, by focusing on the fairies, I ignored the real fear. That somehow those shuffling nightmares had been attracted to me because I was one of them.

Dammit, James Bond did *not* have these kinds of problems. Why couldn't I have a nuclear bomb to diffuse?

Duncan rolled his eyes in a passable imitation of Tiffany. "Bloody hell, woman! For once in your life, listen to reason—"

"I am being totally reasonable." Numbness seeped in, not replacing my anger but surrounding, enveloping it. "I'm not taking the chance of someone getting hurt or killed at the mansion because they *accidentally* got in the way of a bunch of walking corpses."

The stone mask dropped, along with his canines. Anger flamed his eyes into raw neon. "You were fortunate last night."

"I know." And I couldn't help but wonder at the weirdness of the role reversal, my voice remaining calm, his rising. "I had three enforcers, a witch and a demigoddess with me, and we could barely handle eight of them. If there are more the next time, we'd be fucked. I'd be fucked. And I don't want my future niece or nephew, much less anyone else I care about, to be following me down that long, dark tunnel." I sucked a huge breath of rare damp air to stave off the tears hovering behind my lids. "With my luck, the light on the other side would be a Red Roof Inn."

No hint of a smile appeared on his face. Maybe it was another twenty-first century colloquialism that sailed over his head.

He threw his hands up. "I cannot—"

"Hey, if y'all are finish necking—"

At the Texas drawl behind us, we both turned to glare at Alex.

"Or not. Dinner's started." The poor vampire pivoted on his boot heels and raced back to the front door at more or less human speed after the matching death glares we shot at him.

"You will obey a direct order, Samantha," Duncan said. I turned to face him again. The stone mask was back in place.

His words should have royally pissed me off. The best I could muster was a half-hearted bird. "You're not my boss."

"Caesar is. Or are you forfeiting his protection?"

The numbness settled deep in my bones. Caesar's protection. With it, Duncan would guard me, not because he wanted to, but because Caesar ordered it. Without that kind of security, I was on my own. I searched his face, looking for a hint of love, compassion. Hell, at this point even a little of the lust from earlier. Didn't he care? Or had our whole relationship just been an act, a way for the Augustine Coven to control a rare resource?

Disappointed at his lack of emotion, I shrugged. "Whatever." The threatened tears disappeared under the weight of losing everything. My job. My so-called life. Duncan. Everything real sunk into a deep morass of non-feeling nothingness.

He muttered something under his breath I didn't catch. Maybe I didn't want to catch it. I couldn't summon the desire to care either. He spun on his heel at my non-response and stomped back into the restaurant.

Standing there in the parking lot, I wasn't sure what to do next. I hardly felt like partying, but the maid of honor should probably have her ass at the rehearsal dinner. A soft breeze ruffled my hair as I tried to decide what to do next. It was difficult to think though, and I couldn't blame that on the lingering headache. Styrofoam worms had invaded my skull, making everything distant, vague.

The faint thump of drums traveled on the wind. Or maybe it was a stereo bass. Tha-thump. Tha-thump. Like a heartbeat. I felt the pounding through the pavement more than heard it. Some idiot with more money than sense who'd turned the entire rear of his over-sized vehicle into one gigantic sub-woofer. The sound/feel seemed the only thing connected to reality.

I took a step backward. I should go inside to the party. Then someone called my name.

Pivoting slowly, I scanned the parking lot. Nothing there, except one of the valets taking a smoke break. And he was too busy puffing away to have spoken.

Another difficult step backward, but I could have been wading through cotton. The pounding became more insistent. Not a request, a demand. It must be followed.

I shook my head. *My imagination. I'm letting last night's creepies get to me.*

But I couldn't move. The numbness I felt while talking to Duncan turned into a deep lethargy. I tried to will my feet to move, but it was almost like my brain had short-circuited. Were the nanites malfunctioning? Was I finally dying?

No curiosity, much less fear.

I felt nothing. Nothing, except . . .

Need arose. A desire to follow that strange beat swallowed whatever thought I might have had. I started across the concrete, passing the valets and their little traffic cones. Something summoned and all I knew was that I must answer it.

Chapter 14

The screeching brakes and annoying honk should have made me jump. In the back of my fuzzy awareness, the noises meant danger, but I couldn't gather the strength to heed the signs. Headlights flashed in weird colors, chocolate pie and lemon meringue. The flavors in my eyes were much more interesting.

A head popped out of the driver's window of the Mercedes. I waited for the pie dough skull to fall on the pavement from the weight of obsidian-framed diamonds covering its eyes. A single finger rose, bisecting the length of black and white.

The universal gesture registered.

A director. One I should know, but I couldn't think past the pounding beat in my gut, in my blood, in my head. All I knew was the little man in his car and all his desserts were in my way. Another high-pitched beeping. My ears hurt. Centipedes in the shape of music notes crawled out of the metal box, and hands slapped over my ears in a vain attempt to keep them from flying into my brain. I struck the metal box making the irritating cheeps. Steam rose and I kicked the red metal box aside.

I continued on, leaving the raspberry sorbet lights behind. I didn't belong with the sweet lights anyway. I belonged in the dark, the rich earth swallowing me. A satisfying meal of succulent meat and steaming blood as I returned to my real mother's welcoming arms. Wet greenery and decay filled my nostrils, the scent of home.

Dark figures rose around me, surrounding me, welcoming me as one of their own. I could sleep now, safe and warm.

A lightning flash of pain. I screamed.

And woke up from the dream in the middle of a nightmare, surrounded by zombies trying to rip me apart.

I lashed out with my left fist, my right arm useless. I didn't want to think about the white gleaming in the middle of the shredded bicep. Dust exploded along with a skull. Unlike the party at the Rio, these things were so dead they weren't juicy anymore.

Sickly black diamond and red haze played along the edges of the zombies. I elbowed another corpse. Amid the mold and powdered flesh I inhaled was the acrid smell of ozone. *Damn it, Bebe!* It *was* magick that animated these freakin' things!

I kicked, jabbed and clawed, but it was useless. They tore into me, ripping my dress, leaving bloody furrows in my skin. A couple of them even left their brittle fingernails embedded in my body.

Don't panic! A scared giggle burbled in my throat while I popped another skull off a crumbling neck. Ford and Arthur never encountered zombies in their hitchhiking adventures.

An eerie silence enveloped the whole bizarre scene, punctuated by my grunts as I fought them. I tried to yell for help, only to have some elderly woman shove her entire desiccated fist into my mouth the second it opened. I gagged, trying to spit out the bones and dried flesh even as the hand, severed when I jerked my head away, struggled to yank out my tongue.

I couldn't even call out telepathically, my head still aching from the incident at the Rio. Where was the fucking prince who was supposed to rescue me? I'd settle for a duke. Duncan had been a duke once upon a time. Why wasn't he here?

Because I told him to go away, that's why.

I swung and flailed, blocking the attempted gouging of my eyeballs. Desperate to stay upright, because if I went down now, I was a goner.

The nanites couldn't keep up with the injuries the corpses were inflicting, though the tiny robots kept me on my feet in the chaos. It turned to my advantage because the zombies started having trouble grasping my blood-slicked skin. I kicked one guy's knees out. He landed with a crunch, breaking into several pieces on the damp concrete.

My few seconds of luck didn't last. One of them landed a nasty blow on my back, and I crashed to the cold, hard pavement. Another stomped on my calf when I tried to roll clear. The bones broke with an audible snap.

Pain twisted into fury. I snatched a thigh bone of the zombie I'd knocked over and started swinging with everything I had left. My offensive cleared enough space for me to climb awkwardly upright on my one good leg.

"C'mon, you motherfuckers!" My voice croaked with the dust I hadn't been able to cough out. "You want another piece of me? Come and get it!"

With each swing of my makeshift weapon, I'd scream, "Die!" Okay, it was more of a hoarse whisper, but the words added to my temper as I whaled and smashed the zombies. Bits and pieces flew around me. They didn't belong here. It was a freaking time of celebration, of life. Tiffany's face, stark with terror, flashed in my mind's eye, begging me not to let them kill her baby. I didn't stop pounding them. Not until—

"Sam?"

I whirled. Mai stood there, her eyes wide with fear, her semi-automatic in both hands. Pointed at me.

I looked around me. The zombies weren't moving. Not even a twitch. Just body parts scattered over this little corner of concrete behind the restaurant's dumpsters.

Then I looked down at my body. Blood mixed with grave grime to coat what was left of my skin. My dress hung in tatters off my shaking shoulders. I had no clue where my sandals were. The adrenaline started fading, leaving pain in its wake. I knew it was about to get worse. A hell of a lot worse. Not like the time I'd been shot point-blank in the chest two months ago. The nerve receptors in my brain weren't a repair priority with a fist-sized hole between my breasts. My pain perception had changed since then. The crushed lower leg bones and black spots in front of my eyes announced how much.

Maybe I'd get lucky tonight and pass out first.

Facing Mai again, I croaked, "Get the Normals out of the banquet room. M-my parents can't see me like this."

Rubber on wet asphalt squealed behind me. Mai rushed past me and dived through the shrubbery. I hopped on the one intact leg behind her, the small branches digging into my raw flesh. The boutique next door was dark, except for taillights as a sedan peeled onto the street. Mai leveled her gun at the escaping car, but I pushed it down with my good hand.

"Never mind. I saw the license plate." And the two assholes in the car and I were going to have a very serious talk about the misuse of magick when I got a hold of them.

Mai holstered her gun and reached out to sling my left arm over her shoulder. With her help, I limped to the kitchen door.

And this time I knew it wasn't my imagination. Mixed with the odor of grilled steak, tilapia and grave dust was the distinctive musk of werewolf.

<h1 style="text-align:center">Chapter 15</h1>

I flashed Anthony Monroe a weak but sincere smile when the restaurant owner set another bottle of Jose Cuervo Gold on the floor next to where I sat. Thank God, the zombie attack had happened at a Family-owned establishment. Tables were shoved aside in the private room where the aborted rehearsal dinner had started to make room for me and my impromptu trauma team.

I shoved my sixth bottle into Anthony's waiting hand before I put the seventh to my lips and chugged. With a sigh of resignation, I set the empty down on the floor and wiped my mouth with the back of my hand. The room gave a lazy merry-go-round spin. I was pretty close to human drunk with my nanites overloaded from the zombie-inflicted injuries.

Trying not to look at my bizarrely angled left leg, I reclined on the plush carpet. "Do it." I really could have skipped the torture, but if James Bond could survive it, I could, too.

Bebe shoved a thick silicone cooking spatula between my teeth. Biting down, I closed my eyes against what was coming. Hands braced my shoulders and the less damaged leg. One of the vamps, from the room temperature touch on my injured leg, twisted the half-healed bones.

I jerked as they broke again, my scream turned into a muffled groan as I bit through Anthony's expensive utensil. I could feel Bebe working quickly to realign the leg so it would heal straight this time. As fast as the nanites could regrow bones, she wouldn't bother with a healing spell. It didn't exactly make my next five minutes Disneyland though.

Cool hands held me still as the pain raged through my body. Cool, except for the warm touch on my right shoulder, which had to be Phil. She whispered in my ear, but the agony turned her words into gibberish.

When the pain faded to a bearable ache, I blinked the tears out of my eyes and spit the rest of the spatula out of my mouth. At Bebe's nod, Caesar, Anne, Alex and Phil released me. My stomach chose that moment to rumble. Loud and strong and continuous.

Phil and Alex help me into a chair, and I started shoveling food into my mouth before Alex had scooted the chair to the table.

It felt like something inside me would gnaw its way out. I couldn't eat fast enough. The second I cleared one plate, someone thrust another in front of me. I didn't know what I was eating, only swallowed and took the next bite. Anthony's voice called back to the kitchen, but the words were vague in the all-consuming hunger. There was no taste to anything I half-chewed before swallowing. I didn't bother with forks or knives, ripping, tearing and stuffing with my bare hands. Anything to quell the monster growling its displeasure in my gut.

"Damn. I thought my pups could eat."

I looked up, realized I had half a quail hanging out of my mouth, and pulled it out before I reached for a napkin.

John Lannigan, Packmaster of the Los Angeles werewolves, stood there, grinning at me. If Caesar reminded me of a young Marlon Brando, then John was Harvey Kietel. Average height, with thick graying hair and naked power in his frame. So secure in that power, he didn't bother with an escort. One of those men who could be your best friend as easily as your worst enemy. His piercing brown eyes examined me.

I swallowed the last bite of quail before turning my gaze to Caesar. "What's he doing here?"

John's eyes narrowed. "If there's a rogue wolf in my territory, it's my business, little girl."

I reached for another dinner roll, but kept an eye on the werewolf. "How do I know he's a rogue?"

John stepped forward at my insult, threat obvious in the subvocal growl. All he needed was his hair standing straight up.

I'd had enough though. Enough beatings in twenty-four hours. Enough grave crap in my mouth and under my skin. Enough pain.

Simply *enough*.

I shoved back my chair and stood, meeting his glare. The effect was probably diminished by the roll stuffed in my mouth and the fact I tottered on one leg.

Caesar stepped between us. "Sam. John." His head swiveled back and forth, catching our eyes. "Until we know what exactly is going on, no one is going to do anything stupid." His smile wasn't meant to be reassuring with the bared fangs.

I chewed the roll slowly. John, I could take out before he shifted, even with the half-knitted leg bones and most of the meat on my right arm missing. Caesar was another story. He was the oldest and most powerful vampire on the North American continent. Even the other two U.S. vampire masters would think twice before going mano a mano with him.

I sank back into the chair and reached for the bowl of steamed broccoli Anne handed to me. But I didn't take my eyes off John for a second as I alternated bites of quail with the vegetables.

Bebe sighed and wiped her hands on another napkin. "If you two can remain calm, I'm going outside to have a look at those remains." Caesar gave her a quick peck on the forehead as she passed him. And the look he gave her reminded me too much of the one Duncan gave me earlier.

Duncan. He'd charged out into the night when Mai half-dragged my butt into Anthony's kitchen. Not a word of comfort. Not even asking if I was okay.

All right. I had to admit that was a stupid question given my mangled state at the time. But dammit, after that kiss he'd given me during the rehearsal, he could've at least pretended to care.

An uncomfortable silence filled the room while I finished the bird and nibbled on the broccoli. At least I was eating at a semi-reasonable rate now. When those disappeared, Anne passed a plate of cream puffs to me. The pastry I bit into was delectable, the first thing I really tasted all night. The monster had quieted. I looked over at the two tables next to me. Dishes were piled two feet high on both. Two months ago, the sheer idea of eating that much in one sitting would have made me puke. The last time I'd eaten like this was after Mallory's guards had shot me during my escape.

The night I died.

Apparently deciding I was no longer a threat, John glanced at Caesar. "Where's Ziva? I thought she was coming."

"Here, darling!" Ziva Epstein swept into the room, her husband, Ben, a cheerful shadow to her flamboyance. His dark trousers and white dress shirt contrasted sharply with her neon pink running suit. "Where's my baby?"

Of course. In any kind of incident, the Silver Bear High Priestess's first priority would be her granddaughter, Bebe.

"Out back." Anthony inclined his head toward the rear of the restaurant. "I'll show you."

"And check those mushrooms too," Caesar added as Anthony led Ziva out of the banquet room. She acknowledged him with a backward wave and disappeared around the corner.

The mushrooms. "Oh God," I groaned. "Did anyone else eat them?"

Alex grinned. "Just your mother. And only because Tiffany said they smelled funny."

It finally registered that Max and Tiffany weren't in the room. Good. My brother had the common sense to remove his pregnant fiancée from the line of fire, though the vamps probably had to hog-tie her and toss her in the back of the car for him.

"But your mother didn't suffer the same effects you did," Anne said. She took the plate I had unconsciously cleaned of puffs and set a huge helping of tiramisu in its place. "And Bebe stopped anyone else from eating them after Duncan's concern over your behavior in the parking lot."

Their reassurance produced a small wave of relief, but it lasted less than a second. Whatever had drugged me hadn't affected any-one else, and there weren't many pharmaceuticals that affected me. This was so not good. I picked up a fork and dug into the cake and cream.

A thoughtful expression passed across Alex's face. "Though your father may have appreciated a mindless, unspeaking zombie for one night."

Phil gave a wry smile. "We all would have appreciated Elizabeth in such a state for the next twenty-four hours."

The instant Phil realized she was sharing a joke with Alex, her face fell. I didn't know what had gone on between the two of them before, but I was making it my mission to find out and fix it, assum-ing I survived whatever the hell was going on now. For folks as old as they were, they were being utterly ridiculous.

Of course, everyone else in the room probably thought the same concerning Duncan and me after Alex had narc'd about our fight in the parking lot. I didn't lower my shields to find out for certain everyone deemed me an idiot. Our fight was part of the excuse the supernaturals used for my absence, adding for good measure that I'd taken off in my car after the fight. Mai got the valets to move my Accord behind the building before Mom and Dad walked out the front door.

Ben sat on the chair to my immediate right. White fringe danced a semi-circle around his bald head. Sparkling brown eyes peeked out of crow's feet. In contrast to Caesar and John, he came across as the sweet grandfather next door. The type who kept a lookout for the little kids in the neighborhood and passed out the good candy at Halloween.

But it didn't mean the old witch exuded any less power than the vampire or the were.

He peered into my eyes. "You okay, kiddo?"

I had the sneaking suspicion he was trying to read my aura, get a handle on my physical state. But every witch who'd tried eventually gave up. According to Bebe, my aura was pure black. Black as death itself.

Or ultimate evil.

The fairies voted for door number two.

At my nod, he examined the mess that was my right arm. As the Water Elder of Silver Bear, his forte was healing. I dropped my good hand on his as he reached for the terrible wound.

"It's okay, Ben. The nanites are doing their job." I gave him what I hoped was a reassuring smile. And sure enough, now that I'd eaten and they'd finish repairing my bones for the second time that night, the tiny robots set to work on the flesh of my mangled arm.

Under our watchful gazes, skin and muscle rebuilt and stitched itself back together. By the time the enforcers and the witches returned from their examination of the scene of the attack, not even a scar remained from my formerly mangled arm or the zillions of scratches and cuts I'd received in the fight. Absolutely nothing to show for the night's activities, except for the blood, sweat and zombie dust coating my skin.

Oh, and the fact that my secrets were more exposed than Victoria's.

Anthony interrupted that realization when he followed the supernatural CSIs into the room. In one hand, he carried a bottle of Jack Daniels, which he set in front of Bebe who had plopped in the chair across from me. Walking around the table, he handed me the cloth bundle, which turned out to be a pair of navy sweats and a matching t-shirt.

"Thanks, Anthony." I flashed him a grateful smile.

"*De nada.* I learned a long time ago to keep extra clothes here." He shot Bebe a glare before he thumbed over his shoulder. "You can use the bathroom in my office."

I raced out of the room and around the corner. Bless him, he had real towels and washcloths on a little shelf over the toilet as well as a corner shower stall. The hot water felt so good, but I couldn't enjoy it like I wanted. I needed to hear what Bebe and the enforcers discovered. After rinsing off the worst of the corpse grime and dried blood, I jumped out and pulled the soft cotton over damp skin. The remains of my poor dress and underwear I wadded up and stuffed in the trash.

I jogged back to the banquet room in time to catch Bebe saying, "—not sure what this residue is."

"What residue?" I asked.

Everyone, even John jumped at my voice and turned to stare at me.

"What residue?" I repeated. I didn't want to think about the fact that I'd snuck up on the major leaders of the Los Angeles supernatural community and the equivalent of their police. If I could do that, it might alienate the few people left on my side.

Bebe cleared her throat, a soft delicate sound. "There's a type of energy residue on the remains of the corpses you destroyed."

"Magick residue? From the spell that animated these fuckers? And you can trace it, right?" At her fidgeting, my anger reared its ugly head again. "Don't you dare tell me it wasn't magick! I could smell the freaking ozone! And the funky light show surrounding them—"

"I'm not saying it wasn't, Sam." Bebe's voice held that same patronizing tone all doctors had when confronted by an irate patient. She sucked in a deep breath.

God help me, this was going to be bad. Really, really bad.

"The residue may have come from you," she said.

"What!"

Familiar masculine sandalwood washed over me before the British accent murmured in my ear. "Sam, let her finish." Duncan wrapped his arms around my waist and pulled me against his hard, strong chest.

I should have been pissed at him, but I wanted his touch so bad I didn't object. Hell, after the last two nights of mayhem, you couldn't pay me enough to object.

Underneath the sandalwood though was a slight tinge of ash. In the two months I'd known him, I'd never smelled fear emanating from him. I twisted to look up at him. "The license plates—"

"I ran them," he said, his eyes filled with worry. "The automobile was reported stolen earlier this evening by the owner. A Normal with no Family connections."

Shit! I closed my eyes. I'd depended too much on that little tidbit of info.

Opening my eyes again, I turned back to Bebe. "How could magickal residue have come from me? According to you, the nanites rewrote my DNA to match vampires."

Bebe downed a shot of whiskey, so Ziva answered instead. "We're eliminating the obvious. It's not witch magick, sweetie." She held up a hand to forestall my protest. "It's not elf magick either. We're not sure what this energy is. Mai . . ."

The old witch hesitated, and I looked at the enforcer.

Ramrod straight as always, Mai met my look squarely, but there was unease in her sharp features. "You were saying something with each strike against your opponents. I couldn't hear the actual words, but with each blow, there was a, a—" She blinked rapidly as she grasped for the words. "A flash of nothingness."

"Huh?" I stared at her. "Are you sure you didn't eat one of those funky mushrooms?"

"That's the other problem, sweetie." Ziva was young by witch standards, only seventy-five, but right now, she looked every inch a Normal of the same age. "Someone laced the stuffed mushrooms with devil's horn."

"Huh?" My conversational skills were rapidly declining.

"Datura," Bebe said. "It's a hallucinogenic plant."

I blinked and tilted my head. "But drugs don't work on me. The nanites negate the effects too fast."

All three witches shifted uncomfortably in their chairs.

"Out with it," I commanded.

"According to the old stories, devil's horn is used by Voudon sorcerers to raise the dead," Ziva said.

I looked at Bebe, who was suddenly fascinated by the shot glass she rolled between her palms. Returning my attention to Ziva, I said, reasonably politely, "I've been told zombies are impossible to conjure."

"There's always been rumors about the New Orleans and Haiti covens," Ben said quietly. "But no real proof. They've flaunted their abilities in public over the last couple centuries, but nothing serious. The rest of the covens chalked it up to boasting for profit. Enhancing their status among the Normals in order to separate the public from their money." Ben shrugged. "Of course, the New Orleans folks have been quiet lately, their hands full with other problems since Katrina."

Something wiggled in my overloaded brain, a connection I wasn't making. Or maybe the nanites were still dealing with the devil's horn in my system. "So why'd this drug work on me?"

"It was spell-enhanced," Bebe said, her voice so soft I could barely hear her. "It was targeted to affect you specifically because—" She took a deep breath and released it. "Because you're dead." She finally met my gaze. "It made you highly susceptible to such magickal influence and clouded your rational mind."

"So my mom's going to be okay?"

She nodded. "Elizabeth may have some weird dreams tonight due to the hallucinogenic properties inherent in the drug, but no, it won't do to her what it did to you."

Relief swept through me. Despite our differences, I didn't want my mom ripped apart by the undead.

Looking back at Mai, I said, "Thanks for your help. How'd you know I was back by the dumpsters?"

Mai shrugged. "I didn't. When Bebe discovered the doctored mushrooms, Duncan said you had eaten some and you hadn't returned, so we spread out to search the facility."

Duncan hugged me tighter. "Kensai and Jamal have taken the corpses to the crematorium for disposal. Though you seem to have eliminated any animation by your destruction."

"I did save some of the remains, boxed and sealed," Bebe added. "Stan and Harry are already on their way down, so they can check them before daybreak."

My stomach clenched at the thought of the San Francisco enforcers. "Are you sure you want them to check this out? They're half-fairy—"

"Samantha," Duncan said, his breath tickling my ear, "the Gryf-fudds' allegiance is to Caesar for that very reason. They are persona non grata as far as the Courts are concerned, and they will not lie about their examination."

I still didn't like trusting any fairy, half or not, even if they were enforcers and reported to Duncan. But I wasn't getting anywhere by throwing a—

The memory of what I'd done shot home, even if it was a little fuzzy. "Oh crap! There was a car in the parking lot. Scorse—"

"Marty and his wife are fine," Caesar said. "We had to alter their memories, but as far as they're concerned you and they had a fender bender in the parking lot, which resulted in damage to two additional vehicles. Restitution has been made to all parties, and your car is on its way to our mechanic's—"

"You didn't." That little vampire shit was leaving me stranded!

"It was my idea."

I jerked free of Duncan's arms, whirled, and smacked him in the chest. "You didn't even ask!" *Smack.* "You never ask what I want!" *Smack.* "You didn't even ask if *I* wanted to move to Las Vegas." *Smack.* "You just make the decision—" I overbalanced on the last swing and would have landed on my ass if he hadn't caught me.

"If you are finished with your temper tantrum?" Amusement glinted in his eyes.

"I haven't even begun, buster!"

Chapter 16

In the end, my temper tantrum made no difference. In a way, I was a little embarrassed. James Bond wouldn't have thrown a tantrum. He would have just shot the person holding him back.

But what could I really use to threaten a vampire? Not proud of myself, I switched to begging. Not even my pleas concerning the need of a car for wedding preparations swayed Duncan. He gave me a choice of following Caesar's orders to stay at the Brentwood mansion or he'd have the witches trap me in a protective circle. My so-called friends and John volunteered to hold me down while Bebe and her grandparents cast the spell.

I had pouted and snapped while Alex and Mai escorted me in his truck to my place to collect some things. Ziva and Ben followed us in their car to the apartment complex and then back to Caesar's mansion as an additional precaution.

Alex pulled into the gated drive, and Ziva leaned out the car window, yelling "See you at the wedding!" as they drove past. The taillights of their Caddy disappeared into the night.

I *heard* Alex's exchange with the guard on duty, a vampire I didn't recognize. The gates slid open with the barest whisper of metal on metal. When the pick-up pulled to a smooth stop behind the house, I grabbed my overnight case and jumped out before Alex or Mai could say a word.

When I stomped into the kitchen, Bebe sat at the island sipping from a cup, one of her herbal concoctions from the flowery odor. "Which room?"

She eyed me, waiting a couple of heartbeats before she answered. "The usual."

"No." I shook my free index finger at her. "No fucking way. I want the guesthouse."

"Jean-Pierre and his escort are using the guesthouse." She peered at her watch. "They should be arriving any minute." Vamps.

"Then I'll use the east wing."

"Virginia and her party are already here." More vamps.

"The downstairs mother-in-law suite."

"The Polks and their entourage." Werewolves.

My bag dropped to the floor. "This is just fucking peachy." I so didn't want to spend the night in Duncan's room. "Can't I bunk with you or Anne?"

"I like you, Sam, but you're not my type." She took another sip of tea. "And my cousin, Alice, is rooming with Anne along with Mai and Miko. If it makes you feel better, he probably won't spend the day here."

My eyes narrowed, and I considered trying to throw a psy-bolt at her out of spite. That's when I realized my head didn't hurt anymore. No pulsing behind my eyeballs. No nagging ache in my frontal lobe. Nothing.

Bebe must have misinterpreted my expression because she hopped off her stool. "What's wrong, Sam?" Golden light danced along her fingertips.

I frowned. "My headache's gone."

"You're sure?" Bebe's magick played along the edges of my body. After a few experimental tries over the last few weeks, she'd figured out how to check my vitals without her aura getting sucked into mine.

"I still had it during the rehearsal . . ."

Our eyes met, and Bebe's forehead creased even more. "Before you consumed the laced mushrooms."

I nodded. "Could the devil's horn—"

"Datura," she corrected. "And I doubt it. You said you started hallucinating shortly after—"

"I know, I know." My hands waved aside her objections. "But what if it's the plant itself that's the painkiller? My funky mind trip could have been the spell."

Brunette curls flew when Bebe shook her head. "I'm not experimenting. Your health and safety is my first priority as your physician."

"I've heard that before." My pout was back. All those claims that my safety was Duncan's first priority? *Ha!* Instead he left me in the tender care of his boss's girlfriend and his minions. "Where is the rat bastard?"

"Following up some leads." Alex strode into the kitchen and headed straight for the fridge. A bag of blood was quickly emptied into a large mug and placed in the microwave.

"He said the getaway car was stolen." I glared at the back of Alex's blond head.

He punched in the time and pressed the start button, before turning to face me. "Yup."

"So what leads are you talking about?"

He shrugged and leaned back against the counter. "Dunno."

It'd be so easy to fall for the easy-going Texan if I weren't already obsessed with Mr. Tall, Dark, and Asshole. I opened my shields, trying to get a hint from Alex's surface thoughts.

Alex grinned at my amateur probing. "And that's exactly why he didn't tell me and Mai what he was up to."

I needed a new plan. *Anne might know and she might even tell me.*

"No, she doesn't," Bebe said. "She and Jamal are heading up tonight's security detail."

Damn, I hated it when I accidentally transmitted my thoughts.

Bebe smiled. "Only when you're this tired. It's not unusual in young witches and new vampires. Go get some rest. You've had a rough night."

I opened my mouth to protest.

"Don't make me lock you in the conservatory for the night." A titanium will lay behind her words. And spending the night on the marble floor of the room she used for spell casting was about as appealing as spending it in Duncan's room.

At least, Duncan had a mattress.

I grumbled under my breath all the way upstairs. Alex and Bebe were laughing in the kitchen, which meant Alex, with his super-vamp hearing, repeated every insult I uttered.

I woke to a familiar hardness snuggled against my back. The arm hugging my waist wore the same jacket sleeve it'd been wearing at the restaurant. The clock on the nightstand silently blinked from "10:00 AM" to "10:01 AM." Last night's anger sat in my stomach, a lead weight on top of a dull ache.

"Phillippa and Tiffany have arrived. Bebe and Anne are trying on their bridesmaid dresses first. It should give you a chance for breakfast." Duncan's warm breath hit the sweet spot behind my ear.

Warm tingles in my pelvis decided to argue with the lead weight. "So they sent you up as their errand boy?"

He ignored my insult. "I volunteered." A slight hesitation marred his voice. "But essentially you are correct."

"Well, that just makes a girl feel special."

A soft sigh ruffled my hair at my sarcasm. "I wanted to make sure you were all right. And . . . I did not want you to think I was lying, even by omission."

"What a token apology." The lead weight crushed the tingles. I flung the covers and Duncan's arm aside and sat up to shoot the evil eye at him. "That's all I get this morning? A half-assed apology for waking me up?"

He sat up as well, the stone face in place. "What do you want from me, Samantha?"

"I want you to quit telling me what to do."

His voice rose to match mine. "I would not have to if you would use the sense God gave to a horse."

I jumped out of the bed. His bed. And planted my fists on my hips. Otherwise, they'd be planted on his handsome mug. "Are you calling me a horse?"

Vampire speed had him towering over me in less than a blink. "A mule is more like it. You are the most stubborn, infuriating—" His long fingers raked through his hair and yanked. Surprisingly, no clumps came out. His voice lowered with his next words. "Someone is trying to kill you, Samantha. Permanently, this time."

"No shit! I don't need some half-assed vampire detective telling me that!"

The door slammed open to reveal a scowling Alex in his tighty-whities. "Would you two mind keeping it down? Some of us are trying to sleep."

"Fine." I shot Duncan a dirty look. "We're finished anyway." I stalked past Alex and headed for the stairs.

Hellfire! She was not avoiding this discussion by running away again. Duncan started to follow, only to have Alex hold up a hand. The younger vampire leaned back to check the hall before facing him.

She's right. You're being a prick.

Duncan's lower jaw dropped. *She is totally disregarding her safety, and you're taking her side!*

Alex shook his head. *You just don't get it, do you? She wouldn't be this difficult if you hadn't been making plans behind her back.*

I did not do anything behind her back!

Alex crossed his arms and cocked his head to the side. *Vegas doesn't ring a bell?*

Mouth snapping shut, Duncan glared at his second. *I was waiting for her decision concerning her parents, and there is a difference between having a contingency plan and outright lying.*

Then why'd she have to find out your little contingency plan from Jamal instead of you? At Duncan's silence, Alex wiped a hand over his pale face before shaking his head again. "I can't help you if you're this clueless. I need some sleep." He turned and ambled in the direction of his room.

Duncan clenched his fists. He wanted a life with Samantha. She refused his proposal. So he had swallowed his pride and common sense. She refused his offer to live together. He tried to protect her, and now she refused to even have a civilized conversation with him.

All he wanted was to make sure she had a place to go to if she chose the Supernatural Protection Program. Las Vegas was a perfect choice. She could still work for O'Malley under an alias and have a multitude of celebrities to harass. It was fairly close so they could visit Tiffany, Max, and the baby. And . . . and . . .

Anger drained from his blood as Duncan contemplated Alex's pointed observation. Samantha knew none of this because he hadn't said a word to her. And now, she wouldn't listen to anything out of hurt feelings. In Tiffany's words, he'd royally fucked this one up. He wished desperately he had an earthly clue on how to make amends with Samantha.

Chapter 17

Still fuming, I stalked into the kitchen and into organized chaos. Emily Polk, the San Antonio pack's alpha female, had commandeered Caesar's kitchen for those guests looking for a non-liquid breakfast. She shoved a plate full of egg and cheese sandwiches into one of my hands and a glass of orange juice in the other.

"Go," she said with a shooing motion. "The girls are trying on the dresses in the conservatory. I'll have lunch ready for y'all between fittings and make-up."

Bless her heart. And I really meant it. Emily had witnessed my gargantuan appetite after my transformation two months back, and not only had taken it in stride, but had provided for me. I shoved half a sandwich in my mouth and chewed as I made my way down the hall to the back of the house.

And nearly dropped everything in my hands when I reached the doorway.

Three impossibly beautiful women fluttered around Tiffany, who stood on a stool and looked impossibly beautiful herself in an impossibly white outfit reminiscent of something a Greek goddess would wear. Gold trim sparkled in the late morning sun. A crown of white flowers nestled in her black hair and anchored a veil of the same whisper-thin fabric. Contrary to Antoine's opinion during the disastrous shopping expedition last week, the robes brought out the lovely, translucent pink shade of her skin.

She smiled at me, a radiant expression that would have dazzled me even if it wasn't such a contrast with her usual Goth accoutrements. "How do I look?"

My mouth opened and closed several times before my brain caught up. "Stunning." I took a deep breath. "Max is going to fall ass over heels when he sees you come down the aisle."

She blushed. She actually blushed. Smoothing down fabric across her still flat abdomen, she turned to look in the full-length mirror. "Do you really think so?"

Sucking in another deep breath, I noticed the strange odors from the three women arranging the folds of fabric draped across Tiffany's petite form. It took another whiff to identify oak, pine and what I thought might be sassafras.

Something wasn't right. They wore the same casual clothes any California twenty-something would wear. Then it hit me. Little motions of the three ladies were disjointed, out of place. One cocked her head in a birdlike manner while she examined the hem. Another fussed with nonexistent lint in quick, squirrelly motions. The third fluffed the veil streaming down Tiffany's back in the slow dreamy gestures of a butterfly spreading her wings.

A sharp clap spoiled my concentration. I turned to find Phillippa standing near me, a look of motherly pride on her patrician features.

"All right, ladies. Let's get started on Sam since she finally crawled out of bed."

Within seconds, the women, or whatever they were, had Tiffany off the stool and undressed. As Butterfly Woman hung the bridal dress, Phillippa divested me of my breakfast and the other two divested me of my jammies and underwear.

Before I could protest, they covered my nakedness in an outfit made of the same gauzy material as Tiffany's. With deft, sure motions, the women wrapped silver cords across my breasts and around my waist, eliminating the need for a bra.

Not that I needed one anyway with my pitiful B-cups.

Then I caught sight of my image in the mirror. Pale pink set off huge sapphire eyes in a startled face. My face.

Tiffany whistled and flashed a thumbs-up gesture. I turned to Phil to find a frown marring her face. Glancing down, I checked the material. Nope, no crumbs or juice stains.

I looked back up at Phil. "What's wrong?"

She opened her mouth, then shut it before giving a sharp shake of her head. "Nothing."

I would have let it go if her three buddies didn't share the same expression of discomfiture. Planting hands on hips, I swiveled to face them. "What's going on?"

All three of Phil's helpers ducked behind her before peering over her shoulders. Yeah, right. Like I was the one who could throw lightning bolts.

Phil muttered to them in a language I didn't recognize, and the women darted out the door. Tiffany's head swiveled, confusion smeared over her face, but Phil didn't bother to elaborate.

And I wanted some elaboration. "Phil—"

She held up a hand. "Don't start with me. I'm not sure . . ."

The anger simmering since I woke up hit a full roiling boil. "Then don't take that holier-than-thou tone with me, Little Miss Demigoddess. What the hell is going on?" When she remained silent, I added, "Your friends saw the same thing you did. Who are they? Forest creatures you made human to help you with your goddaughter's wedding?"

"Don't take your anger at Duncan out on me." Lightning flashed in her eyes, a not-so-subtle warning.

I waved my hands, the only way to express the exasperation that threatened to turn my anger into a steam explosion. "I'm sick to death of everyone keeping secrets from me."

Tiffany snorted in a vain attempt to swallow her laughter.

"What's so fucking funny?"

My snapping didn't deter her. "You're sick to death." She collapsed to the floor, rolling in hysterics.

I rolled my eyes, but her humor served to dispel the literal storm clouds swirling around Phil and me.

Phil smiled before she said, "I'm sorry, Sam. I don't—" Her attention flicked to the sunshine streaming through the window again before returning to me. "I called in some favors from the local nymphs to help with the dresses. As for what we saw—" Her expression grew pensive. "We're not sure."

Concern drank the steam of my exasperation and anger. No, not drank, sucked it down like an alcoholic on a binge. Mai had the same worried look last night Phillippa had now. "You mean, the nothingness Mai reported, or the strange magick the witches detected?"

Phil shook her head, curls from her loose bun bobbing in an erratic motion. "That's just it. It was neither of those things. It was more like—"

"Pure beauty."

We both faced Tiffany at her oddball words. She shrugged. "I don't know what else to call it. Do you?" She shot accusing glares at us.

A thoughtful expression crossed over Phil as she tapped an index finger on her cheek. She slowly nodded. "Yes, you're right. Sam's whatever-it-was reminded me of Aunt Aphrodite's glamour—"

I held up my hands. "Whoa, whoa, and whoa. Mai described the end of existence, and now you two are talking about me throwing off sex goddess vibes?"

Tiffany shrugged again. "Makes sense. This could be how the nanites manifest their version of vampire mojo."

"But—" I spluttered. "You're girls!"

"Geez, Sam." Tiffany matched my fists-on-hips pose. "It's not like we jumped you or anything."

Phil smirked. "Besides, you've seen the effect Duncan has on other men."

I snorted. Unfortunately, they were right to a point. "Jimmy the waiter is gay, and David Head's bi, so it's not like he converted . . ." My brain went into overdrive. The were musk I picked up both in Vegas and at Anthony's restaurant in Beverly Hills. I *had* smelled it before. Head's buddy at the party last week. "Shit!"

I jumped off the pedestal and raced through the door, gauze trailing behind me. The tree nymphs darted out of the way from their eavesdropping positions as I plowed past them. *Duncan!*

He was in front of me, pulling me into his arms before I cleared the hallway. "What is it? Samantha?" His gaze darted around, looking for a foe.

His worried tone cleared my shakes. Except I wasn't sure if it was anger or fear causing them. "The scent I told you about last night? I knew I smelled it before. It's the werewolf who was with David Head last Friday. That doesn't make sense though. Why would he be after me?"

Warm sandalwood covered my body, my thoughts. *Breathe, Sam.* Strong arms guided me to the kitchen and a chair. "Emily, would you please make a cup of tea for Samantha?"

I shot him an irritated look. "Coffee." I swear. How on earth do I keep picking tea-totalers?

The alpha bitch's husky laugh filled the kitchen. "No sissy drinks for my girl." Two seconds later, a mug radiated its reassuring aroma in front of my nose. I scalded my throat gulping it, but I didn't care. I needed some semblance of normalcy.

I stared at my liquid love, hoping to find answers in its velvety sienna depths. "It doesn't make sense. What the heck did I do to have a were send real zombies after me?"

"Were? What the fuck is she blathering about?"

I glanced up at Emily. Her brows pinched into an ugly scowl. I shuddered. I'd been on the receiving end of her claws once, and she'd only been mildly irritated that time.

Duncan's eyes glowed, another not so good sign. "What do you know about a were that accompanies David Head?"

"The New Orleans basketball player with the crazy hair?" Emily's eyes unfocused while she thought. "One of the Cajun pack's pups works for Jean-Pierre. He might know." She whistled, a sharp, piercing noise that had both Duncan and me wincing.

A tall, rangy man with reddish brown hair appeared in the doorway leading to the dining room. "Yes'm?"

"Marvin, who's the cousin on your mamma's side working for Jean-Pierre Rousseau?"

"Frankie?" The big were's attention flicked from the pack mistress to me. I didn't like the guilt flashing in his eyes.

Emily snapped her fingers. "Yeah, would he know what pup's hanging with—"

"That'd be him." Damn werewolf had been eavesdropping. "Frankie's just a runt. How could he be any threat to—" He waved a hand in my general direction.

I stood. How, I didn't know because the shakes were back in full force. "What. Did. You. Tell. Him. About. Me?" My voice had dropped a full octave.

"I—" Hair sprouted across his skin in response. "Pack Mistress." His head canted to reveal his throat. "Everyone's been talking about what happened at the Mallory Labs' shareholders meeting. I didn't mean nuthin' by it."

A pissed expression filled Emily's tight features. "Answer the girl's question." If my voice had deepened, hers was an outright growl. I glanced down past her waist. Crap. Claws extended from her furry hands.

A canine whine spilled from the were's throat before he answered. "We were just havin' a couple of beers over cards." Whites shone around his irises. "I told him how the Augustine queen had died, who did it, and why. And I told him about the metal zombie girls Mallory created, what they smell like and how she—" he jerked his head in my direction "—took out the other one."

This was probably the most stupid thing I've done in my death, but I stepped between Marvin and Emily. I laid a hand on his shoulder, and he flinched at my touch. "It's okay. Nothing's going to happen to you."

Emily wasn't quite as forgiving. "Get out of here!"

Marvin slunk out of the kitchen. Lucky for him, he hadn't morphed all the way. It'd take a month to get his tail out of his ass.

"Of all the stupid—"

"Let it go, Emily." Focusing on the empty doorway, I tried to process the why of everything. "Marvin's right. Everyone's talking about me these days." I sure didn't like being on the other side of the gossip column, but there wasn't a damn thing I could do about it.

I looked at Duncan. "Think Jean-Pierre knows one of his boys is hooking on the side?"

For once, his stony enforcer face had been replaced by an analytical expression. He blinked. "'Hooking on the side?'"

I crossed my arms in a vain effort to quell the shakes. "What are the odds Frankie's trying to collect on the fairies' bounty?"

Duncan nodded. "The thought had crossed my mind, but it does not explain the presence of zombies, much less how they came to be."

Tiffany appeared in the doorway. "Dammit, Sam! You are so not spilling coffee on that bridesmaid dress." I let her drag me back to the conservatory. I had to focus on one major crisis at a time.

Yvonne's hands shook as she sorted through her luggage, trying to decide what to wear to the Normal wedding. The last time had been Mother's second wedding, and the daisy print she'd worn as a ten-year-old would hardly be appropriate at an elite Los Angeles function. Being back in this house where that lunatic stalker had tried to kill her baby brother did not help her nerves either.

She laid the clothing out on the bed. A fingernail tapped her chin as she examined the five outfits she'd brought with her.

She tried to talk Davy into coming with her, but he pointed out the wedding was a business function and Jean-Pierre needed her. Then he stormed down the hall and disappeared into his bedroom. It did no good to speak with him when he was in one of his funks, but she'd hoped to distract him from whatever trouble he and Frankie were involved in.

"How long has the ex been living here?"

Nylons and panties flew from her hands in every direction. She turned and glared at Frankie. "Can't you knock?"

He rapped on the open door, a wry look on his face. "How long has David's ex been living here?"

She should have known the were would pick up the fresh scent, but there hadn't been time to come out and cast a spell to cover it. Not without both Davy and Frankie knowing. She still wasn't sure what prompted Davy to leave the hotel. He hadn't been inside this house in nearly two years, not since the night he and Brandon broke up. The same night the stalker broke in.

His flippant answer about not wasting money on the hotel contrasted sharply with his normal spendthrift ways. But then he'd never bothered to sell the house either. Like he hoped Brandon would come back to him someday.

Plucking undergarments off the floor, she stacked them in the open drawer. "Brandon needed a place to stay while he looked for a house here. It's only been a couple of weeks."

Frankie shook his head. "You shouldn't be keeping secrets from your brother, *chére.*"

She slammed the drawer and whirled to face him, beads clacking her anger. "I shouldn't be keeping secrets? What about you and Davy sneaking out at all hours and not one word about where you were? I know damn well it hasn't been your usual partying." When the were didn't say anything, she flung a hand upward. "What? No answer? How surprising."

Frankie crossed the bedroom, weariness hanging from his frame, and sat on the bottom edge of her bed. His gaze never left the open doorway, his body poised to bolt. "He's practicing again." The admission hung in the silence.

She edged around the bed and sat next to him, rolling and unrolling the stockings she had rescued from the floor. A deep sigh spilled from her. "And you've killed again."

The chartreuse shame rushed from his aura, nearly pulling her under in his despair. "Yes." The acknowledgement didn't even qualify as a whisper.

What a trio they made. None of them could outrun the mistakes they made as children. Maybe they were fated to repeat them over and over again. Linking his cold fingers in hers, she squeezed in gentle reassurance. "Jean-Pierre's here for the Augustine wedding. He'll know what to do."

Frankie leapt away. The sudden motion shook her. His face elongated into a snout. Hair sprang from every pore. "No! You can't!" The garbled words were more barks than English. "He said if it happened again, he'd turn me over to the pack."

She hated giving voice to her own disturbing suspicions. "Not if Davy forced you. How long has Davy known the binding is no longer holding his powers?"

Desperation and hope warred in Frankie's golden eyes. Then his snout sank to his chest. "He didn't make me do anything, Yvonne. I'm not hanging him out to save myself." Sorrow laced the gruff words.

Yvonne kept her voice gentle. "I won't say anything about you. But I need to know, Frankie. How long has Davy known that his *full* powers were back?"

Fur receded back into his skin. His despairing gaze flicked to the window before returning to her. Good. He'd stay, and Goddess knew she needed all the help she could get.

"I don't think he knew for sure until two days ago." He shrugged. "That's the first time I've seen him try to cast a complex spell."

She snorted. "Except for shorting out security systems."

Frankie nodded. The boys' penchant for sneaking out hadn't changed in all this time.

Her finger resumed tapping her chin. The binding spell was supposed to last Davy's lifetime. But from the ancient scrolls and books Jean-Pierre had acquired for her, it was nearly impossible for a binding on a true necromancer to last. Something about them being a fundamental force of nature. And that force of nature was now loose in Los Angeles.

She sucked in a deep breath. "Last night the first time he's raised the dead?"

Frankie shook his head. "Night before too."

That explained the absences. Damn it all, why couldn't the two men simply have gone to a brothel? *Aizan, what should I do?* But the loa was silent.

Yvonne rubbed her sweaty palms on her slacks. "I'm meeting Jean-Pierre in a couple of hours. Maybe he'll have an idea of how to contain Davy." The loa knew she had none. She didn't have the raw power alone to bind her brother, and the Lord knew he wouldn't quietly submit. Not this time.

She would need assistance. Maybe Jean-Pierre could petition the Silver Bear coven on her behalf. Frankie stiffened at her words, but she held up her hand. "Don't worry, I'll keep quiet about your situation, but we can't have Davy running around, animating every dead body in Los Angeles."

The were's head bobbed in silent agreement.

Fuck 'em both! David gunned the engine as the rental tore down the street. Good thing a house intercom was right outside Yvonne's room. His suspicion than Frankie would narc on him had been right. Dammit! He would have covered the were's ass for the murder of that girl. Frankie was practically blood. Knuckles tightened on the steering wheel at the blatant betrayal.

Maybe after he took care of that zombie chick, he'd deal with those backstabbers. Yeah, once she was in tiny pieces, then he'd clean house. And he knew just what would convince her to come to him. Alone. This time she wouldn't have her friends to protect her.

The car shot through a yellow light before whipping into the Hollywood Cemetery driveway.

Chapter 18

Once again, I piled into the limousine behind the girls, Mai at the wheel. This time though we resembled a series of pale moths, not jeweled beetles. The mood was quiet compared to two nights ago. Tiffany's hands trembled when she smoothed her veil back.

"You can still call it off. Max'll understand," I whispered.

If possible, her eyes would have shot daggers. Or No. 2 pencils.

"My baby is *not* going to be illegitimate. And quit foisting your commitment phobias on me."

The rest of the gals carried various expressions of annoyance. Time to back off. Besides, I hated to admit the kid was right. I prayed my own nerves were due to my own relationship issues and not my worries over another zombie attack. All we needed to do was get Max and Goth Girl hitched and on the plane for the honeymoon.

Except I couldn't call her Goth Girl anymore. She'd let the nymphs apply a delicate, natural-looking make-up, not the stark black and white stuff she normally favored. The kid looked absolutely freaking unbelievable. The maiden bride. A mother-to-be.

"Would you quit staring at me? I swear, Sam—" Tiffany jabbed a finger over the bouquet of white lilies and blue-green carnations she held.

I grinned like an idiot. "Max is a lucky man."

"Damn straight he is." Then her own idiotic grin lit up her face. "He's going to shit when he sees me, isn't he?"

"Yup." She joined me in a round of giggles.

When we finally stopped laughing for lack of air, she pinned me with a shrewd look. "You're breaking his heart, you know."

"Max?"

"Duncan, you moron."

"We're different than you and Max."

Her eyeroll wasn't as dramatic without the black eyeliner and mascara. "Yeah, you're both stubborn. And self-pitying. Oh, boo-hoo, I'm not Normal so I can't have a *real* relationship."

Now, Phil, Bebe and Anne were staring at us while Miko covered her mouth to hide her grin. Tiffany shot each of the supernatural women a disgusted look. "Oh, *puh-lease*. You all do it, and you know it."

She turned back to me, her fixed look sealing me to the limo seat. "Every relationship has problems. Pregnant at twenty wasn't *my* first choice, but condoms break." She shrugged. "I love Max and we'll figure out how to make it work. *You're* not even trying."

I couldn't answer her, couldn't even look at her. Damn, I hated when the kid was right. I stared out the window at passing head-lights. Duncan and I, in a brief moment amidst the flurry of prepa-rations, had agreed to talk after Max and Tiffany were on their plane tonight. How'd things get so complicated? I wanted him, but I was afraid of losing myself in his expectations. Just like I almost had with my parents. I locked my fingers so I wouldn't twist the stems of my own bouquet.

It wasn't just his expectations; it was my irrational need to rebel against any expectations. And Duncan hadn't said one word about me having to leave my job or my family. He left the decision up to me, despite making his contingency plans behind my back.

Was that what I was really angry about? That he didn't dictate terms, so I had nothing to protest? That he was trying to give me alternatives? That he actually cared enough to give me a choice?

I swallowed the lump gathering at the top of my throat. And I was pissed at him for what? Having an undead life I hadn't chosen? It wasn't his fault. Just my own pig-headed nature for not letting go of a story that had been bigger than I could handle.

A deep breath calmed the growing butterflies. One thing at a time. Get Max and Tiffany hitched. Catch the were rat-bastard trying to kill me. Then maybe Duncan and I could find a tolerable compromise.

Yvonne twisted the beaded evening purse as she paced in front of the gated estate. Augustine security had refused to admit her into the Brentwood mansion without an invitation. Not that she blamed the two blond half-fae watching the dark street. The beads slickened under her sweaty hands. Where was Jean-Pierre?

When Yvonne hadn't been able to reach him on his cell phone, she'd ordered the driver he'd sent for her to come to the Augustine estate instead of the wedding location in Beverly Hills. Had she already missed him?

A familiar essence, sandalwood and sea salt, filled her mind the same moment headlights appeared in the driveway. The iron gate began to slide open. She dodged through the narrow gap and ran to meet the SUV—as best as she could in heels.

The vehicle screeched to halt in order not to hit her, and the two front doors sprang open. Arms cabled with muscle caught her, and she writhed in a vain attempt to escape the half-fae's grasp. "Jean-Pierre!"

A familiar figure slid from the vehicle's passenger side. "Let her go, *mon ami.*"

The comforting face loosed the tears she'd been trying to contain the last two days. The second the imprisoning grip disappeared, she leapt into Jean-Pierre's arms.

"What's wrong?" No vampire suggestion in his smoky voice, just raw concern.

"It-it's Davy. He came out here b-because he thinks he's in love." Tears soaked the front of his dark purple suit jacket. The skull and crossbones tie clip dug into her cheek, but she didn't dare let go. To do so meant facing the ugly reality.

Warm comfort slipped into her mind, *seeing* the reason why she came with David to Los Angeles. A soft chuckle rumbled beneath her ear. "*Chére*, there's nothing wrong with love."

"The b-b-binding's dissolved."

The vampires, the half-fae, even the night around them, stilled. A world holding its breath at the news a necromancer had been loosed upon it.

"Where is he?" He resumed stroking her braids.

"I-I don't know. He may have overheard Frankie and me talking about him. We heard tires squealing in the drive and the rental's gone."

"And where's Frankie?" The deep, dark bass fed reassurance into her soul.

"Out looking for him."

"Shifted?"

She nodded. "He said he'd have better luck as a wolf."

Patoi swear words rang in her ears. A soft buzz filled her mind as Jean-Pierre fed the information to someone approaching them.

"Yvonne?" There was no mistaking the authority in the Greek accent behind her.

Hating to leave the haven of Jean-Pierre's embrace, she broke away to face Caesar Augustine. Golden eyes glowed as he regarded her, followed by the brush of a master vampire's mind against hers.

"Why is your brother trying to kill Samantha Ridgeway?"

A deep breath didn't banish the tears, but it did ease some of her shaking. "The person he's in love with is Duncan St. James, and St. James told Davy he's engaged to Miss Ridgeway."

Mold and rot filled David's sinuses, perfume accenting the heady power. Firelight danced shadows across decaying skin. His neck and shoulder muscles ached with the strain of holding so many zombies in his thrall. He needed more, but his efforts pulled at the fraying threads of his aura.

More power, heh? I'll take something else in trade. Low-pitched laughter followed the words in David's head.

Dammit. He didn't have anything else. Fingering the bloody blade, he racked his mind for something he could use to bargain with.

What's that slinking behind you?

At Papa Ghede's question, he twisted to find canine eyes reflecting the firelight. Most of the shape was hidden behind a pedestal. The angel on top of the grave raised its hands in supplication. Relief and wariness swam through his blood at the familiar head. "Frankie?"

The dark figure whined, a plaintive sound in counterpoint to the sharp crackle of flames. He crept forward on his belly, inching across the disturbed earth. The acrid stink of fear rolled off the wolf. He reached Davy, shoving a cold nose in the crook of his elbow.

Don't do this, man.

Davy shoved the wolf's head away. "You've got no right telling me shit."

Frankie's sharp yellow eyes flicked from the blood dripping from Davy's arms, then back to his face. *Yvonne's gone to the wedding. She'll tell Jean-Pierre what you're up to. They'll be ready for you tonight. You won't get near that stupid reporter. Let it go.*

Davy stood and glared down at Frankie, anger reigniting. "Sis wouldn't have jack to tell him if you hadn't blabbed." The zombies shuffled restlessly in response to his emotions.

Ears flat, Frankie cringed at the nearest corpse stepping closer to him, but he didn't run. *She already knew you were practicing magick.*

Bitterness flooded David's mouth. "Bullshit! You were ready to run to the vamp, too. I heard you."

Frankie rose to his paws, teeth bared. *I fucked up, too. You think I want both of us executed? I'm trying to help you.*

A glacier spread over David's fury. "Thanks. I appreciate that." The wolf got the hint, but too late. Claws and teeth were no match for the avalanche of corpses falling on him.

Frankie thrashed and bucked, but with legs and head pinned, he wasn't going anywhere. One golden eye rolled to meet David's. *Maybe I deserve this, but don't seal your fate with my death.* Weariness laced his mental tone, not the pleading David half-expected.

"I want you to know I always admired you." He plunged the knife into Frankie's chest. The wolf jerked once, twice.

Harsh laughter filled the bright, noisy Los Angeles night. *Done.*

The bee buzzing of rapid telepathic communication hummed outside and around my old bedroom at Mom and Dad's. Phil and Bebe primped the bride, but they couldn't disguise the split-second worried look they shared. I glanced at Anne, who resembled a Sixties flower child in her lilac dress and straight brown tresses. Complete with the acid trip look on her face.

Anne? What the heck's going on?

The faraway look disappeared, and she met my gaze. *There was a problem at Master Augustine's estate with one of Jean-Pierre's party.*

With her Amish upbringing, the vampire couldn't lie worth shit. Even telepathically. *Don't mess with me, girl.* In bare feet, I towered over the diminutive woman. *If you don't tell me—*

She checked Tiffany, but the kid was totally oblivious. Anne flashed fangs at me in warning. *Duncan doesn't want Tiffany to know. We are* not *ruining her wedding.*

Before I could add my opinion of Duncan's orders, a sharp rap brought everyone to their feet. My heart skipped a beat as the man in question entered the room. The sandalwood and spice that was uniquely Duncan filled the room. For once, he wasn't dressed in his ever-present black and gray. The pale azure suit matched Phil's dress, but where her outfit flowed, his hugged all the right places. The tie, a darker hue than the suit, knotted at his throat while the platinum tie pin winked at me. But his loving smile was solely for the bride standing before him.

Damn, would he look that good if this was our wedding?

"I believe you need something old." He fished in his pants pocket.

Tiffany shook her wrist so the gold and lapis lazuli beads on her bracelet tinkled. "Phil's bracelet stands for both borrowed and old."

He pulled out a gold locket from his pocket. "You should have this."

"But—" Tiffany's eyes were wide with shock. Actually, we all mirrored her expression. Duncan *never* took off his sister's locket.

"Your great-grandmother Margaret would want you to have it."

Tiffany bent her head and pulled the veil out of the way. "Just add fifteen more 'great's there, Uncle Duncan." Her smartass comment didn't hide the emotion in her voice as he fastened the locket around her neck. She fingered it before whispering, "Thanks."

Duncan smiled at her while she fluffed the veil back in place with Phil's help. "Everything is in place. Are you ready?"

Tiffany's big brown eyes grew even bigger, but she nodded.

An instant of the insect sound filled my head as he relayed the news downstairs, then he held the door while we traipsed through. Just when I didn't think he'd acknowledge my presence, his long fingers encircled my arm. Cool lips brushed mine.

It isn't Head's were behind the attacks. I'll tell you the rest after the ceremony. And then we'll discuss our future.

I must have been struck dumb. By the kiss, the news or the offer to *talk*, I wasn't sure. All I could do was nod. It didn't make sense. Why was there were musk all over the zombies that had attacked me the last two nights if Head's buddy wasn't involved? And why is Duncan acting Mr. Attentive all the sudden?

Trying not to read too much into the kiss or the promise of disclosure, I carefully maneuvered down the stairs in the freaking long dress and joined the girls behind the drapes leading to the patio.

Instead of last night's rehearsal fiasco, every step of Anne, Miko and Bebe was precise as they each strode down our makeshift aisle. Shoving my problems aside, I bent and gave Tiffany a quick peck on the cheek. "Break a leg, kid."

She squeezed my arm, and then I joined the parade. The patio concrete still held a hint of afternoon sun beneath my soles, but all too quickly gave way to cool grass. Guests sat on mismatched folding chairs. I tried to ignore the curious gazes and whispers coating my skin. And the sniffs as vamps and weres who hadn't met me marked my unusual scent. Nerves tingled and my face warmed at being on the receiving end of the gossip mill.

Mom and Dad sat to my left. Dad's face glowed with pleasure while Mom examined me with a critical eye. I gave them a smile as I approached.

Ahead of me stood Max, a ridiculous grin plastered to his face. His white suit glowed under the jury-rigged outdoor lighting. Thank God, Tiffany hadn't asked him to wear a toga. Those scrawny pale legs of his would have blinded the guests. I flashed him a thumbs-up as I joined the girls in front of Reverend Mitchell.

The trio of vampire musicians broke into the Bridal March, and the crowd rose. Flanked by Duncan and Phil, Tiffany strode down the aisle, head high and expression radiant. My eyes stung at the picture they presented, family no matter the circumstances. A small green monster snorted its displeasure. I couldn't see myself doing the same with my parents. Mom would claim it wasn't traditional for the mother to walk down the aisle with her daughter.

From the corner of my eye, I could see Max. His mouth hung open. It took him a couple of tries before he could close it. I knew the moment his and Tiffany's gazes met. His face held such an expression of utter happiness I wanted to hate him.

Tiffany and her guardians reached the altar. Duncan and Phil presented Tiffany to Max, and to my embarrassed pleasure, Duncan winked at me before they took their seats. Everything else receded into a wash of white noise as the minister droned on about the responsibilities of spouses to each other. Despite the boredom, I had enough presence of mind to exchange Max's ring with Tiffany's bouquet at the appropriate point.

I breathed a sigh of relief when Reverend Mitchell finally reached, "I now pronounce—"

I should have known better.

All the electric lights exploded.

Chapter 19

The screams of the Normal women swallowed the crack and sizzle of the shorted halogens. Somehow, Mom hit the daughter disappointment note by being one of them. The woman could bitch out the CEO of a Fortune 100 company for taking her parking spot at the country club, but a few blown bulbs sent her in a tizzy. Okay, not a few bulbs. Every light inside the house had failed, too.

The entire assemblage on Tiffany's side rose as one, spreading out in a defensive stance. As if they had expected something like this. Maybe they did on a regular basis considering how many supernatural leaders stood on Mom and Dad's lawn.

Goosebumps rippled over my skin at the other possibility. But dang it, the lights hadn't gone out at the Rio or the restaurant.

The electrical failure didn't leave us totally in the dark. A nearly full moon floated on ambient city glow. Multitudes of candles bobbed in the pool. Tiny blue flames wavered under the buffet's warming pans. Animal eyes reflected the light balls and fireballs glowing in many witches' hands as the weres started stripping off clothing to Change. Neon colors sparked where vampires interspersed themselves between the shifting weres. Ozone from the electrical surge mixed with that from the witches' spells.

The fact that the power outage was serious enough to disregard supernatural rules about exposing their abilities in front of so many Normals sent my heartbeat into overdrive.

Duncan stepped between me and Tiffany. Reverend Mitchell

thrust his crucifix at him. Not that I blamed the shaking minister. With fangs fully extended and eyes glowing neon green, my guy was an awesome sight.

"Be gone demon of Satan—"

Tiffany reached out and slapped the minister. "With all due respect, Reverend, shut the fuck up."

Duncan pressed his keys into my hand. "Get to my vehicle. Stan made sure it is at the end of the drive."

"But—" I glanced wildly around. Dad pushed his way over to Max, who now clutched Tiffany to him. Not that she looked real happy about him doing the he-man protection thing.

Duncan shook his head. "Do not argue with me this time, Sam. They will follow you. Mai!"

The enforcer jumped to my side, weapon drawn.

"LAX. You should be able to outrun the zombies to the airport. Get Sam in the air."

Anxiety nibbled the edges of my sanity. This was different from the last two attacks. I dug fingers into Duncan's arm. "What if they don't follow us?"

A flash of green light and a sonic crack swallowed Duncan's reply. The harsh grumbling of stone warned we were too late.

The fae shield's fallen! Bebe's warning echoed in my head.

Fallen, my ass. Those two bastards probably let the zombies in the front door with a bow and a smile.

In the wake of the good doctor's telepathic shout, the witches, both guests and catering staff alike, raced and darted, trying to encircle the crowd. An all-too-familiar moaning filled the air, but instead of the earth shaking beneath our feet, the masonry of the estate walls rippled and cracked. With a roar, a large section behind Mom's new foliage collapsed inward. Rock shrapnel flew at us and carved through the outer ring of witches before they had a chance to get their protective circle up. Cries of pain ripped the air, followed by the metallic scent of blood. Bebe's grandmother shouted orders, attempting to stitch the magickal ring back together, but too many of her people lay on the ground.

A flicker of movement caught my eye. Silent as ever, the corpses crawled and clambered over the rubble of the estate wall. Silent except for the rub and scrape of decaying flesh and bones against stone and trees.

"RUN!"

Duncan's combined vocal and telepathic yell almost knocked me over. Mai clutched my arm, dragging my stunned body toward the house. Bile ran thick in my throat at leaving Duncan and my family behind. But I couldn't fault his logic. Those things had been fixated on me both times before, and that many corpses would crush anyone in the way. The only chance the guests had was for me to draw them away.

Stan, one of the half-fae enforcers, met us in the kitchen. He supported his partner, Harry, with an arm under the smaller man's shoulders. Both men were covered with gouges and cuts under equally shredded clothing. I hurt just looking at the thigh-length slice on Harry's leg. Moldering flesh clung to the silver short swords they both carried. Any question I had about their loyalty to Caesar and Duncan dripped away with their blood onto Mom's immaculate white tile.

Stan shook his head, red droplets flipping from the ends of his blond buzz cut. "Bastards are in the front yard, too."

"Duncan's vehicle?" Her gun was steady, but Mai's arm shook as it held mine.

"Can't get to it." Harry gasped out the words. "Too many of them."

"What if I clear a path?" All three enforcers stared at me like I'd lost my last marble. Maybe I had.

"Those things are obsessed with me. They'll follow me. If they don't, I can use a psy-bolt to knock them out of the way. Once you get to the SUV, I can outrun them and meet you on the street."

"Using one at the Rio—" Mai started. Like she had to remind me of the blinding migraines.

"No time to argue. Go." Stan waved his sword in the direction of the front door.

Now, I was the one pulling Mai through the house, leading the guys back to the front door. She was right though. I wasn't sure I could pull off another telekinetic stunt. My head no longer ached like a sonuvabitch, but it didn't mean I'd regained the mental strength.

Odd thumps from outside rattled Mom's knick-knacks on the wall shelves, and scratching assaulted our ears. Knowing what made the noises didn't help my nerves, but I charged forward anyway. It helped that three enforcers were covering my butt. I stopped in the entrance hall long enough to hand the keys to Mai. "Don't stop for me no matter what. Just get to the wheels."

Whites shown around her irises, but she gave me a curt nod. Drawing on her professionalism shoved my own gnawing fear out of the way. No more people were getting hurt on my account. I sucked a deep breath and launched myself forward.

Kicking open the front door knocked over two zombies. The third one lost his skull with a well-placed right hook. I jumped over the stairs, bowling over a few more in the move. Black terror rose when I got a good look at the front yard under the moonlight.

Zombies packed the lawn. The section of stone wall to the right of the gates had been destroyed on this side of the house, too. More of them stumbled over the blasted rocks and clambered over the vehicles lining the drive. A rancid, coppery odor mingled with the ozone, and a thick, ugly black diamond and red haze surrounded the corpses.

This definitely wasn't like before.

Gibbering panic tried to drive me back to my childhood bed-room. *Hide under the covers where the monsters can't get you.* Except I knew such an act wouldn't save me. No, the zombies'd just pull the house down around my ears before stomping my liver to shreds and eating my brain.

"Move, woman!"

I jumped at Stan's shout. Snatching up one of the stupid concrete garden gnomes Antoine insisted Mom needed as a yard accent, I flailed at the closest zombies. Dust and gooshy body parts flew around me as I whacked the undead out of my way, making progress across the grass. A bullet whistled past my ear and blasted the face off a corpse I'd missed. I twisted and flashed Mai a grateful look.

"Pay attention." Coinciding with her reprimand, she aimed the semi-automatic at my head and fired. No, not my head. The upraised arm of the zombie about to bean me. The bone snapped with a dry crack, but the fallen hand grasped the blades of grass to crawl toward me. The gnome smashed through the torso of the still-standing corpse, and my heel crushed the inching finger bones.

We were half-way to the gates. But it was getting harder to swing the gnome without hitting one of the enforcers. The boys were having the same problem with their weapons. Mai had given up on her gun as well. Two slim swords gripped in each hand hacked in a vain attempt to clear us some space, but corpses pressed us together.

"Sam?"

The tremor in Mai's voice kicked my fear up a notch, and I pulled all that yellow emotional sludge into a massive ball. Facing the gates, I yelled, "Fire in the hole."

The psy-bolt slammed through the zombies in front of me, shattering many and knocking apart the rest. Despite the amount of power I expended, I didn't collapse under a wave of agony. A ghost of the leftover headache from Thursday nagged my head instead of the full-blown migraine I'd normally get using that much telekinetic force. I wasn't about to stop and analyze the situation. The four of us raced the remaining yards for the SUV. I threw the poor garden gnome at the zombies ambling toward us before I grabbed Harry from Stan and tossed him in the backseat. I scrambled in after him.

Mai shifted into gear before the vehicle doors slammed shut. The Suburban jerked when Mai mowed over the first couple of zombies who reached us. It rocked again as tires rolled over the fallen front gates. Then we were clear of the estate and racing down the street.

I peered over the backseat. No. That could *not* be right. I blinked and focused again, a new iciness filling my veins. More zombies shambled over the rubble and into the grounds. Not one of them looked in my direction.

"Mai, stop!"

She slammed on the brakes, and the SUV squealed to a halt.

"Are you fucking insane?" Harry's eyes widened beneath his crimson-soaked bangs.

"They're not following us!" If I hadn't been afraid before, gut-churning horror filled me now. As one, the others looked out the rear window, and their eyes reflected my fear. Dammit, I couldn't leave innocents behind to be slaughtered by the undead.

There was no question or vote. Harry slid into me as we tilted on two wheels when Mai whipped the Suburban in a U-turn. The engine revved as she punched the accelerator, and we raced back to the house.

Chapter 20

Mai plowed over more upright zombies, gunning the Suburban up the driveway. The boys and I hung on as best we could with all the bumps and jerks. Swerving past guest cars, she cut across the lawn. In her wild careening over the grass, she hit as many walking corpses as possible while still making progress toward the back of the estate. The SUV tires churned soil and body parts when Mai whipped it around the garage in a slick ninety-degree turn and slammed on the brakes.

Splashes of lightning and fireballs illuminated the scene. Wolves raced, leaped and dived, using guerilla tactics to pull down and shred zombies. The three vampire masters and their people formed a protective ring between the Normal guests and the zombies not engaged by the werewolves. But in their panic, the Normals were more of a threat to the vamps than the zombies. Screams and the smell of burnt sandalwood filled the air. Dammit. The Normals had figured out the effect of silver on the vamps. Another group of zombies surrounded a clump of people by the temporary pulpit.

There wasn't enough room to get past the pool without dunking the Suburban. We piled out and charged toward the carnage. Okay, three of us charged. Harry limped to the driver's seat, revved the engine and mowed down the corpses shuffling around the garage to keep them from joining the backyard fray.

Mai tossed me one of her swords, and I waded into the mess, swinging and hacking. We couldn't reach one of the vamps in time.

Two zombies played taffy pull with him. His head popped off, followed by the stench of rotten meat when the vamp's body dissolved into goo.

Sorrow and anger raged at the waste. With a single chop, I sliced the zombie on the right in half. Mai did the same on the left. Stan hacked his way through the clump at the altar, shouting Bebe's name.

I couldn't take the time to figure out the half-fae's plan. A sharp shove sent me crashing backward over one of the buffet tables. Three zombies stomped through steaming broccoli and green beans, reaching for me. In the seconds it took me to untangle the sword from the tablecloth, bony fingers arched and slashed across my neck.

Bright red arterial blood spurted up and over me and the zombies before I could slap a hand over the deep cut. Rotten tongues snaked out to taste the splashes. One of the zombies removed the aviator glasses dangling from his intact ear and slurped red liquid off the rims. My stomach heaved at the sight, but the three were no longer interested in me, instead licking as much of my blood off their arms and hands as they could. I waited for them to explode into silver dust like Sierra Mallory had when she tried to drink from me.

Nope, I wasn't going to get that lucky. They were real zombies, not cybernetic wannabes like Sierra and me. The three licked each other's body parts out of reach of their own tongues. In a gross and unsettling way, the picture reminded me of the time Max sprayed catnip all over me, much to our cat DC's delight.

The blood seeping beneath my fingers slowed as nanites worked to repair my sliced carotid. I rolled to my feet to face more immediate concerns, only to catch sight of a zombie punching Tiffany in the stomach.

She fell backward, her head smashing into the coffee urn at the end of the line of tables. *No!* All her fears spoken in the limo ride home from Vegas were coming true. I ran, but somehow, Max beat me to her. He swung a music stand at the corpse coming after Tiffany. The zombie caught Max's wrist and squeezed. Max's howl didn't block the crack of bones breaking. The zombie raised its other fist.

No, no, no! "No! Go back to hell, you fuckers!"

I yanked the zombie off Max. Just like last night behind Anthony's, I punched and kicked with every scream and swear word emphasizing my emotions. The zombie disintegrated under my blows, and I stamped its entrails into Dad's formerly pristine lawn.

I bent and wheezed, trying to catch my breath. Exhaustion blackened the edges of my vision. It didn't make sense. Beating one freaking zombie shouldn't have sapped my strength, unless it was a delayed reaction from the telekinetic stunt I'd pulled in the front yard. My skin prickled and I looked around.

Everyone in the yard who was still conscious stared at me. No sound whatsoever except my harsh gasps for oxygen. And the zombies . . .

They lay scattered around the people and wolves, all of them in the same state as the one I had just pummeled. My heart lodged in my throat. They weren't the only ones not moving. Quiet sobs rippled the air. Mobile guests knelt next to prone figures, helping where they could, covering the bodies where they couldn't. What had been a joyous occasion had been turned into a carnage scene out of a horror movie.

A tap on the shoulder made me jump. I whirled to find one of the zombies who'd attacked me at the veggie table. Except his flesh was no longer hanging off his bones. Pink skin surged with blood. Vitality. Life.

"Ya wouldn't happen to have a stogie, would ya, toots?"

Chapter 21

I blinked blood and sweat out of my eyes. Nope, he was still there. In fact, his two buddies joined him. I blinked again. I wasn't seeing things. No aggressive moves, just looking at me as their desiccated skin knitted back together and filled out while I watched.

"By the way," Zombie Number One waved at the chaotic scene, "where are we?"

Eyeballs plumped and cartilage elongated the nose once again. *No, it couldn't be.* He shoved the huge aviator glasses back on his restored nose. *Dammit, I covered his funeral last fall.* I blinked for the third time, and any air I'd reclaimed left in a whoosh.

Mortimer Stern stood before me. Uncle Morty. Mr. Comedian, himself. The man. The myth. The rejuvenated corpse.

Like my death could get any stranger.

Uncle Morty waved a hand in front of my face. "You okay, toots? You're kind of pale." His eyes traveled down my body, taking in my blood-drenched gown and gore-encrusted feet, before working their way back to my boobs. Figured. The man had been a notorious lech in life. "What kind of production are you working on, toots?"

"Who's the kid?" Familiar red hair haloed around the face of comedienne Lily Bell. And behind her stood the Nose himself, Bill Faith. Three major stars from my grandparents' generation in front of me. Three major stars looking like they did in their prime instead of wrinkly old people. Okay, three dead major stars dressed in their moldy burial clothes, and I couldn't think of one coherent thing to say.

Bill Faith leaned over to whisper in Uncle Morty's ear. "She mute?"

"Don't know. Hey, toots? Can you talk?" He lifted a hand and pantomimed a moving mouth. "You know, talk?"

I relaxed my jaw muscles and muttered, "Stop calling me 'toots.'"

"Sam!"

"Stay here." I jabbed a finger at the ground and took a step away. They didn't so much as twitch, the curious expressions remaining on their restored faces. After shooting another glare at the trio, I stumbled the couple of steps back to where Max huddled with an unconscious Tiffany in his good arm. The right one bent at an un-natural angle that churned my stomach.

"Where's Bebe?" Tears coursed down his face. Ashy fear leaked out of every pore. "She's—"

I bent and checked Tiffany's pulse. It was there, and she stirred under my touch. But . . .

"This is all your fault!" Mom's screech rent the air. She stomped over to where I crouched next to Max. "You just couldn't let Max have his day, could you?"

Caesar grabbed her shoulder. "Stop." She sucked in a breath to yell. "Now, Mrs. Howell," he finished. No *suggestion* at all, but from the look in his neon yellow eyes, his bloodlust was barely in check.

I prayed Mom would get a clue, but she was just getting her groove started. She shook an index finger less than an inch in front of his fangs. "Don't you think you can scare me with your vampire act, you undead freak."

I rose and joined Caesar. "Mom, shut up. We've got to get the in-jured to the hospital."

She opened her mouth.

"I said stop, Mom." Everyone around us froze. Ri-i-ight. Like I was scarier than the Prince of Vampires.

The ugly stench of fear rolled off Mom, but she disguised it well. Her familiar haughtiness filled her eyes. "Or what? You'll smash me like you did all the zombies?"

God help me, I had done it. Just like last night. I couldn't worry about this new ability right now. Instead, I matched Mom's nasty look. "Don't tempt me."

"Duncan? Max, where's Uncle Duncan?" In the silence, Tiffany's hoarse voice carried across the crowd. No one answered her plaintive plea.

I took in the various piles of sludge that formed vampire remains. I reached out with my thoughts, but met with empty blackness instead of the familiar warmth. No. No, this couldn't be happening.

My heart stopped before it broke in two.

The vinyl waiting room couches in the Maura Lannigan wing of Good Samaritan Hospital were Federal blue instead of the avocado of Los Angeles Memorial. It didn't make them any more comfortable. For the second time in two months, I slouched in crappy cushions, mourning the death of someone close to me.

At least Fred Nguyen's assassination back in January had been a normal death. Not that a van smooshing my LAPD source into road pizza was a good thing for him or me. His death had been the red pill for my trip to the supernatural wonderland.

A trip made more surreal by the events of the wedding. The Los Angeles leaders pulled strings to get their people, both supernaturals and Family, transported here while the non-Family Normals were sent to Cedars-Sinai. Probably with a little memory-erasure during the ambulance ride.

As far as the outside world knew, this wing specialized in treating rare forms of cancer. The cover of John Lannigan's late alpha female allowed money to be donated by the supernatural community. The

hospital board never questioned the only stipulation for the dona-
tions, that Bebe supervised, and had sole discretion, over the wing.

The fingers of Max's good hand twined around mine as we sat. I'd
offered to sign his cast, but he murmured, "Later."

There was nothing worse than waiting in a hospital. Dad shoved a
cup of coffee in my free hand and dropped a few packages of cheese
crackers he'd scrounged for my growling stomach in my lap. Mom
took up the role of pacer when he took the chair next to Max and me.
My trio of restored zombie comedians perched on the couch across
from us, and for the most part kept their mouths shut. No one knew
what to do with them, so Caesar ordered them to stay with me until
Bebe could examine them. Right now, our witch doctor needed to
care for the living.

A few yards away, Caesar stood in a whispered conference with
the other two vampire masters. Jean-Pierre wouldn't meet my gaze.
Virginia shot me withering looks from time to time. She was the only
vampire master with a bodyguard, a tasty hunk with straight blue-
black hair and cinnamon-flavored coloring. A witch I didn't know
stood with the vampires, an eclectic from her simple ball studs and
hoop earrings. A multitude of braids were gathered at the top of her
head, each ending in a bead of a different kind of stone. From the
way she inched closer to Jean-Pierre under my watch, she probably
worked for him.

Closing my eyes, I leaned back against the couch. I'd been so ex-
cited to talk to Virginia. When Caesar had arranged for me to interview her after the wedding for the vampire histories he wanted me
to write, I'd been ecstatic about talking to one of the first Europeans
born on American soil. When I told Duncan, he said to tread lightly
with her . . .

Tears streamed from beneath my lids. Damn, I'd gone almost five
minutes without thinking about him. I wanted to believe he wasn't
one of the piles of vampire sludge scattered around Mom and Dad's
back lawn. God, how I wanted to believe!

The naked, raw silence reigned in my psyche.

Max's hand slipped from mine, and he tugged my head to the crook of his shoulder. "They'll find him."

I sniffed, shooting for a subject change to keep the floodgates in check. "You need to worry about your wife and your baby."

A dry chuckle thrummed through his chest. "You mean fiancée. The ceremony wasn't completed." His voice dropped to a whisper so Dad wouldn't hear. "And I think the vampires have already erased Reverend Mitchell's memory."

I would have laughed if I didn't have a lead weight sitting on my chest. Swiping my nose, I said, "It's probably for the best."

Max stiffened underneath my cheek. "Me and Tiffany not getting married?"

Blinking gummy, swollen eyes, I looked up at him. "No, I mean Reverend Mitchell. He almost stroked out when Duncan—" The words jammed in my throat.

Max sighed. "Maybe Tiffany was right. The civil ceremony at the court house would have been less—" He stared at the operating room doors for a long time before he finished. "Just less."

I squeezed his knee. "Tiffany'll be fine. They'll both be fine." Now, if Bebe would come out and verify my wishful thinking . . .

With a pneumatic hiss, the doors at the other end of the corridor opened to reveal Alex. Compared to my gore-crusted gauze, his jeans were pristine. It made me wish I'd had a chance to clean up. Gross was becoming my natural state. And my tears would be a little less obvious in the shower.

Cowboy boots tapped a somber rhythm as he strode down the hall to report to Caesar. A status report Duncan should be giving to the coven master. Alex glanced our way, but wouldn't meet my eyes either.

He kept his voice low, but damn it all if he didn't switch to French for his update. I should have paid more attention to the private tutor Mom insisted on in high school. If I had the energy to care, I would have given Alex hell for hiding stuff from me. All I could do was stare at the floor.

At Alex's mention of Jamal, my head jerked up to see Caesar's still expression. Eerily still expression. The last time he had that look had been two months ago. The night Duncan had killed Caesar's twin sister to save my ass.

Oh God! Even my exhausted brain could put two and two together. Jamal was dead. His laughter flickered through my memory. He and Kensai had been together nearly four centuries. How the hell was Kensai dealing?

This was all my fault.

I couldn't breathe when Alex flicked a look in my direction, then whispered something else.

"What do you mean he's missing?" Mom's voice jerked me out of my wallowing. She strode over to the vamps, arms crossed.

From the looks she got from the vamps, I would have thought she'd grown another head.

"*Oui, je parle francais,*" she snapped. "Now, what do you mean Duncan's missing?"

My heart jerked. Missing? The vinyl crackled when I rose. Or it may have been the dress. Caesar and Alex shot worried looks my way before Caesar's expression turned imperious.

"This is a private conversation, Mrs. Howell."

Mom's arms loosened and a manicured index finger waved underneath his nose. "Don't you dare take that tone with me, you undead freak." Weird. The sounds she made weren't her normal high-pitched screech. More like Mr. Cuddles growling a warning.

I couldn't bear to let go of the tiny sliver of hope. "Mom." I crossed to them and laid a grimy hand on her arm. She didn't so much as flinch at the possible stain on her designer suit.

Instead, she met Caesar's mojo head on. "And don't you dare try that mind control shit with me." Her body shook, but her voice remained steady. "My grandbaby may be dying in there. The last thing poor Tiffany needs is for you to lose her uncle's body, too."

"Mom."

She turned to me. Unshed tears shimmered under the ugly fluorescent lighting. "Don't defend them, Samantha. You and Max should have told me."

What? She never blamed both of us for anything.

Caesar's sharp voice sliced through the frigid hospital air. "This isn't your business."

"Listen up, you undead son-of-a—"

"Mom!"

"Stay out of it. Samantha."

"Mom, they're not undead. I am."

Mom's head turned toward me in slow motion. Total blankness that had nothing to do with her Botox injections filled her face.

I sucked in a harsh breath, trying to get air past the lump of grief in my throat. "I am, Mom. I-I died two months ago. Duncan tried to save me, but—" There. I finally said it. After agonizing over my decision for two freaking months, I blurted the truth out in the middle of a hospital waiting room after zombies crashed my brother's wedding.

Horror dawned on her face, and a fist rose to her mouth. "Oh, my God. He turned you into one of them?"

"No, Mom."

The fact that Dad stood behind her, hands gripping her shoulders, finally registered. "What happened, honey?"

Within two minutes, the *Reader's Digest* condensed version spilled from my lips, including my kidnapping, death and transformation at the hands of billionaire Tyrone Mallory and Caesar's twin sister, Selene, as well as Duncan's rescue of me.

"Wait a minute." Dad held up an index finger, a puzzled look on his face. "Did you die from the nanites or the gunshot wound while you were escaping?"

"Well . . ." My dirty toes brushed against the formerly sterile linoleum. "We're not sure."

"But surely the Mallory girl—"

"Um—" The wheels in my brain turned furiously, but there's no easy way to admit you've committed homicide to your parents. "I kind of stabbed her through the heart after the nanites had been injected into her."

"You what?" Mom's mouth dropped open.

"With a wooden spoon. I couldn't reach the butcher knife." If Mom's eyes could have jumped out of her skull, they would have. "It was self-defense. She was choking me with a fireplace poker," I finished lamely.

"Dr. Zachary didn't have a chance to examine either Sam or Sierra Mallory between the introduction of the nanites and their mortal wounds." I didn't notice Max had joined us until he spoke.

Mom's shrewd gaze shifted from Max to me. "So what really happened to Sierra Mallory? The rumor around the club was she had cancer. Or is that a cover story for you killing the poor girl?"

Nice to know things were back to normal between us. "She did have cancer," I said with gritted teeth. "I was the guinea pig for the cure. The nanites eliminated the leukemia, but somewhere along the way, Sierra turned psychotic. When she sucked my blood, both of our nanites hit a programming glitch, and she exploded."

"She exploded?" Not even the Botox treatments could keep Mom's eyebrows from climbing halfway up her forehead.

"But you're saying you're a zombie, right?" Poor Dad. From the furrows in his forehead, he was trying to accept this. Maybe it hadn't been such a good idea to tell them.

"Damn. After that load of bullshit, I need something stronger than a cigar," Uncle Morty muttered.

In unison for once, the entire family turned to Morty and said, "Shut up."

"No." Mom shook her head. "No, I don't accept that. You're nothing like those things." She jabbed a finger in the vampires' direction.

I rolled my eyes. "Of course not, Mom. Vampires aren't dead. They just have a chronic disease. I'm a zombie, and yes, I am dead."

"But you're not like the ones that-that—" Dad cleared his throat.

I shook my head. "Because of the nanites, Dad. Those were real, summoned-by-magick zombies."

A snicker sprouted from the other couch. "With that story, it sounds more like she's the bride of Frankenstein."

I turned to Bill Faith. "Opinions of the 'normal'—" My fingers made air quotes. "—zombies are not welcome. So keep your mouth shut unless you want to end up as Dad's new lawn fertilizer."

Bill's jaw snapped shut, and he went back to flipping through a *Better Homes and Gardens.*

I couldn't deal with everything at once. Wrapping my arms around my body, I took stock. Jamal was dead. Tiffany was still in surgery. It wasn't like I could help either of them, so the next priority was Duncan. My attention focused back on Alex. "Spit it out. What's going on?"

The tall Texan twitched. It sucked being the bearer of bad news, but I wasn't about to let him off the hook. I had to know, so I gave him the Siamese stare-down I'd practiced for years on our cat DC. And it wasn't like Mr. Psychoanalysis-for-everyone-but-him to avoid the truth.

At a slight nod from Caesar, he met my eyes and took a deep breath. "We've been able to identify all the remains through personal effects." *Jewelry and watches mired in goo,* my mind filled in. "We haven't found anything that we know is Duncan's. Not even his sister's locket." His eyes closed in resignation, then opened with a pleading look.

Like he needed my forgiveness. Hell, I was the one who needed everyone's forgiveness. If I'm the one animating the dead as Mai suggested . . .

Then his statement of evidence registered. "He wasn't wearing Margaret's locket." Caesar and Alex jerked at my revelation. "He gave it to Tiffany as her 'something old' right before the ceremony." A small blister of hope developed on my heart. God, it was going to hurt when it popped.

"This one?" Max dug awkwardly with his left hand in his suit trousers. Blood had dried in reddish-brown spatters across the white legs. He pulled out the handful of jewelry Tiffany had worn during the ceremony. "Bebe took these off her in the ambulance." In his open hand lay the simple gold wedding band, Phil's bracelet, and the locket.

I reached for it, only to have Jean-Pierre's eclectic slap my hand away. "No. Don't contaminate it any more than it is. I may be able to trace where my brother's taken St. James."

My overloaded gray matter finally regurgitated Ralph's story. David Head's sister was Jean-Pierre's eclectic. And before the wedding ceremony, Duncan said it wasn't Head's were buddy behind the attacks . . .

"You bitch!" I reached for her throat. She scrambled away, running for the doors.

Except I never touched her. Caesar and Jean-Pierre grabbed my arms when I was millimeters from her neck. Writhing and yanking, I tried to reach her, but the master vampires' grip might have been concrete for all the good it did.

"Stop it. Samantha, stop. Killing her won't help Duncan." Caesar's words penetrated the red haze covering my vision.

I gasped and stopped fighting the men. "Okay, fine. I won't kill her." Caesar and Jean-Pierre's hold relaxed. Shooting her a murderous look, I added, "Yet."

"Tracking spell?" Alex's words floated somewhere behind me, and the bitch nodded. She didn't take her eyes off me, or release her death-grip on the door handle.

I shook my head, vigorously enough Jean-Pierre's hand tightened on my upper arm. "No, Bebe'll do it. Not her."

"I'll do what?"

With our little homicidal tableau, I don't think anyone in the waiting room heard Bebe and Ben Epstein come out of the operating room. She turned and gave her step-grandfather a one-armed hug. "Go get some rest. And thank you."

He patted her on the back. "You too, little girl." Dark circles ringed his eyes, and their normal twinkle had been ground under the foot of exhaustion. Giving everyone a curious look, he shuffled past Head's sister and out the doors.

Ignoring the eclectic's advice, Max pressed the jewelry in my hand and approached Bebe with an anxious expression. "How's Tiffany?"

"She'll be fine." Bebe pulled off her operating room cap, and wild curls sprang everywhere. "We got the internal bleeding stopped and healed. Same with the concussion." She gave Max a tired smile. "A few days of bed rest and she'll be back to her charming self in no time."

"The baby?" Fear tinged Max's voice. Mom stepped closer to him and wrapped an arm around his uninjured side.

Bleakness filled Bebe's face. "It's too early to tell."

"What kind of doctor are you?" I could hear the sneer in Mom's voice.

Bebe's posture stiffened. "I'm sorry, Mrs. Howell. They don't cover zombie assaults in med school." She turned to Max, her body language freezing Mom out. "The first twenty-four hours are critical after this kind of physical trauma to the mother. Ben and I healed the damage, but the body still registers it." She sucked in a deep breath. "If Tiffany's body doesn't spontaneously abort, she should be able to carry to term just fine."

Max shrugged off Mom's embrace. He reached out and pulled

Bebe to him in an awkward one-armed hug. "Thanks," he whispered. Lilac gratefulness mushroomed in a cloud around him.

She nodded. "You can go on back and sit with her in recovery." When Max disappeared behind the doors to the operating section, she strode to where the guys still stood between me and the eclectic and eyed me. "Now, what do you want me to do?"

Rapid-fire buzzing brushed my mind as Caesar filled her in.

She sighed, her relief palpable. "And here, I thought you people wanted something difficult." She held out her hand, and I untangled the chain from the bracelet before dropping the gold in her upraised palm.

"You need to set a circle—"

Bebe eyed Head's sister. "I don't need jack, little girl." She paused and grinned. "I take that back. A fat bottle of Mr. Daniels would be highly welcome after the night we've had." Her mood sobered. Eyelids dipped and ozone spiced the air. After a couple of seconds, her eyes blinked open, and she dangled the locket in the air. "Here you go, Sam. Just hold it in front of you, and it'll point the way." The locket swung on its chain for a second before hovering to the right. "It'd be best if you—"

A scream choked off her words. Her body convulsed and shook, collapsing to the floor. I reached out to help, but the moment I touched her, black diamond fire seared my skin and incinerated my mind.

Chapter 22

Agony racked Duncan St. James skull, driving him away from comforting unconsciousness. Tiffany's wedding. Samantha in danger. The desire, the need to chase those thoughts drove him. Unfortunately, full coherence lay in the same direction of his pounding head. Resigning himself to the inevitable, he opened his eyes. The darkened bedroom seemed vaguely familiar, but recognition escaped him, and not because of his blurred vision.

Instinct said it was after sunrise, but the heavy drapes blocked the fatal rays. He blinked, tried to lift his head to check his surroundings. Cheeky idea. A spike of pain drove the wave of dizziness, and sweat trickled into his eyes. Maybe Tiffany would have suggestions on combating the swirling nausea.

Another tactic then, but trying to raise his right arm seared his flesh. An ugly odor confirmed the burning long before he could gather the strength to look. Silver encircled his wrists. A painful glance down showed similar shackles on his ankles. Not to mention he was stark naked.

How humiliating.

Last night. He closed his eyes, trying to concentrate on the previous evening's memories. The attack on the wedding. He'd sent Sam out of the Howells' estate with an enforcer escort. He turned to Tiffany and then . . .

And then . . .

One of the zombies must have bashed in his brains, considering the level of discomfort and lack of memory. Bloody hell. Where had he been taken? He took a deep breath to calm the nausea. Sharp, acrid ozone coated with ginger and an earthy masculine scent wafted through aching sinuses.

David Head. His home in Los Angeles? A possibility since the hotel said Head and his party checked out Friday morning. Yvonne was right. The boy had gone off the deep end if he was kidnapping vampires in addition to trying to kill Samantha.

Duncan jerked the manacles again, only to have the silver fry more skin. God only knew where Head was. The throbbing made detection of anyone else in the building difficult. He had to escape, find Samantha before Head—

No, the idea didn't bear any more scrutiny. She was a resourceful and clever woman. If she could escape Selene, she could escape Head. Those thoughts didn't make his current predicament any more palatable.

Metallic noises reached his ears. It took precious time to recognize a key in a lock. Head was returning. He renewed the painful efforts to extract himself from the manacles.

Brandon shoved the key in the lock. His therapist was right. Running away from admitting his identity hadn't solved his problems. Neither was using Yvonne to touch and not touch the man he still loved. He needed closure with David, even if it meant David kicking his ass. He turned the key and entered.

The odor of something burning smacked him in the face.

He raced for the kitchen. No, stove and oven both were off. He ran down the hallway, the acrid odor worse with every step.

Oh shit! Had David left incense or candles burning? His carelessness with both had been an ongoing source of irritation when they were together.

He hit the master bedroom door at full speed, and it slammed open. His mouth opened in shock. In the near darkness, a naked man lay in the middle of David's custom-made bed, spread-eagle and chained. Brandon flicked the light switch. The stranger blinked rapidly, but it was Brandon's stomach that did a queasy somersault. Around the cuffs on the man's wrists and ankles, ugly burns oozed blood and mucus.

"Who the bloody hell are you?"

Brandon absorbed the sight. Longish, black hair, one heck of a body, and a British accent. Yeah, he could understand why David might want to chain the stranger to his bed. But the David he knew wouldn't hurt someone. Not like this.

"I said—"

"I'm Brandon." He almost added "David's boyfriend," but that wasn't true anymore, hadn't been true for a long time, and he didn't think the stranger would appreciate the comment. Not the way those intense green eyes practically glowed. "Brandon Tyler."

"Find the bloody keys!" Somehow this guy was freaking intimidating while chained to the bed and stark naked.

Brandon crossed to the bureau, set down his keys and the plant he'd brought for David, and yanked open the top drawer. Yep, David still kept his toys in the same place. He rummaged through various lotions and plugs until his found a key on a slender silver chain.

"Here we go." Reaching the top post, he unlocked the first cuff. The stranger hissed when the metal brushed the top of his right hand. Ugly redness spread across the skin, and small blisters popped to the surface.

"What the—" Brandon checked the manacle, then his own hands. Cool metal and unmarred pale skin. "Are you allergic to this?"

"Yes, you imbecile!"

Brandon glanced down. If he didn't know better, the stranger's canines were longer, too long for a normal mouth. He took a step back.

Air whistled as the stranger sucked down a lungful of air and released it. "I apologize for calling you names. My head aches, and—" He glanced down his body before giving Brandon a rueful smile. "This is not normally how I meet a young gentleman. I am Duncan."

"Um, sure." *Figures.* This Duncan was just someone David picked up at a bar or something. "Where is David, by the way?"

Duncan's eyebrows rose. "You do not know?"

He shook his head and released Duncan's ankle, holding the appendage away from the silver as best he could. "I came over, hoping to talk to him." Dang, the man had cold feet. What the hell was the attraction when frozen toes were one of David's pet peeves? He walked around the bed.

"Hey, Duncan, I've got tea, scones and—"

Brandon whirled to find David standing in the doorway, holding two bags and a drink tray. Chocolate eyes widened as David took in what he was doing. He took a tentative step toward his ex. "David?"

Steaming tea spattered over the hardwood floor and bags flew. David dropped to his knees, his hand slamming down on the silver piping near the doorway. Blood orange light sizzled across Brandon's eyes. When he blinked the spots out, David was gone.

Brandon strode to the open doorway and literally hit an invisible wall. Banging on the nothingness in the doorway produced no sound, no knock, nothing. It was like the air itself was solid. His heart skipped a beat. No. All David's stories, all those insane tales told in dark nights as they held each other couldn't possibly be true.

Turning back, he tripped over one of the paper sacks. A plastic bag full of scarlet liquid poked out of the top. He knelt and reached for it. And nearly threw up.

He looked back at the bed. The stranger had unlocked the last two manacles and now stood beside him. Neon green eyes met his. Fangs extended in a snarl. And his stomach convulsed at the knowledge of just what his ex-boyfriend had locked in the bedroom with him.

Chapter 23

The beast inside me roared, howling its hunger for all to hear. Meat, bloody and raw. The smell, the desire, It wanted the rich flesh, to savor the juices.

"Sam?"

"Goddess dammit, Jake! Stay back!"

The voices meant nothing. Not when the hunger was all that mattered. Then a wedge entered my mouth, not the delicious odor that teased, but something else. The beast didn't like it. Not this wimpy, pale imitation.

Cold, dead fingers stroked our throat. "C'mon, toots, swallow."

We shook our head, but the fingers and the voice persisted. Our throat convulsed and the mouthful slid south.

"C'mon, toots, another bite." Meat, hot, but not the right hot.

The beast grumbled its displeasure. A heartbeat. Two. It gave in and grudgingly accepted the offering. Then we devoured everything shoved at us.

I hiccupped and looked down. A zillion Big Mac wrappers lay on top of hospital blankets on my lap. Twinkie boxes stood open with only scraps of cellophane in them. And they weren't just the regular supermarket variety boxes, but the mega boxes you get at the wholesale cost clubs.

I lifted my head. My three zombie comedians were closest to the bed, obviously the ones who'd fed the beast within me. Mai stood between the bed and the door, Stan behind her. She holstered her gun as I took in their presence. The defense to my possible zombie rampage. Tiffany sat in the opposite corner next to the window, her semi-automatic pistol in her lap. Max stood next to her.

Just like last night at the restaurant, everyone in the hospital room, except Bebe and Mai, alternated between staring at me and the food debris left in my wake. My brain kicked into gear and sped past the satiated beast. Stan hadn't witnessed one of my gorge-outs, and this time wasn't like the ones Tiffany and Max had seen in the past. I blinked. And what the hell was Goth Girl doing in a wheel chair so soon after surgery?

And Jake . . .

I pointed at my ex who peered over Uncle Morty's shoulder. "Holy crap! What's he doing here?"

A lazy, sardonic smile spread across his face. "Thanks a lot. Maybe I was worried about you."

Bebe elbowed Bill Faith out of the way and lowered the safety railing. "She's coherent. Let me check her vitals." When I shot her an inquiring look, she snorted. "Two of John's boys were on duty downstairs." She glanced at Jake and turned back with a disgusted look. "Your *boyfriend* here said he was Family."

Uh-oh. I wasn't sure if she was angry at the security weres for screwing up. It's not their fault they didn't have telepathic abilities in their human forms. Or if she was furious at Jake for figuring out how to finagle his way past the guards. Or pissed at me for, well, involving a civilian in this mess. An ex-boyfriend at that.

"Actually it's the asshole who tried to fry my brain who's ticking me off," she muttered.

Oops. My head ached a little, but nothing like the previous migraines. Still, with Jake here, I needed to be extra careful with stray thoughts.

Instead of using magick, Bebe wrapped a blood pressure cuff around my bicep. I winced when she jerked the pressure cuff a little tighter than necessary. "If it wasn't for you and your minions, I don't know what would have happened." Her wave indicated the zombies hovering beside the bed.

I twisted to find Lily Bell sitting behind me stroking my hair. Uncle Morty clutched the raised railing in one hand, a bag of Mickey Dee's fries in the other. And I don't mean one of those itty, bitty paper envelopes, but the small bags used for Happy Meals. Full to the top. An unlit cigar dangled from his mouth.

I turned back to examine the doctor. The circles under Bebe's eyes were bigger and darker than Ben's had been. With a jolt that had nothing to do with the air-filled plastic pinching my skin, the memory of the waiting room slid into view.

I grabbed her arm. "Are you okay?" No wonder she wasn't using magick to examine me. The doctor was lucky her brain wasn't barbequed.

She nodded and slid the flat end of the stethoscope through the neck of my hospital gown before she shushed me and said, "Breathe in."

I inhaled. Mother of pearl, it hurt. My entire ribcage seemed constricted to the point my lungs had no room to expand.

"Again."

"You're a fucking sadist, Zachary," I muttered, but I sucked in another pain-filled lungful anyway.

She snorted. "Yeah, I'd say you're fine." A sober expression drove away her amusement. "Thanks for saving my ass last night."

"Last night?" I croaked. No, I wasn't out that long, was I?

I must have accidentally transmitted again because Bebe nodded. "Yeah, you've been out a little over fourteen hours."

"What happened?" I glanced at Jake before I waved a hand. "You did the . . ."

She grimaced. "Someone anticipated the tracking spell."

"Huh?" A quick check showed my ex with a nonchalant expression, considering Bebe had just admitted she's a witch.

Tiffany rolled up to the bed, and over Bill's toes from his curse as he jumped back. "Like a computer hacker spiking a trace. Whoever took Duncan put a spell on him, so when Bebe tried to find him with Grandma Margaret's locket, boom!" She smacked a tiny fist into the opposing palm, her endearing homicidal look fixed on her sharp features. "A magickal back surge to liquefy her brain."

Joy flooded through me. He was alive. Duncan was alive.

A wild grin replaced the nasty look on Tiffany. "Yeah, he's alive." A shadow fell. "For now."

"When you touched Doctor Zachary, you went into convulsions too," came Lily's smoky husk from behind me. Her tender strokes through my hair were far more comforting than I wanted to admit. It was something a real mother would do for a troubled daughter. I hadn't missed the fact Mom was nowhere to be seen. Neither was Dad.

"We could *see* you pulling the spell out of her." Lily's voice held a touch of wonder.

Bill gave a quick nod. "Yeah, it was like we knew you were trying to ground out the power, but you were having trouble. We jumped in to help." His wave indicated the other two dead comedians.

Uncle Morty plucked the cigar out of his mouth and tucked it in his jacket pocket. A pocket connected to a brand new suit jacket. Nice to know my little zombies weren't wearing their moldy grave clothes anymore. "Doc, here, was a little shaken but fine. You took the brunt of the surge. We couldn't wake you up for anything though." A handful of fries replaced the cigar, and he chomped away.

"But the spell still worked, right? We know where Duncan is?" I glanced from Tiffany to the rest of the group gathered around me.

"That's the problem, Sam." A scowl twisted Stan's features. "We know where he is—"

"But Caesar nixed any rescue missions," Tiffany finished with a snarl.

Chapter 24

Duncan brushed past the trembling Brandon and tried not to think about a certain infuriating blonde. She damn well better have survived the zombie attack. He couldn't bear contemplating the alternative. The dryness of his throat prevented him from swallowing his guilt. Why didn't he deduce David was behind the zombies? He knew the boy's history, and he'd put Samantha, everyone, in danger with his ineptitude.

The smooth nothingness of a witch's circle met his touch. He knelt at the doorway, but the ring of silver burned with just a fleeting brush of his fingertips. There was no getting a telepathic message through the shield. David had planned well. Too well.

With a grunt, Duncan rose. He needed to prioritize the actions he might accomplish, to prepare for his next encounter with David and find an escape. A quick examination of the room resulted in an empty phone jack. Not that the line would have worked with an activated circle intersecting it, but it had been worth the try.

Returning to the center of the room, he considered the next step. The tea was a total loss, so he snatched up the plastic, red-filled bag and tore it open with his teeth before upending the contents. The taste nearly gagged him.

Human.

Well, that was just bloody perfect. What the hell was Head thinking? He considered flushing the contents down the toilet.

A slight movement caught his eye. The Normal boy had wedged

himself between the dresser and the table holding stereo equipment, crouching there with his back plastered against the wall. His fear flooded the room, setting Duncan's fangs on edge.

No, he'd have to drink what David had brought. He couldn't risk losing control of his thirst with an innocent trapped in the bedroom with him.

Steeling himself, he swallowed the contents of two of the three bags. He knelt and stashed the third bag in the mini-fridge tucked under the nightstand. No sense in being a pig. Only the Lord on High knew when David might return.

He stood and flexed his wrists. The blood was already doing its work. The pain of his burnt skin eased. He turned to the boy shivering in the corner. "Brandon?"

The ammonia-stench of urine filled the air.

Duncan sighed and raked a hand through his hair, the strands stiff under his fingers. Probing further, he found the tender spot on the back of his skull, all that remained from his zombie-inflicted injuries. "I believe I will shower first. After you have a chance to clean yourself, we will talk."

The only answer was a squeak of fear.

He scowled. "I am not the one who sealed you in his bedroom."

A step toward the young man produced another squeak. Duncan held up his hands. "I will not harm you."

"Y-y-you—" Brandon pointed at the trashcan where the blood bags had been disposed.

Duncan shrugged. "Beggars can't be choosers." The lightest of mental touches eased the boy's tangled emotions. Truly, his actions were for his own relief. Canines retracted at the lessening of the boy's fear scent. "Are you hungry?"

Brandon's eyes widened and his ashy scent sharpened.

Duncan swallowed another sigh. The boy was totally useless. He retrieved the soggy pastry bag from the puddle of tea and glanced inside. The heady smell of cinnamon and sugar wafted into the room. The waxed paper had saved the contents from a thorough dousing. Pulling open a dresser drawer, he yanked out a white t-shirt and used it to mop off the dark brown liquid that trickled down the sides of the little sack. After being kidnapped, he couldn't feel guilt over permanently staining his abductor's clothing.

"If you change your mind," he said, placing the bag on top of the stereo. On reconsideration, he should have let the tea drip all over David's expensive components.

The boy didn't budge unless one counted the quaking fear.

Duncan gave up and strode into the bathroom.

"What do you mean he won't let us rescue Duncan?" My words came out in a throaty growl, more animal than human. Dammit, I couldn't even picture Caesar leaving any of his people, much less Duncan, to the mercy of another supernatural. "Where is he?"

Tiffany glared back, the anger in her eyes matching mine though not aimed at me. "Duncan's at David Head's mansion in Malibu."

I glanced between the furious Bebe and the equally seething enforcers by the door. "What are you talking about? He's an eclectic. He's got no fucking standing in Los Angeles. There's no reason we can't bash down his door." My hands wrapped around the guard-rails. Metal squeals filled the air as my fingers twisted the metal into new shapes in my efforts to escape Lily's arms.

Stan's glower promised someone would be hurting once the half-fae got his hands on the culprit. "Head made a deal with Duke Millanthropas."

With his words, I froze. This was so not good. "Why would a Seelie duke deal with an eclectic witch?" My tone matched Stan's frigid voice. "Especially one under a vampire coven's jurisdiction?"

Bebe covered my right hand. "Jean-Pierre repudiated Head after

Lannigan's pack found a dead were in the Hollywood Cemetery. His heart had been cut out. A couple hundred graves disturbed."

A blood sacrifice to raise the dead. The zombies that had crashed Max and Tiffany's wedding. All one hundred Twinkies surged in my stomach. "Not one of his?" *Please, God, not one of John's people.* Maybe I didn't totally trust the Los Angeles packmaster, but I wouldn't wish that kind of death on anyone.

The doctor shook her head. "The runt from the Cajun pack who works—" Her eyes closed as she corrected her words. "Worked for Jean-Pierre."

The image of the short were from Duke's party flashed through my mind. A formerly living, breathing were. The one whose scent I'd detected on the other zombies. I swallowed hard, trying to keep the Twinkies contained. "Head killed his own bodyguard? To raise those zombies?"

Another nod. Teary eyes opened to meet mine. "He knew Jean-Pierre would call a death hunt on him for the murder. So he went to Millanthropas."

A death hunt. Acid coated the back of my mouth. The supernaturals were great believers of capital punishment, even here in California. If Jean-Pierre Rousseau leveled an execution order on one of his people, Caesar had every right to carry it out if Head was still in his territory. In fact, he'd be required to if he didn't want to start a war with the southeastern vampires.

The nanites put the food I'd gorged on to good use because neurons began firing, trying to make two and two equal four. "If Rousseau's called a death hunt, why would the fairies get in the middle of an internal vampire matter . . ."

Everyone in the room, except Jake, gave me the "duh" look.

Jake raised his hand. "Hey, someone want to explain it to the dumb mortal here?"

Max took pity on my ex. "To the fairies, Sam's the equivalent of Saddam Hussein."

I rolled my eyes. "No, Caesar's Hussein. I'm more like the alleged WMDs hidden in the desert, except I'm real."

Jake's eyes still had an incredulous look.

"The steel in the nanites," I pointed out.

Understanding registered on his face. "So they'd want a necromancer in their back pocket as their assurance the vampires won't launch a first strike."

Mai's quiet voice filled the hospital room. "Except Head doesn't have the control over Sam he would over other zombies."

The scene behind the restaurant surged to the forefront of my thoughts. "He had enough control over me a couple of nights ago."

"Only because he was able to slip a drug into your food. He won't catch you that way again." Mai's pain and rage simmered behind her eyes. Jamal was her family. For someone with no extra gifts, she could be freakin' deadly in her own right.

Just one problem with the enforcer's theory. I looked up at Bebe. "What about Head's sister?"

The doctor snorted. "She claims she doesn't have the necromancy talent like David. You can't just bind one aspect of a witch's power. According to Jean-Pierre, David confessed to raising the dead so the New Orleans coven bound only his powers."

I eyed Bebe. While I believed her, Rosseau's story was suspect just from his and his eclectic's body language. There was definitely an emotional attachment between them, even if she wasn't one of the new witches who were immune to the vampire virus. "Then why was she kicked out of the coven?"

"Because she knew what her brother was doing and didn't try to stop him or report him to the coven." A sad sigh followed Bebe's statement. "Sam, Yvonne's waiting outside to talk to you." She held up a hand when I opened my mouth to argue. "I think you should hear what she has to say."

A new beast growled inside me. Bebe was making a mistake trusting this woman. How could we be sure Head's sister wasn't involved in Duncan's kidnapping? She had already been found guilty of complicity in Head's actions by her own coven.

There was only one way to find out, and if she refused me, I'd have my answer.

I nodded my acquiescence. Bebe's shoulders eased, but just a hair. Good to know I wasn't the only one who didn't trust the New Orleans witch.

Stan poked his head out the door. A soft voice with a Caribbean lilt answered, one I recognized. I wound my fingers in the standard hospital blanket, not trusting myself to keep my hands from her throat.

She slipped into the room, the clicking of her braid beads the only sound. Stan held out his hand. She hesitated a moment before handing the designer bag slung over her shoulder to the enforcer.

"Jewelry too." Mai's hand on the butt of the gun on her hip indicated her seriousness.

Fear flashed in the woman's eyes, but she complied without a word, handing necklaces, rings and a billion bracelets to Stan. Mai still didn't remove her palm from her weapon.

Through it all, the witch never took her attention from me.

Bebe cleared her throat. "Sam, this is Yvonne Head."

Head took a step closer to the bed. Uncle Morty dropped the half-empty bag of fries into my lap. The former comedian moved to block her before I laid a hand on his arm. He glanced at me. I shook my head slightly. His body language remained tight as his attention returned to the woman, but he didn't take any further steps. I'd have to sort out the whys of the dead comedians' protective streak later.

Once I had Duncan back.

There was something incongruous about the whole situation. Here I was in a hospital bed, surrounded by a pile of fast food wrappers and with my ass hanging out of one of those standard issue hospital gowns. Meanwhile a beautiful, and no doubt powerful, witch stood in front of me, dressed in the latest designer-wear, twisting her fingers like a kindergartener caught picking a booger in class.

I took a really good look at her. Her expertly applied make-up didn't cover the dark smudges under her eyes, much less the blood-shot whites or puffy skin. Manicured nails ended in jagged tips. Ashy splotches showed on the skin of her neck and arms. The signs of someone under a hell of a lot of stress. I almost felt sorry for her.

It was an emotion I couldn't afford right now. Not with Duncan's life at stake. "Why are you here, Ms. Head?"

She jerked at my lowered voice. Her attention fell to her twined fingers. "I-I want to help you, and I need your help in return."

The space between my eyebrows tightened. "You want me to help you how?"

Her head rose, naked pleading in the tears trickling down her cheeks. "I need help saving my brother."

Tiffany snorted. "A little late for that." Max shushed her.

Head's attention flicked from my almost sister-in-law in the corner and back to me. "I don't have anyone else to ask." She sniffed and swiped at the wetness on her face. "The fairies don't care about him, and he's—" Her gulp was audible before she met my eyes. "He's sick. The binding the coven elders placed on him has failed. I can't bind him alone. He's too powerful."

Granted, her brother had rattled my clock with the magickal feedback, but she probably wouldn't make sense anyway. Was she really trying to plead the insanity defense for Head? I stared at the nervous witch. "What do you expect me to do?"

She flicked a look at Bebe and sucked in a deep breath. "He's as much a danger to himself as to everyone else. I spoke with Dr. Zachary—"

That earned Bebe an ugly look before I focused back on Yvonne. "And?" I prompted after too many seconds of silence.

"Instead of relying on a binding, you could take away his powers."

My mouth dropped open. Lily tensed behind me, her hands

gripping my shoulders. I floundered a few times before I found my tongue. "How the hell do you expect me to pull that rabbit out of my ass?" My attention turned to Bebe.

Her arms were crossed, a thoughtful expression on her round face. "The same way you destroyed the spell animating the zombies."

A quick peek at Yvonne standing there with a hopeful expression on her face didn't help my nerves. I glared at Bebe. *Are you fucking insane? Did you see what happened to the zombies when I broke the spell? I don't have that kind of finesse!* As much as I despised Head's guts at that moment, I couldn't conceive of smashing him to bits. I barely handled the nightmares from the three times I'd killed in self-defense.

She winced at the mental shout. "Stan and I can tutor you. David's not going to hurt Duncan. Not if we keep our distance before we're ready to strike."

"You've got no guarantee—"

"David's in love with St. James."

My head whipped around at the surety in Yvonne's voice.

What game was she playing at? My eyes narrowed. "Tell me something I don't know. But if he's as nuts as you say, there's no reason to believe he wouldn't hurt Duncan."

In return, her eyes widened and blinked several times. "How-how did you know about his feelings?"

"David smelled like roses when we ran into him at Duke Miller's party." I took a deep breath and released it. "I want to read your mind."

Horror spread across Yvonne Head's angular features. There was no other word for the expression. "W-why?"

Muscles tightened as I hardened my expression. "That's the price for my help. For all I know, you're setting me up so he can knock me down. We both know there's no love lost between your brother and me since I'm the one who outed him. So let's cut the bullshit."

All my cards lay on the table. Getting into Head's estate would be easier with her help, but not impossible. I was gambling Duncan's life that her concern for her brother's would outweigh anything else. Then I'd know for sure what the stakes were.

Or she could fry my brain if I screwed up.

I tried very hard not to think of that possibility as we locked eyes for a very long minute.

Finally, she nodded. "I will submit, but—" A diamond glint flared in her light hazel eyes. "I want your promise you will not kill Davy."

I nodded as well, but I had the terrible feeling I'd just told the biggest lie of my life.

Chapter 25

Humid air followed Duncan out of the bathroom. His eyes fell to where his fellow prisoner sat in the same spot. The boy still had his arms wrapped around his knees, his chin tucked. But instead of shaking in fear, he rocked, trying to comfort himself no doubt.

Duncan gestured to the open door. "I am finished if you would care to use the facilities."

The boy's head rose. Bloodshot, puffy eyes stared from between the dark locks hanging in his face, a suspicious cast in them. He said nothing.

"Has David come back?" It was a moot question since he would have heard, but it was the most neutral subject he could conceive at the moment.

The boy shook his head.

Gripping the towel wrapped around his waist, Duncan knelt next to the boy, who tried to become one with the wall again. At least this time he didn't squeak in fear.

"Brandon, right?" Duncan tried to inject as much calm and patience he could muster into his words and mind-touch.

The boy nodded.

"Those damp clothes cannot be comfortable. Please, clean up."

Brandon's posture tightened further. He remained silent.

"I promise not to harm you."

"You're a vampire."

The boy's choked words were spat at Duncan's feet. It reminded him too much of his earliest years. Of Margaret's fear upon her discovery of his transformation.

"Yes."

"You want me alone and naked so you can do perverted things to me." Anger replaced the fear in Brandon's eyes. All in all, a good sign if his words didn't cast aspirations at Duncan's manhood.

Amusement twisted his lips. "As my fiancée would say, I do not swing that way." Duncan rose to his feet. Was David's abduction of him due to the young athlete's infatuation with him? Or was he bait to lure Samantha to her permanent death? Experience already answered that question. *Hellfire!* With Selene's demise, he'd simply traded one obsessed, not-exactly-sane suitor for another.

He tamped the growing concern and kept his tone light. "Frankly, you would be far worse off if you were trapped in here with her." Pulling open a drawer, he rooted for something to wear. Nearly everything David owned was far too colorful for his taste.

"You mean, girl vamps are worse than guy vamps?" Brandon's posture eased. A dread curiosity filled his youthful features.

"She is a zombie, not a vampire." Duncan held up a pair of black athletic shorts. As much as he detested the feel of synthetics, they would suffice.

"Z-z-zombie?"

Duncan glanced at the boy while he worked the shorts over his feet and up under the towel. "I would not be too concerned." He grimaced. "She prefers Taco Bell over human brains." A shrug as he tossed the damp towel on the bed. "There is no accounting for taste." He resumed rummaging for an acceptable shirt.

"Is there anything worse than a zombie?"

"Oh, yes." Duncan tugged a gray t-shirt over his head. "My niece is mortal, but she would have shot you out of spite by now." He eyed Brandon as he smoothed the Sabretooths logo over his chest. "And that is without suffering the effects of her current morning sickness."

I twined my vanilla hand around Yvonne's chocolate one. Damn, less than ten minutes and I was already thinking about food again. Sucking in a deep breath, I closed my eyes and lowered my shields. The rich scent of loam and mulch filled my head. Sparkling green swirled behind my eyelids.

My eyes popped open. I wasn't in the hospital room. Instead, I stood on a chair, my hand on a spoon stirring a bubbling liquid. Warm colors filled the kitchen. The stove before me looked older. Maybe a '50's model like the one in Grandma Neel's house.

My hand, but not my hand. A melodic voice behind me said, "Now baby, what's next?"

"A teaspoon of dragon's blood to amplify the power?" I glanced up at the woman. The exotic cheekbones were familiar. I knew her and didn't at the same time. Warmth and affection suffused her smile, a pride and acceptance I'd never received from my own mother.

She gave me a teasing look. "Be sure, Yvonne. A spell works as much from your will as it does the ingredients."

"Man, the kitchen smells like girl farts." A boy stood in the doorway. He appeared to be around seven. His short hair was its normal dark brown, not the day-glo colors he would affect years later.

"Davy." My voice wailed in protest.

Mama turned, a stern look on her face. "David Jebediah Head, that is no way to speak in my house."

He waved a tiny hand in front of his nose. "When's supper?"

"When Daddy gets home." I stuck out my tongue.

"Yvonne."

At Mama's admonition, I turned back to the boiling pot. After carefully measuring out the dark red powder from the jar on the counter, I dumped the spoonful in the mixture. Pink steam puffed from the addition, and I resumed stirring.

"I'm hungry."

Davy's plaintive whine struck my last nerve. "You're always hungry."

"Can I have a cookie, Mama?"

"One." She held up her index finger for emphasis. "And I'd better not hear you complaining you can't finish your dinner."

He fished a molasses cookie from the jar before disappearing back into the living room.

A sharp knock on the front door, and Mama reached for the towel to wipe her hands. Confusion bent her brow.

"Mama!" Davy raced back into the room, his eyes wide, the half-eaten cookie in his hand forgotten. "There's a policeman at the door."

And I knew. Daddy wasn't coming home tonight. He wasn't ever coming home again.

Green tilted, and David's voice was older but still hadn't cracked with adolescence. "I'm tellin' ya, he's evil."

"David." Mama's admonishment didn't hold the strength it used to. "He's your father."

I blinked my eyes to clear the green spots. We were in a different house, smaller. Mama's bedroom. She sat in front of her dressing mirror, stroking make-up over the new bruises. Pain wrenched my heart. Mama wouldn't let me heal her split lip. It would only make Mr. Jenkins more furious.

And I wouldn't call him "Father" no matter how many times Mama lectured me or he beat me.

"He's not my father!" Davy swiped furiously at his tears, embarrassed he'd let them slip.

I shared his anguish. Reaching for her hand, I whispered, "Please, we need to leave before he hurts you bad."

Mama closed her eyes and said nothing.

Another green shift. My stomach wrenched. Mama lay at the bottom of the stairs, eyes staring at nothing. I flung my body next to hers. Her aura faded from green to dark gray. Reaching for her wrist, then her neck. No thrum. No beat. Nothing.

"Davy, call 9-1-1!"

No hint of movement. I looked up at my baby brother.

Murderous fury darkened his eyes, his face, his aura. He stared up at the top of the stairs.

Jenkins stood there. No remorse, no concern on his blank face.

"Davy." No one moved at my whisper, not even me. Mama's aura turned black, then disappeared completely.

A green flash.

"You murdered her!" My throat burned from my screams. Arms and hands ached from hitting and slapping him. I didn't care anymore. No one believed me and Davy. Not the police. Not Bishop Samuel. Not even Grandmama.

"Shut your mouth, bitch!" Another blow to the face. My head slammed into the doorframe and rebounded into Jenkins's fist. I couldn't focus, couldn't think of a spell, couldn't find the strength to pick myself up before he grabbed the front of my nightgown. The fragile cotton ripped under the weight of my limp body.

An ugly gleam appeared in his eyes, one he showed before he and Mama disappeared into their bedroom. His attention flicked over my naked bosom, making me feel awful and dirty. He reached for me. "Guess you do have some magic after all."

"Leave her alone." Davy's voice cracked and broke.

Jenkins and I both turned. Davy stood in the hallway, his aluminum baseball bat in both hands. He gave an experimental swing. "Wanna play ball, *Dad*?" A dangerous anger filled his face.

Jenkins rose to his full height. He still towered over Davy, but not by much. "This is my house."

Davy took a threatening step forward. "Not tonight."

Eyes darting between the two of us, Jenkins muttered, "You'll get yours, boy." He spit on me before he wheeled and marched down the stairs. The front door opened, then slammed shut.

I clutched the torn nightgown over my nakedness. "He'll be back."

Arms reached around me, helped me to my feet. When had my baby brother grown so strong?

"We'll be ready for him," David said as he guided me in the direction of the bathroom.

I blinked to clear the green spots. We sat in the stifling attic. I eyed Davy's set-up. "I don't think this is a good idea. We don't even know if it'll work."

"It will." His voiced broke again as he poured a measure of whiskey.

"How do you know?"

He wouldn't meet my eyes. "I brought Mr. Whiskers back."

Hot air caught in my throat. Jenkins had strangled our pet bunny two months ago after Mr. Whiskers had chewed up one of his slippers. "Y-you did?" I was afraid and impressed. Davy sucked at most spells.

"Yup."

For the first time, I really looked at his aura, to *see* the black sparkles underneath Davy's pretty salmon. Not the sad black of Mama's death or the tainted black of Jenkins's fury, but a beautiful diamond pattern.

My breath left in a whoosh. Baby brother was a real live necromancer.

He gave a sharp nod. "You ready?"

Anxiety welled again.

"Yvonne?" He looked at me. "I can't do this without your help. You in?"

I matched his nod. "What do you need?"

"Just a little blood." He pulled out the hunting knife Jenkins had used on a couple of the neighborhood dogs stupid enough to do their business on our lawn.

I swallowed the hard lump in my throat and held out my hand. He pricked the tip of my index finger and squeezed a few drops into the glass of whiskey. After performing the same operation on his own finger, he set down the knife and chanted. A cold wind swept through the small space, cold enough to set my teeth chattering, even though it was deep summer in New Orleans. Something whispered at the edges of my awareness. I watched Davy's eyes close. A smile lit his face.

"Now, we just have to wait," he said in his cracked voice.

A crash downstairs jolted me awake. Shouting filtered up through two floors, but the words were so slurred, I couldn't understand them.

"Davy?" I sat upright, pushing braids out of my face.

"It's okay." He patted my knee.

I may not have been able to understand the words, but I recognized the voice all too well. Fear solidified into a lump in my gut.

A gunshot cracked so close my heart paused. More shouting, nearer this time. Another shot. A hole appeared in the attic floor less than a foot from Davy's makeshift altar.

"I can smell your shit up there, you bastards! Get down here!" The third shot ripped through Mama's Book of Shadows, sending shreds of paper into the air.

Davy climbed to his feet and headed for the fold-up ladder.

I grabbed his ankle. Clammy flesh and damp socks met my touch. "Davy, don't." I barely breathed the words. "He'll kill us."

"Maybe." An oddly confident boy grinned down at me. "I doubt it." He eased the trapdoor open and shouted, "We're coming down."

Jenkins met us at the bottom of the steps. The reek of alcohol, smoke and old sweat wafted through the hallway. He waved the gun in the direction of his and Mama's bedroom. "In there."

I shot a glance at Davy. Didn't he realize what terrible things Jenkins would do in there before he killed us?

When neither of us obeyed, Jenkins aimed the gun between Davy's eyes. "I said move!"

Pink floral print flashed at the other end of the hallway. Chemicals and mold rolled through the hot air in a noxious wave. My eyes widened. "Mama?"

Jenkins turned and his mouth fell open. Mama stood at the top of the staircase. Her burial dress was stained and filthy, her shoes missing. Gray tinged her skin. Purple filled her bloated lips, black stitches tugging the swollen flesh.

Oh, sweet Oshun! What had we done?

Mama, or rather the thing that had been her, shambled forward.

An explosion rattled my ears, and I collapsed to the floor.

A wisp of smoke drifted from the barrel of the shotgun Jenkins now aimed at Mama. A clear liquid oozed from the neat round hold in her forehead, but no blood. She took another step forward.

Whites appeared in a solid ring around his midnight eyes. He pulled the trigger again and again. Some of the bullets hit Mama. Others left scars on the walls. She didn't stop. Jenkins made an odd sound, almost a pig squeal, before he bolted for the big bedroom. The door slammed, then I heard the harsh scrape of furniture on hardwood.

"Mama?" I reached for her, but cold skin brushed past my outstretched hands. A whimper escaped my throat.

Hands stroked my hair, my hot, wet face. "It's okay, Yvonne. It'll be over soon."

I looked up at Davy. Puce lay underneath his mahogany skin. My own stomach heaved.

The bedroom door shattered under the first blow of Mama's fists. A shove sent the antique dresser sliding across the floor. Jenkins's terrified face disappeared as Mama stalked him out of our view.

Then the screaming started.

I buried my face in Davy's t-shirt and clamped hands over my ears. His arms wrapped around me, but nothing shut out the awful squishy ripping and the pain-filled howls. When quiet reigned again, I dared to look.

Mama stood in the smashed doorway. Bits of unnamed things added their own stains to her once beautiful dress. Crimson slicked her cold, dead skin and dripped from her fingertips. She stumbled toward us.

Davy released me and rose.

Terror filled my mouth. I clutched his leg. "No!"

"It's okay." He shook free, but not before I saw the queasiness in his face. Striding forward, he said, "That'll do, Mama. That'll do."

She halted. My own nails dug into my thighs. This wasn't my mama. It was something unnatural. A scream rose in my throat as I waited for my mother's corpse to tear Davy and me apart as well.

"Sleep in peace, Mama." He reached out and closed the filmy, unseeing eyes. The body collapsed to the hardwood, a meat puppet with its magickal strings cut. Then Davy fell to his knees and puked all over the dirty, bloodstained floor.

Chapter 26

Sitting before the silver ring embedded in the floor, Duncan pulled apart the remote and flipped the batteries onto his palm.

A freshly showered Brandon watched him from the edge of the bed where he rolled up the legs of the overlong sweatpants he'd found in David's bureau. "Whatcha doing?"

Duncan set one battery aside. "Attempting to escape." Using the tiny file on a pair of nail clippers he found in a drawer, he pried the casing off the remaining cylinder. His breath hissed and fire flared in his nerves when a white flake landed on the base of his thumb. Not as damaging as a silver burn, but he needed to be more careful with the scarce resources on hand.

Concentrating, he scraped the potassium hydroxide out of the battery. If he could break the circle before David returned, they'd have a chance to summon help. He pushed the white powder into a line across the silver using the clippers.

Feet thumped to the floor behind him. "How's the insides of a battery going to help?"

Duncan held up a hand and Brandon halted. "The chemical is highly caustic." He stood and eyed the boy. "I am retrieving water. Do not touch anything."

Brandon took his bared fangs seriously. The boy retreated back to the bed and held up his hands. "No problem, man."

As he filled the glass from the tap, Duncan tried not to think about why David hadn't come back to the house yet. Too many possibilities, most of which ended with Samantha never smiling again.

Damn it all to hell! He resisted the urge to throw the glass against the mirror. This whole scenario was something Selene would have concocted. He really had traded one sadistic bitch in his life for another.

Taking a steadying breath, he returned to the bedroom doorway with the crystal tumbler filled with water and a toothbrush. *St. Simeon, protect your fools.* Dipping the toothbrush in the liquid, he dribbled a tiny amount on the line of white powder. Heat slapped his face as the potassium hydroxide dissolved.

Movement whispered behind him again.

He didn't bother looking. "Brandon, if you do not wish to have lye burns, I suggest you retreat to the bathroom." Soft pattering told him the boy obeyed.

Noxious fumes burned his eyes and nostrils. Retreating to the bathroom as well, he prayed the alkaline solution would work.

Brandon gasped at the fumes working their way into the bathroom when the hissing metal dissolved with a soft *pop*. Duncan crossed the tiled floor and released the catch on the frosted glass window. Wrapping his arm and hand in a clean towel, he pulled it open. Fresh air flooded the area, brushing away the ozone from the spell along with the alkaline fumes. He took a grateful breath and reached through the opening with the encased arm. No circle.

And despite the high, bright sun, his reach didn't extend past the shadow of the house.

Summoning all his will, he targeted a mental shout. Nothing but a tinny echo came back. Bloody hell! Head must have another circle around the estate. But how could a witch with his minimal talent cast that size of a spell? Odds were a larger circle shield would be far weaker than the one that had imprisoned him and Brandon in the bedroom. If so, it could be broken with enough force. He shook his head. Best to deal with one problem at a time.

The problem was the noonday sun. He turned and examined Brandon. The boy was his best hope, but he would be vulnerable to whatever traps David may have set on the grounds.

A shudder rippled through Duncan at the memory of zombies climbing the walls and shambling across Ted Howell's precious lawn. Whatever David Head may have been two years ago, he'd grown in his abilities. Dangerously so.

"Did you come in your vehicle?"

Brandon nodded. "If we can get past David, we can make a run—" Crimson spread up his neck and lit up his ears. "You can't go outside, can you?"

"Not right now anyway. Not unless you have UV film lining all the windows of your automobile."

The crimson migrated from ears to cheeks. He shook his head.

A bitter smile twisted Duncan's lips. Daylight was more of a cage than anything David could devise. "Do you know where Anthony's Restaurant is?"

Brandon's snort resembled one of Tiffany's so much Duncan had difficulty restraining a laugh. "Only one of the hottest places in the city? I think I can find it."

"When you reach the restaurant, tell the staff it's an emergency Family matter and you must speak with Anthony's Uncle Caesar. Tell Caesar everything that's happened here." He paused. The last thing he wanted was to frighten the boy more than necessary, but he grabbed Brandon's shoulders and looked him squarely in the eye. "You may be pursued. Do not stop for anyone. Do you understand?"

Despite the ashy fear scent rolling off the boy, he gave a sharp nod. "No stopping. Get help at Anthony's." He hesitated. "Caesar's l-like you, isn't he?"

"Yes." Duncan smiled as wide as he dared to reassure Brandon. "He will not harm you. And this may be your only chance to escape."

"David wouldn't—" Brandon sucked in his cheeks and looked away. "Never mind."

Sympathy for the boy filled Duncan. He'd learned the hard way as well that someone he thought he cared for could have a horrible, vindictive, selfish side.

Still no sounds of any living thing inside the house except for those made by the two of them. He released the boy. "David's not inside the house. You need to go." He clapped Brandon's shoulder. "Now."

The boy trotted from the bathroom, stopping long enough to shove his feet in the leather loafers he'd originally been wearing and to snag his keys and wallet. After stepping carefully over the still smoking gap in the silver ring, he glanced back. "Will you be okay?"

"I will if you hurry."

Guilt passed across Brandon's face before he turned and ran down the hallway.

Duncan followed at a more sedate pace until he reached the living room. Sunlight flooded the huge room. The rapid slap of the loafers ended with the creak of a door opening. He blinked watery eyes and stayed in the edge of the shadowed hallway. Then with a prayer, he indulged in one of Tiffany's childhood quirks and crossed his fingers.

Outside, an engine purred to life then dipped in tone. When the vehicle was about a hundred yards away, shouting began. The engine whined as if a foot pressed the accelerator to its limit. A clang. A thud of metal on flesh. Screams of pain but none he recognized as Brandon's voice. The roar of the engine as it moved further away.

A smile tugged his lips. The boy did better than he expected.

A door slammed. Heavier footfalls, rubber on hardwood. David Head appeared in the opposite entrance to the living room, panting. His wrist flicked with a mumbled word.

The floor heaved under Duncan, tossing him into the air. He rolled with the landing in the sun-bright room. Gaining his feet, he expected the bite of UV charring skin. Only seconds to take down Head before he was incapacitated by the radiation.

Nothing.

No pain. No burning. Not even an itch.

Fangs extended, he launched himself at the witch. Despite the extra inches Head had, he didn't stand a chance. In less than a second, Duncan pinned him to the floor, both arms wrenched behind his back. "Why are you trying to kill Samantha Ridgeway?"

David wiggled, trying to find an opening. If the situation weren't so dire, Duncan could almost admire the man's tenacity.

He pressed a knee against the witch's neck. "Answer me."

"He's not your real problem, vampire."

Ozone filled the air. Green and yellow lights exploded in Duncan's vision. He couldn't move, couldn't breathe, couldn't do anything except fall headlong into a black tunnel.

Chapter 27

Green spots cleared from my vision. Worms twisted my intestines in intricate knots. I bent over, trying to deal with the shit in my head. Oh God! Yvonne . . .

I straightened at the tight clasp on my hand. The witch still held my palm in hers. Tears ran down her face, washing away the make-up she so carefully applied before coming to see me.

"I'm so, so sorry." I squeezed her fingers lightly because my lame words were so fucking inadequate.

She said nothing, merely squeezed back and swiped at the wetness on her cheeks with the back of her free hand.

I cleared the hard lump out of my throat and eyed the rest of the assemblage. "You guys need to get out of here."

A resounding chorus of "No" slammed into my eardrums, along with a "Fuck you, bitch" from Tiffany.

"Look, guys," I said, trying to meet everyone's eyes. It was a little hard with Lily still sitting directly behind me. "Head wants me dead." After everything, Yvonne showed me, I couldn't blame him. The shit he'd dealt with before he'd ever left middle school explained a lot of his screw-the-world attitude. And the failure of his last relationship rested squarely on my shoulders. I'd never faced the fallout of one of my stories. Never really saw the aftereffects.

I swallowed hard and focused on Duncan's face in my mind. Because if I didn't remind myself of the consequences to the man I loved if I didn't face Head, I'd chicken out.

There. I admitted it. I loved Duncan.

Another swallow. "Head'll do a trade if I show up, but not if the cavalry follows me." My hand shot up to forestall the beginning protests. I eyed the doctor. "Bebe, so far this mess is between the vamps and fairies. You can't drag your family into it." She gave me a reluctant nod. If nothing else, she had a practical mind.

Not so for others in the group. When I turned to Tiffany, her mouth was already moving. "Don't you even think of cutting me out. He's my uncle. My family!" A French-manicured nail shot in Yvonne's direction. The incongruity of the missing black lacquer nearly derailed my thought train. "If she's going, I'm going."

"What about my niece or nephew?"

At my quiet point, her mouth snapped shut. A single drop trailed from the corner of her eye down her murderous visage.

My attention switched to Max behind her. He held up his uninjured hand. "I know, I know. I'm worthless in a fight. I'll keep an eye on them." He laid the hand on Tiffany's shoulder. She buried her face against him so the rest of us wouldn't see the tears.

I looked at Jake.

A shit-assed grin filled his mug. "You're not cutting me out of this one. I want to meet my replacement." He shrugged. "Besides, if Head's expecting a lot of woo-woo stuff, I'll be your ace in the hole."

He made sense as much as I hated to admit it. Jake could give Mai a run for her money in fighting and weaponry. I turned to the female enforcer. She stared back.

I started to say something and found I couldn't. That stare of hers made me uncomfortable, so uncomfortable I couldn't meet it any longer. I shifted and plucked at the blanket. "Mai . . ."

"My sister is still in ICU and Jamal is dead." No inflection on those words. No emotion. No argument.

"Ok-a-a-y then." I turned to Stan.

A pale blond eyebrow rose, almost meeting the edge of his buzz cut. "Do you really want to walk into Head's without a sidhe ally yourself?"

"You're half-fairy," I spat back.

"And my cousin Harry's still in the hospital too, thanks to Head." He shrugged boulder-sized shoulders. "Bebe and I have been working on some magick combinations." He inclined his head toward Yvonne. "Give me a couple of hours with her."

Yvonne returned his acceptance with a gracious nod of her own.

I was now officially worried. From the little Bebe explained to me, witch and fairy magick could be a lethal mix, usually to the casters. We had no clue what my peculiar black light crap would do to such a mix. And speaking of my unknown abilities . . .

I pivoted on my butt to face the three zombie comedians. "You three need to stay with Bebe."

Uncle Morty gave a sharp shake of negation. "We're with you, toots." Bill and Lilly nodded in support.

I sighed, more from sympathy than exasperation. I hated to be left out of the loop, too. "Look, guys, I appreciate the thought. I really do. But—" My voice hardened at the memory of the rehearsal dinner fiasco. "Head controlled me once before, and I almost didn't break the spell in time." Hell, I still wasn't sure how I'd broken it, or if I really had. Maybe Head let it slip so he could enjoy my pain and fear while his zombies were skinning me alive. "The bastard pulled you out of your graves. I'm not putting you at his mercy. Not again."

Bill shuffled, the eyes behind the famous nose shifting with uncertainty. This was a man who'd done USO shows in combat zones, and he obviously didn't like the fear he was feeling. Lily's expression was solemn, contemplative. I couldn't read the inscrutable emotion in her eyes. However, Morty's eyes glared with ferocity. "Just a damn minute, toots—"

I reached for his hand, grabbing warm, living flesh. "Please, Morty. I've attended your funeral once. Don't make me do it again. Not yet."

Morty plucked the unlit cigar from his pocket. Fingers searched for a light. He finally gave up and returned to glaring at me. "Don't get yourself killed, toots."

I smiled up at him. "Don't plan to. Didn't like it the first time." I let go of his warm grip and handed the greasy bag of fries to him. "Besides, these things will kill me faster."

Brandon shivered in the dimly lit back room of Anthony's restaurant. Not sure if it was the temperature or the company, he stammered through his story. The man, no, the vampire seated across from him listened as he told the tale of David imprisoning him in the bedroom with Duncan, the British vampire's ingenuity and his subsequent flight from the estate. Occasionally, the vampire Duncan had referred to as Uncle Caesar asked for more specifics. Otherwise, the vampire stared over his steepled fingertips at Brandon with those oddly yellowish eyes.

Two other people sat across the table with the vampire. The graying, middle-aged man with a predatory air kept looking at him like he was something to be dissected. The older woman kept giving him reassuring nods as he related the story. He had the impression neither of them were vampires but just as dangerous.

"And then these creatures, uh, people," Brandon amended with a nervous glance at Uncle Caesar. "They seemed to melt out of the shrubbery and jumped at my car. I-I think I ran one of them over, but Duncan said not to stop for anything." He should feel guilty over that, he knew he should, but he was just too damn grateful to be alive. The arrow sticking out of the ruined stereo reminded him of that on the reckless drive to the restaurant.

The vampire sat, looking at him. Another shiver stole over the raised goose pimples covering his arms. The guy appeared close to Brandon's age, but the vibe he gave was older. Much, much older.

Finally, Uncle Caesar lowered his steepled fingers. "Thank you for your assistance, Brandon." He sighed. "For your own safety, I think it's best that you don't remember any of this."

Cold sweat broke out on his forehead. "Wait a minute. You don't have to kill me. I won't tell anybody. I swear!" He couldn't stop the rising pitch from scraping his vocal cords raw.

"Don't be silly." The woman waved a manicured hand. "We're not going to kill you."

A cold, iron vise clamped onto his arm. Brandon looked up.

An Asian guy dressed in black jerked him up from the chair. "I shall deal with him, Master." At Caesar's nod, the other vampire dragged Brandon from the room.

"Please, man, don't do this!" He yanked and pried, but the Asian guy's fingers might as well have been iron chains for all the good his struggles accomplished.

"Hush," Asian Guy hissed. He dragged Brandon to a covered unloading dock and shoved him into a black Ferrari waiting in the shade.

Brandon threw his weight at the door and yanked on the latch. No luck. A flick of the switch showed the window was secured as well. Before the thought of climbing over the console and out the driver's door fully formed in his brain, the vampire climbed in and turned the ignition key.

Asian Guy eyed him. "Put on your seatbelt."

Brandon hesitated a moment before reaching for the strap. It didn't make sense. Why would the vampire be concerned about his safety if he had been ordered to kill Brandon?

"I'm not going to kill you." The vampire's growl acted as a counterpoint to the purring Ferrari. He accelerated around the building and whipped the car into traffic.

"Wh-what are you going to do to me?" Brandon swallowed a screech at a near-miss with a produce truck when the vampire changed lanes. Fingertips dug into the soft leather armrest. Then again, he may die as a normal Los Angeles traffic fatality before the vampire could drain his blood.

"I'm taking you to Yvonne."

Fury surged. How could this vampire ninja wannabe know about Yvonne? "Don't fuck with me, man."

Darkness filled the vampire's profile. "David Head is responsible for my lifemate's death." Glowing yellow eyes glared at him before returning their attention to traffic. "While I would take great delight in exacting my revenge on you, Yvonne has convinced Samantha of your usefulness."

Bile surged in Brandon's throat. David, or at least the David he thought he knew, wouldn't have harmed a soul. Maybe a little jostling on the court in a heated game, but not deliberate murder. And from the furious look on the vampire's face, anything he wanted to exact on Brandon was bound to be painful. *Focus, man. Focus.* "W-who's Samantha?"

"Samantha Ridgeway." An evil smile curved the vamp's lips, exposing elongated fangs. "Our resident zombie."

Oh God! Not her! Acid billowed and the vampire grimaced as Brandon bent over and heaved chunks on the floor of the Ferrari.

He sat up and wiped his mouth on the shoulder of the oversized t-shirt he wore. David's t-shirt. As if the fear and weirdness of the last few hours weren't bad enough, now he had to face his worst nightmare. The woman who destroyed his career. Destroyed the one real relationship he'd ever had. Destroyed his entire fucking life.

And he couldn't even kill the bitch because she was already dead.

Chapter 28

Another round of pain greeted Duncan as he swam toward consciousness. He lay still, praying for the ache behind his eyes to subside before he tried to open them. The constant assaults were becoming bloody inconvenient. If this is what his wedding to Sam would be like, maybe she had a point in refusing such a ceremony. He reached for his skull, only for a dollop of searing agony to halt his wrist. Forcing his eyes open, he raised his head.

Damn it all to Hell!

Once again he was chained spread-eagle in David Head's bed. His only consolation was this time he was still clothed.

At the rustling of the bedcovers, the villain himself looked up from where he knelt next to the doorway. "This is just cold, man." David gave a sad little shake of his head when he bent to continue examining the damage to the silver circle. "Do you know how hard it is to cast a ring of silver this big? Do you have any idea how much something like this costs?"

"I can imagine," came Duncan's dry reply. Bracing himself against the pain, he tugged experimentally at the right manacle. No give. He relaxed the muscles, trying to wrap his mind around anything else besides the burning skin on his wrists and ankles.

Patience. He needed patience, but the gut knowledge that he had hours to go before sunset screamed in outrage. "If you release me, I can go to the bank before it closes. Reimburse you for the damage."

David chuckled and climbed to his feet. Tension in Duncan's

body ratcheted as the witch crossed the room and sat on the edge of the bed. "Maybe tomorrow. When the bank's actually open." His focus shifted to the floor. His hands clenched and released but he made no move to touch his prisoner. "This isn't how I meant everything to go down, you know."

It took Duncan a few seconds to realize David was weeping. With an effort, he kept his voice low, soothing. "You can still fix it. Release me. I will speak with Caesar and Jean-Pierre. We can work out some sort of arrangement."

David gave another shake of his head and swiped away the wetness on his face. "Too late for that."

Queasiness filled Duncan's abdomen. Too late? What had happened while he was unconscious? *Please, Lord, let no harm have come to Samantha.* He chose his next words carefully. "Both masters are fair. Recent events—"

David faced him squarely, and the words jammed in Duncan's throat. The odd light in the witch's eyes sent an uneasy frisson through his body.

"I love you. This all started because I love you."

An odd combination of horror and sympathy swept through Duncan at the boy's whispered declaration. He sorted through everything he could possibly say, and there was nothing, absolutely nothing, that wouldn't shatter David's fragile ego. "I appreciate the sentiment, but I—"

"You love that bitch. Why else would I want her dead?" The statement held so much bitter resentment it was difficult for Duncan not to flinch.

"I was under the assumption you were still angry over the pictures she took months ago."

A dark expression shadowed the witch's face. "Hell, yeah!" He rose and began pacing along the foot of the bed. "How'd you like pictures of you and a lover in a private moment plastered all over the fucking country?"

Everything fell into place. David blamed Samantha for two losses. Not sure how to counter the angry glare, Duncan sighed. "You are correct. I would not."

"Damn straight." The witch gave a sharp nod. "This whole situation is so totally fucked up. Brandon shouldn't have run off either. I wasn't going to hurt him. You'd think he'd want to be in on this. She hurt him more than she did me. Totally fucked up his music career."

During David's rant, Duncan took a good look at him. Dark circles marred the skin under his eyes. Had the boy slept in the last three days? He gambled on information Yvonne had given Caesar shortly before the aborted wedding ceremony and the thick rose scent in the house. A scent that didn't come from David alone. A scent even Brandon's fear could not totally override. "He still loves you."

David jerked to stop, bloodshot eyes wide. "What'd you say?"

It wasn't the reaction Duncan expected, but nevertheless David deserved honesty. "Brandon still loves you."

The witch strode to the head of the bed, fist raised to strike. "Shut the fuck up!"

Duncan didn't miss the flare of hope under David's furious visage. "I am conveying the truth. Do not toss this chance away. Release me. Let me help you."

"He's lying, David."

The familiar mellow voice from the bedroom doorway smashed the glimmer of belief in the witch's eyes. Duncan turned his head to find Duke Millanthropas. The fae no longer dressed as the effete persona he affected on stage. This time he was decked in the leather and silver mail of a sidhe warrior. As Samantha would have said, this so was not good.

Focusing on the truth was the best option, and Duncan aimed his next words at David. "Brandon's scent coats this room. Read my mind if you do not believe me." Inviting a possibly insane basketball player inside his head wouldn't have been his first choice, but it was his only chance to break whatever hold the sidhe had on the young witch.

Millanthropas crossed his arms. A raised eyebrow on his sharp features conveyed his disbelief. "Then why did Ruby track your Brandon to Anthony's where he met with Augustine, Lannigan and Epstein?"

"I sent him to the restaurant for his own safety." Duncan shifted to glare at David on the other side of the bed. The witch was smart enough to lower his upraised fist. "I was not the idiot who sealed the boy in a confined space with a severely injured vampire and scared the piss out of him."

"I panicked when I saw him unlocking the cuffs!" David's protest held a slight whine. "I haven't seen him since he-he—" He could no longer meet Duncan's stare and started shifting his weight from foot to foot, a schoolboy caught in a foolish escapade.

"It doesn't explain why Kensai Osaka disappeared with Brandon shortly after the boy's interview with Augustine." Millanthropas's honeyed voice carried an annoyed hint, his focus solely on Duncan. "And it doesn't explain why two other members of Augustine's inner circle along with your fiancée and David's sister have vanished and we can't track them."

Duncan couldn't stop his smile at the fae's peeved tone. The duke's bodyguards were two of the best trackers of the Seelie Court, which meant Bebe and Stan's experiments to combine witch and fae magicks succeeded. "Given David has made three attempts to take the life of someone under Master Augustine's protection, I am shocked at your question."

Millanthropas smiled in return, but the expression cast an ugly shadow across the fae's flawless features. "And how does one kill something that's already dead?" He stepped closer, his posture far more menacing than the witch's, who was nearly twice his size. "Now where would your master hide his precious little zombie?"

The kitchen in Duncan's townhouse stank to high heaven from the concoction Yvonne stirred on the stove. I considered opening a window when the double beep of a car horn sounded outside the garage. Even with feeling Kensai's presence outside, I waited for Mai's shouted confirmation from the living room. With fairies involved in this mess on top of a necromancer who hated my guts, it paid to be careful. Really, really careful. I'd already parked Duncan's Suburban in the alley behind the townhouse, so I hit the switch on the wall.

Another honk, closer this time, and I hit the switch again. When the rumbling of the garage door stopped, I poked my head in to confirm it had closed properly. What can I say? After the last three days, I was turning into a safety girl.

Kensai had already exited the Ferrari, giving me fewer seconds to drool over Caesar's beautiful machine than usual. He eyed me as he crossed over to the passenger side. "You're cleaning the vomit out of the carpet."

I blinked. Vomit? Please let it be Normal puke. I'd have to replace the carpet otherwise. The last two months had taught me nothing's worse than trying to get bloodstains out of upholstery. Not to mention, I could barely afford my grocery bill on two salaries, much less new Ferrari carpet.

Brandon Tyler's face was as pale as the Caucasian vamps when Kensai helped him climb out of the car. He took one look at me, and he somehow managed a new shade of green.

I raised my fingers in a half-hearted wave. If Head really wanted me dead, he should've sicced his ex-boyfriend on me. The laser-like intensity of his gaze conveyed his hatred almost as effectively as the gagging stench of brimstone filling the garage from the open door to the kitchen.

Kensai tugged the singer forward, and Brandon's hatred switched rapidly to green-gray nausea. Funny how the mental flavor of that feeling matched the physical one. Kensai got the garbage can in front of the guy, but all he produced was dry heaves. My cast-iron zombie stomach twitched in sympathy.

I reached out to steady Brandon when it seemed he was finished. "Let's get you upstairs."

He jerked back. "Don't touch me, bitch."

The miasma of grief at touching Kensai's mind lurched in my gut. *There's crackers and soda in the kitchen.* I wished I had said the words aloud instead.

The Japanese enforcer showed no sign of his inner turmoil, merely nodded in acknowledgment as he escorted the stressed-out singer into the townhouse.

I headed to the wooden shelving Duncan had installed and pulled off carpet cleaner and a package of sponges. With a quick trip into the stinky kitchen, I filled a bucket with water and retrieved some rubber gloves. Kneeling next to the sports car, I started cleaning up another one of my messes.

It was hardly the worst I was responsible for, but it was a start.

Duncan had just better keep his ass alive long enough to appreciate my efforts.

David paced the length of the living room, listening to Millanthropas on his cell phone. At least it looked like a cell phone, but considering the amount of residual fae magick the device exuded, it was something else glamoured to look like a cell. The duke's voice still held a hint of irritation.

The fae hadn't been happy when David had stopped him from plunging his silver knife into the helpless vampire. When the hell had he lost his stomach? Frankie's canine features floated in his mind. He quickly shoved the thought back in the deep dark hole along with memories of his stepfather. Or what had been left of him.

"I understand, my queen." An odd look glimmered in the fae's mahogany brown eyes. "I will look into the matter." Millanthropas snapped the phone shut, his uncanny eyes unblinking. He tapped an index finger on the black casing. "Is there something you wish to tell me, David Jebediah Head?"

He halted, hands flexing. "What're you talking about, man? Are you going back on your bargain?"

Millanthropas stood there, looking at him, his stillness as unnatural as the vampires. Or a raised corpse. The only thing moving was the slow climb of crimson under his dark-fuzzed cheeks.

David stomped across the floor. "She's not alive! I have the right to destroy the bitch for what she did to me!" Hysteria filled his voice. He tried to clamp down on the panic. What the hell was the fae hinting at?

"I am not referring to Samantha Ridgeway. She's as much a danger to us as she is to you." Millanthropas took a menacing step closer. "I am referring to a dead were the Los Angeles pack found in the Hollywood Cemetery."

David spread his hands wide. The duke was no fool, but he'd have to spin this carefully. "I told you Yvonne planned to turn me over to the vamps even though I was in my rights. She sent Frankie to stop me." The remembered smell of bowels and entrails clogged his throat. "I had raised too many, and-and—" He swallowed the hard lump of memory. "I couldn't stop them in time." His gaze dropped to the floor. "It was an accident."

A soft snort from Millanthropas made him raise his head. "I swear. It *was* an accident."

The fae's unnerving eyes bore into him. "Rousseau has called a death hunt on you for Francois Charles LeBeau's death. He's re-

quested my queen turn you over to him." A cool smile spread his lips. "Or present your body."

Ice filled David's veins. "He wouldn't. Yvonne wouldn't let him."

Mild surprise raised the duke's fine eyebrows. "You just said your sister planned to turn you over to the vampires anyway."

David collapsed in the couch, fear chewing on his belly. Where the hell had this thing gone wrong? "Turning me in, yeah, but-but—"

The fae stood over him, rebuke in his voice. "I couldn't care less about the Normal you killed in Las Vegas—"

David's head jerked up at those words, hot anger replacing the fear. "I told you. I didn't kill the bitch." He licked his lips. His best friend was gone, had stabbed him in the back, so protecting him no longer mattered. "Frankie did when she surprised us in the morgue."

Amusement twisted Millanthropas's mouth, and his warm hand clasped David's shoulder. "As I said, we will keep our promise in return for your aid." He squeezed to the point of pain. "As long as you are useful to us, David Jebediah Head."

With those words, he pivoted and stalked out of the room, his footsteps making no sound.

David lowered his head into his hands. Any other time in his life, he'd talk over a problem with Yvonne. She always had an idea, a plan, hell even a clue. Why had she betrayed him? And how in Papa Ghede's name was he going to get out of this mess without her?

Chapter 29

The smell of Yvonne's spell cooking in Duncan's kitchen was marginally better than my gloves and sponges, but not by much. I tossed the reeking cleaning materials into the trash. I peeled the gloves off my sweating hands and quickly tossed them in with their compatriots. Two seconds later, the trash bag was safely deposited in the wheeled garbage bin in the garage.

When I came back in, Yvonne glanced in my direction before turning her attention back to the brew she stirred. "You should talk to him."

I didn't have to ask who she was referring to. Brandon Taylor's rancid anger filtered through the stench of puke and the witch's spell. "What makes you think he wants to talk to me?"

She laid the wooden spoon in the ceramic holder next to the stove and faced me. It was the most action Duncan's stove had seen since Tiffany moved in with Max last month. I bit my lip to keep my wisecracks to myself. This was not the time. I just prayed Head wasn't hurting Duncan because he couldn't reach me.

Yvonne's light hazel eyes tracked my path to the refrigerator as I retrieved a gallon of o.j. and started chugging the contents. I could have read her mind, but we'd both kept our psychic distance since the hospital. I suspected she'd seen my past as easily as I had seen hers. When I didn't think she'd add anything, she said, "You have the rare chance of making amends after your death, Samantha. I suggest you take it." She turned her back to me, picked up the spoon and resumed stirring.

I drank the rest of the jug before tossing the empty plastic into the recycling crate. The witch was right. I'd started this fiasco two years ago by pursuing a story. A legitimate story. Dammit, I hadn't been the one in the wrong.

I hung my head. No, I took away what little privacy David and Brandon had in their fledgling relationship. And now, those closest to me were paying for my story-at-all-cost work ethic.

Stalking through the living room, I gave Mai and Jake a curt nod of acknowledgement. My steps slowed the closer I got to the top of the stairs. What the hell was I supposed to say to fix this?

The muffled voice that answered my knock on the guest bedroom door held a hint of tears. Sucking in a deep breath, I twisted the knob.

Brandon must have been expecting Yvonne because he sat abruptly at my entrance. "What do you want?"

I released the air in my lungs and closed the door. "We need to talk."

The petulant glare he gave me through red and puffy lids would have been funny if it weren't for the circumstances. "I told Kensai everything I could remember about our—" He swallowed and his attention dropped to his clenched hands. "Everything about David's place."

"That's not—" Despite the gallon of juice, my throat dried out faster than a raisin in Death Valley. "I mean, I—" I shoved my hands in my jeans' pockets. "Dammit, why are you making this so hard?"

"Me?" He held a hand to his chest in mock horror. "And how, pray tell, did I wreck your recording career?" He climbed to his feet and padded over to me. "Ruin your love life?" He jabbed a finger at my chest. "Destroy your existence?"

Brandon had maybe an inch on me. So between his bare feet and my Nikes, his bloodshot eyes stared directly into mine. Brimstone filled the air once again. I had to give him credit for not having a mental breakdown after everything he'd been through since this morning.

"Well, I'm dead. If you want a pity party, I've got you beat on that one."

His face stilled. The quick switch between brimstone and cotton candy was the only warning I had before he exploded into gales of laughter. He turned and collapsed face first on the bed, the comforter muffling the noise.

"It's not that funny," I muttered.

Brandon rolled over and sat. "Yeah, it is." Swiping at his eyes, he tried to get his humor under control. "Yvonne gave you the same lecture she gave me, didn't she?"

Face muscles twisted my expression into a frown. "What are you talking about?"

"She gave you the 'kiss and make up before it's too late 'cause life's too short', blah, blah blah." Both of his hands flapped in time to his words.

My eyebrows lifted. "Wow. Braid your hair and you could pass for her."

He rubbed his cheek. "Don't think I can shave that close."

I eased down next to him on the bed, not meeting his eyes and a little surprised he didn't scoot away from me. After sucking in another deep breath and releasing it, I whispered, "I am sorry."

Brandon snorted.

Heat flared under my skin and I glared at him. "Look, I'm trying to give you an apology."

"Only because my ex had your boyfriend chained to his bed."

My mouth fell open, and I tasted his thoughts. Clean cotton. Shit. Kensai had kept that little tidbit from me.

From Brandon's wide eyes, he'd come to the same realization. "Oh fuck. I thought you knew."

Sandpaper filled the back of my throat. "Silver?"

He nodded.

I stood. The thought of going without Kensai crossed my mind, but I'd made enough mistakes lately. And I needed all the help I could get to rescue Duncan. My fists clenched. Sundown couldn't come fast enough.

Heading for the door, I was stopped by Brandon clearing his throat. I looked at him.

Pink flared under the faint peach fuzz on his cheeks. "I accept your apology and—" He found a sudden interest in the area rug under his feet. It took my enhanced hearing to catch his "I'm sorry too."

I crossed back to him and laid a hand on his shoulder. "Brandon, do you think you can talk David out of doing something stupid?"

His head lifted, and his dark brown eyes met mine. "I think so. Maybe." He shook his head. "I'm not sure anymore." He took a deep breath. "I wanna try."

"Stay by Kensai. David'll be gunning for me, so I don't want you in the line of fire."

He licked his lips. "Yvonne—"

"Will be backing me up." I tried to give him a reassuring smile. "Kensai won't hurt you."

"He's a—" Brandon glanced at the door.

I laughed and gave him a reassuring squeeze. "Trust me. It's the witches and fairies you want to stay away from."

He shook his head. "Not all of them." He closed his eyes a moment before eyeing me again. Tears filmed the orbs. "Try not to kill him."

Sobriety filled my head. "I'll do my best."

I was so going to hell for making promises I might not be able to keep.

Millanthropas admired Sapphire's lithe form as she paced a healthy distance from the steel gates but close enough to watch for her sister's return. She must have sensed his presence because she whirled in his direction and crouched, her hand dropping to the hilt of her sword.

Straightening in recognition, she sketched a bow, but her eyes flashed with her emotions. She didn't bother to hide her contempt at the queen's previous command. "Instructions, Your Grace?"

"We wait." He fingered the curl on her cheek that had escaped her warrior's knot. How he missed its leaf green color.

Dark flooded her skin. "The vampires—"

"Are seeking a political solution rather than put their precious weapon at risk." He smiled, and his fingers moved to stroke the tight lines of her neck muscles.

Her slim eyebrow rose. "The queen doubts your assessment of the zombie?"

He shrugged. "It matters not. Samantha Ridgeway is more of a danger to herself than to us. But Head lied to gain our protection."

Humor lit her golden eyes at her understanding. "We are no longer needed here."

Tugging her closer, he pressed his lips to hers. A sigh escaped as her body pressed to his. Her yielding drove his body rock hard with desire. She reached for him, slim fingers cupping, caressing, demanding.

He forced a hand between them, as much to tantalize a soft, full breast as to halt the proceedings. "Have the warriors return to our mound except for a dozen."

Confusion drove away her dreamy expression. "But you're not leaving?"

Another smile tugged his lips. "Not yet. I want to observe how events unfold tonight."

Sapphire blinked. "The vampires will attack—"

He shook his head. "No. They won't. She will come, though. She's marked young Duncan as her own, and she will come for him tonight." Fierce emotion heated his blood at the thought of watching the necromancer and the nestling battle. "Our queen simply doesn't realize she has wagered her throne on the outcome."

Chapter 30

I fingered the paintball gun on my lap, the one now loaded with pellets of anti-zombie potion. It felt weird not sitting in the driver's chair of Duncan's SUV. I glanced at Mai as she focused on traffic. The collective mood molded a grimmer than usual look on her face.

I twisted around and peered at the rest of the group. Brandon and Yvonne huddled in the second seat. Concern over tonight's outcome gave them sour looks that matched Mai's expression. I couldn't blame them. They cared about David, didn't want to see him hurt, but we didn't have a clue what kind of a fight the fairies would put up defending him.

With his pink-tinged cheeks and nasty scowl, Stan resembled a Rams linebacker prepping to throw the first punch after an illegal hit. He did have a clue, and even though he didn't sugarcoat his assessment, listening to someone's war stories was very different than living through a battle. I found that out the proverbial hard way when I was twelve and had the terrific idea of snapping pictures of a riot in South Central.

Kensai and Jake crowded in the back seat next to Stan with near-ly identical stoic looks. Except the muscles in my ex's jaw twitched occasionally. The vampire's face could have been carved from tan marble with neon lights inserted for eyes.

And don't get me started on the flood of scents in such a tiny compartment. I didn't blame them for being wound up, but it was all I could do not to gag as I addressed the troops. "Let's go over this one more time."

Brandon groaned. "Jesus, Ridgeway. You're not fucking Eisenhower, and this isn't D-Day."

Stan snickered, easing the stress lines on his face. His humor was probably due to the fact he'd worked with Ike during WWII.

"And I've had enough people die over this bullshit, so we are going to review the plan." I glared at the pop singer. "One. More. Time."

He fingered a matching paintball gun slung over his shoulder, but the fairies must have scared him enough this afternoon. He dropped the attitude and said, "I stay with Kensai and shoot any zombie that comes our way."

I eyed him.

He gave a dramatic sigh. "And talk David down if he tries to stop us."

The vampire picked up the recitation. "We enter the house, find and release Duncan, and take him back to the SUV."

""Meanwhile, I keep Millanthropas and his troops busy." Stan's bass held a nasty delight, which would have scared the piss out of me in any other circumstances.

Jake shot me a reassuring smile. "Mai and I guard the SUV until Kensai and Brandon return."

"We head directly for Caesar's Brentwood estate." Mai still wasn't pleased about that part of the plan. It wasn't in her nature to run from a fight.

"And if David doesn't interfere with Kensai and Brandon, he's our responsibility," I said, gesturing between me and Yvonne. The odds were our renegade would stick with his murderous obsession to eliminate me from the planet.

Damn it. James Bond went into situations with a better plan even if he was the bait. No, Bond was luckier than me. If he shot a bad guy in the head, the bad guy stayed dead.

Well, at least I had a plan for once. I just didn't have a fucking clue of how to stop one pissed-off, nothing-left-to-lose necromancer.

Morty Stern pressed the non-existent gas pedal on the passenger side floor. "Damn it, Lil! Speed up or we'll lose her!"

Lily said nothing underneath the surgeon's cap still holding in her hair, but the speedometer crept higher as they followed the black SUV.

"We shouldn't have stolen the doc's keys," Bill muttered from the back seat of the BMW.

Morty snorted while he fiddled with the unlit cigar in his fingers. Considering they were all wearing scrubs emblazoned with the Good Samaritan logo and had knocked out the werewolf assigned to guard them, grand theft auto was the least of their problems. "I don't think Doc Z. would've ordered me not to smoke in her car, then left the keys on her desk if she didn't know what we were planning."

"What *you* were planning, moron."

Leave it to Bill not to call him a liar directly. Morty twisted to look over his shoulder. Not too long ago, such a move would have left him wracked in pain from the damn arthritis. Now, he felt forty years younger, and he wasn't about to let go of the second chance providence had granted him.

He glared at Bill. "This jerk is the reason we're not camping out in our graves. Toots is the reason we don't look like George Romero extras. We owe her."

Guilt tugged Bill's face under the passing headlights, and he nodded.

"What do we do after that, Morty?" Lily's voice carried a serious tone under her smoky husk. She glanced at him before returning her attention to the vehicle—and the woman—they chased. "We can't go back to our families."

Leave it to the broads to try to be practical when he was trying to save the damsel. He hadn't thought about what they'd do after they saved the kid's ass. Hell, the doc still had no clue why they were running around, and younger than when they died, in the first place. What would Molly do if he showed up on her doorstep?

He played with the stogie as he contemplated that thought. Interesting that Ex-wife Number Two popped in his head instead of Wife Number Three, who stood by his bedside when he took that last breath.

An audible gulp sounded in Lily's throat. "I don't want to die again. Call me a chicken, but the cancer hurt too damn much the first time."

Bill leaned forward and patted her shoulder. "That won't happen, Lily. Samantha's not that type of girl."

A bitter laugh erupted from Lily. "She doesn't even know how she restored us."

Morty shoved the end of the cigar between his teeth and bit down. Hard. Lucky for them, Lily and Bill had only the haziest of recollections of last night's events. He remembered though. It was all he could do not to puke at the pictures flashing in his brain. How he slashed her throat open. How the crimson liquid sprayed all over the place. How sweet it tasted.

The stogie seemed to suck the spit from his mouth. If Toots's blood was the only way to stay alive, then by God, he'd drink it. But he needed her intact, and that meant facing the bastard who'd dragged him out of his grave.

David's eyes snapped open, and he glanced around the living room. Shadows filled the space, daylight long gone from their depth.

Surprised at having fallen asleep, he sat up and rubbed his eyes. The only sound was the twin hums of the A/C and the refrigerator, but something had awakened him.

No, not the presence of something. The absence. The fae shield surrounding his place was gone.

"Millanthropas!"

One shadow next to the widescreen parted from the rest. "Do you require something, David Jebediah Head?"

One of Duke's bodyguards. He couldn't tell which girl in the darkness. "Where's the shield you promised me?"

Her laughter prickled his skin. "*I* promised *you* nothing."

Panic skittered underneath his puckered flesh. "Your queen did through Duke Millanthropas."

Again, the cold laughter filled the room. "Based on your assertion of innocence." The midnight outline of face, hair and pert breasts moved closer to the couch. "We both know you're hardly innocent, David."

From the purr in her voice, he was dealing with Ruby. And humans were nothing more than toys to her. Fuck. Sapphire at least had some affection for him.

Yeah, Davy, the same affection some rich bitch has for her lap dog.

Funny how Yvonne's remembered words made him feel a little better. Didn't make Ruby any less of a threat. "I want to talk to Millanthropas." He licked his lips. "Now."

Ebony heat slid across his body as she straddled him. "I'll get him." Steel velvet fingers tugged his dick, and honey filled his head. "When I'm done with you."

Fear overrode lust. He shoved at her, but deceptively thin ankles locked under his thighs. Diamonds sparked in his vision. "Get off me, bitch!"

The diamonds exploded, sending the fae ass-first into the TV. Ruby dropped to the floor in a crouch, her normally soundless heels crunching the plastic shards of the widescreen.

"That's no way to treat your only allies, David." Fire laced her voice. Only the static electricity skating across his nerves warned him.

Reaching down with magic, he pulled at the house's slab. Hardwood groaned, cracked and shattered as the concrete underneath the floorboards shifted and molded over his body. It blocked the spell she threw at him.

He counted to two, and Armageddon shook the walls and frame of the house as the two magicks reacted violently against each other. The boom of plate glass imploding rang his ears. His skin baked in his self-made oven. Wild energy cracked the concrete encasing his form.

He waited, but the need to breathe overwhelmed him. A mental shove sent the concrete crashing to the floor. The resulting dust launched a coughing fit.

Once he caught his breath, he noticed the still form by the remnants of the widescreen. Staggering past the smoking couch, he knelt beside Ruby. Her leather and matte black armor had protected everything below the neck. Only a couple of small nicks from flying debris marked the flawless skin of her face.

Then his mind registered the thick wood shard protruding from her left eye. The wide-open right eye stared unseeingly at the ceiling.

He staggered back to his feet. Pissed would be an understatement the minute Millanthropas knew about this. He pivoted, looking for help that wasn't there.

Clenching his fists, he glared at the stupid bitch. What the hell had she been thinking? Anyone with common zense knew not to pit fae magick against a witch. Hot white anger chilled as the missing shield registered. Duke had pulled his warriors and had probably sent Ruby to . . .

Shit.

His sister, his best friend, and now the fucking fairies.

No doubt the vamps were on their way. Well, they would find out he wasn't an easy target. He knelt next to Ruby's dead body once again. A man had resources, and he'd use whatever he had at his disposal. Pulling a silver dagger from the fae's boot sheath, he started chanting.

Glass crackled underneath footsteps on the patio. Wild magick tickled his mental shields. Millanthropas hadn't sent the other fae away after all.

Chapter 31

I staggered and blinked tears from my eyes while white spots continued flashing on my retinas. Ozone filled my nostrils. "What the hell was that?" I had barely climbed out of the SUV at the gate to Head's mansion when my vision and nose had been assaulted by the explosion of energy. The scary thing was the total lack of noise from the blast.

Something grasped my shoulders. No, not something. Someone. Jake, by the Granny Smith odor trickling past the acrid stench. "Sam?"

"I'm okay." I lied. My head felt like it would blow up any minute. The experience wasn't as bad as Head's backfire spell last night, but it came in a close second.

"It was fae and witch magick interacting." Pain laced Stan's rumbling bass.

The damn spots did not help the confusion in my brain. "I thought you guys could work together."

"He means someone's throwing attack and defensive spells up at the house," Yvonne choked out. In addition to the migraine-type pain in my head I was sure she and Stan were also feeling, terror edged her words. The only witch tossing magick up there would be her baby brother. "If the energy's not tuned, it's like throwing a piece of magnesium in a toilet."

Oh, jeez. "Except a lot worse."

"Yes."

Something slithered to my right, and I jerked out of Jake's grasp. Soft honey wafted past the ozone. I raised the paint gun in that direction, even though I couldn't have hit Mom and Dad's garage at point blank range with my blurred eyesight. "Freeze, asshole."

A familiar chuckle rippled across my ears. Duke Miller. "Do you really think you could hit me right now, Samantha Marie Ridgeway?"

I still found it hard to think of him as anything but an R&B star, and that was a good way to get my friends killed. The fact he hadn't ordered his people to attack meant they were as incapacitated as Stan, Yvonne and me. I smiled in the direction of his voice. "I've got a load of witch potion in my gun. Wanna take a chance?"

Icy grief tainted his next words. "David Jebediah Head killed one of my bodyguards. I will not stand between you and your goal."

The spots eased enough I could see two purplish forms a few yards away. From the white lines running across them, they stood on the other side of the gate.

I frowned. Something wasn't right. I'd never seen Duke without both girls in arm's reach. Why would he leave one of the twins alone with Head? Brain cells tried to fire despite the ache. Head hadn't killed anyone without a reason. Granted, his reasoning was totally warped.

A whisper of movement next to me preceded the hint of sandalwood. Not Duncan's rich, woodsy smell, but spice overlaid with the rotten egg smell of grief. Anxiety sent another wash of acid through my stomach.

The *click-hiss* of Kensai drawing his sword came before his words. "Head discovered your betrayal."

Thank god, vampires could only smell magick. Otherwise, he would be blind, too. Bracing myself against the emotional anguish, I reached out mentally for the vampire.

What betrayal?

Ruby has always performed Millanthropas's dirty work, at least for the four centuries I've known her.

Gerbils began swimming in my stomach acid pool. *Who's with Duke besides Sapphire?*

I do not detect any other fae in the vicinity. And the fae shield is down.

That explained some of the weird silence. *Duncan!*

No answer.

"He was alive before we left the house a few minutes ago."

My sight had cleared enough to detect the movement of Duke's mouth at the top of the deep purple pillar of his body. I aimed the paintball gun at the tiny black opening. "Doesn't mean you didn't have Ruby kill him first before she went after Head."

Decaying flowers drifted past my over-sensitive nose. "She didn't touch your mate." The deadness in Sapphire's voice matched her scent. "We have no wish for your attention on us."

"Huh?" The bitch was lying. She had to be. It was no secret the fairy queens wanted me gone. Why would Duke and his minions care about attracting my notice?

The laugh from Duke blew more fear across raw nerves. "What is the human proverb?" The second dragged forever before another laugh. "A bull in a china shop." Sharp white teeth appeared in the black hole of his mouth. "It would be rather idiotic of me to wave a red flag in front of a bull like you, wouldn't it, Samantha?"

Any time someone used my full name it never boded well for me. "Then open the freakin' gate and get out of the way, or I pull the trigger."

Apparently, Duke decided not to call my bluff. The two now-black forms shifted to the left. A quick series of electronic beeps, then the gates swung inward.

My aim shifted to cover Duke and Sapphire as they gave the steel latticework a wide berth. "Where're the rest of your fairies?"

A soft intake of breath came from Duke, then his scent rippled. Putrid lemon and dead roses overlaid his honey. "They are no longer here."

Fuck. There had to be more fae than just Ruby throwing magick at the top of the cliff. "Stan?"

"There's just the three of us anywhere near Head's house. Don't worry." A hint of satisfaction lay beneath the bass rumble. "These two aren't going anywhere."

"Sam." Jake's hand grabbed my elbow again. "You can't go in there." His voice lowered. "You can't see a damn thing."

I swallowed the laugh at his attempted discretion. Reaching for the warmth on my arm, I patted his hand. "You worry too much."

"How many fingers am I holding up?"

I batted at the black thing waving in front of my face. "We stick to the plan."

The scrape of boots drew Duncan's attention away from the shackles and back to the doorway. Silence and darkness had reigned for the last few minutes since the explosion of ozone. Who'd been foolish enough to throw the first spell? Even worse, who had survived the battle?

A lithe form appeared in the bedroom doorway. He peered at Ruby through the one eye not swollen shut by her previous exercises. She stood perfectly still for an instant, then the fae woman shambled toward him.

Bloody wonderful. His good eye closed. No doubt the fairies would try to use him to bargain for Samantha.

The wash of blood and decay swept past the ozone that clogged his sinuses. His good eye popped open. The silver and black mail covering her upper body was gone. Her leather jerkin gaped open, revealing pristine fae flesh smeared with crimson and a fist-sized hole over her heart.

Or where a heart should have been.

Film covered the malicious glitter that normally shone in her eyes. The awkward gait no longer resembled a fae's light step. In four hundred years, few things grabbed his intestines and twisted them like the sight of the zombie fae bending over him. He sent a quick prayer to the Virgin Mary that the zombie wouldn't literally twist his guts before he had a chance to run.

She reached for the silver chains holding his arms. A solid yank snapped the links. She shifted and bent over his legs. At the groan and crack of overstressed silver, Duncan whipped the arm chains forward. The links caught the zombie across the cheek, ripping blotchy skin. She, no, it, Duncan corrected himself. The woman who'd tortured him less than an hour ago no longer inhabited the body that tumbled onto the bed. Using his legs as leverage, he tossed the dead woman across the room.

He rolled off the bed, but muscle weakness from the fae's ministrations and the lack of blood sent him reeling to the floor. Using the dresser, he dragged himself to his knees. Shuffling sounds behind the bed warned him of his fate if he didn't get out of this house. He forced aching bones upright and stumbled through the bedroom door.

The scent of fresh blood triggered the extension of his fangs as he entered the living room. Splatter patterns decorated the floor around the smashed widescreen. The hardwood and concrete had buckled as if an earthquake had centered in the room.

A shadow fell over him. David stood near the shattered floor-to-ceiling windows overlooking the patio and pool. Wetness shone silvery red under the moonlight streaming through the opening and across his naked body.

"Sorry, man. Can't let you leave yet."

Nutrient-starved muscles refused to move at Duncan's command as the fist flew at his face. Beneath the crack of his skull ricocheting from David's blow and crashing into something hard and sharp behind him, Duncan could have sworn he heard Samantha screaming his name. Before he could answer her, the scarlet stars darkening his eyes turned black.

Chapter 32

The four of us started up the drive, Kensai leading me and Brandon doing the same for Yvonne behind us. White spots had stopped exploding in my vision, but the magickal A-bomb still compromised my eyesight. Without streetlights, I'd been reduced to Normal vision.

I'd forgotten how much being mortal sucked. But then from the tension in the hand that guided me, Kensai wasn't happy about moving at regular human speed either.

We'd trudged halfway to the house when something bit me. Before I could slap at the offending insect on my arm, it exploded in a silvery white puff.

"What the hell was that?" Brandon's voice hit the falsetto pitch that had grated my nerves when he was still with his boy band. It didn't sound any better with super hearing.

"A mosquito. Or it was." Kensai shot me a puzzled expression. Or at least it appeared to be. The moon wasn't as full as it had been a couple of nights ago, and its glow along with his gold eyes gave the vampire's face some pretty odd shadows. "What happened?"

The last thing that bit me and blew up had been Sierra Mallory, the only other cybernetic zombie. I shrugged. "The nanites don't like it when something does an unauthorized blood withdrawal."

But the exploding mosquito set off alarms in my head. Bebe had theorized my nanites were incompatible with Sierra's, so when the former heiress started gnawing on me, the robotic smackdown literally consumed her from the inside out.

Except the damn mosquito didn't have any nanites.

A stillness settled on the estate in the few seconds I tried to figure out the exploding bug problem. I blinked, peering through fuzzy eyeballs, but nothing came into focus. Even the mosquitoes stopped buzzing under the building silence. Then the fresh wave of ozone followed by musty decay proved my olfactory nerves were back to normal.

"Run!" Yvonne's scream ripped a ragged gash through the air.

I sensed more than saw the things flying, running or hopping toward us. I twisted out of Kensai's grip to catch the ginger-smelling figure of the witch. Tossing her over my shoulder, I sent, *Grab Brandon. I'll follow you.*

The vampire didn't argue. Brandon was too scared to protest from his silence and the waves of ash rolling off him.

I did my best to keep up with Kensai, but the pavement rolled under my toes, making balance even more difficult. Behind my shoulder, Yvonne whispered foreign words. The ground swelled and receded on both sides of us in time to her rhythm. It finally sunk into my brain she could see the animal zombies on the manicured yard through her abilities and used the sod to crush them.

A zombie rabbit slipped by and latched on my ankle. I stumbled and nearly dropped Yvonne. *Can't go down. I can't go down.* A shake of my leg and the decomposing bunny flew into the air. A wet thump hit the grass. It hadn't exploded into sparkly dust.

The vision of the zombies licking my blood at the wedding flashed through my head. I clamped down on the nausea. We didn't have time to deal with resurrected rabbits. Lungs sucked air as I raced after Kensai.

Unfortunately, Yvonne couldn't do a darn thing about the chitinous bugs dive-bombing us. Brandon shrieked as the things landed on him and proceeded to snack on his exposed skin. I chewed and spit out the few that flew into my mouth. But it was difficult to focus on running, keeping my trap shut, and breathing through my nose as black specks filled the night.

And I really wished my eyesight would go away again when I spotted the resurrected feral cats covering the ground in huge leaps.

Then we were inside the main door. Kensai threw the lock. Brandon crumpled to the floor. Yvonne and I smashed the remaining zombie bugs. Both the vampire and I breathed hard, though the entire episode had lasted less than a minute.

Kensai was still bent over, and I reached for him. He slapped my hand away and growled, "Don't touch me."

He straightened. Neon yellow filled his eyes, and his fangs were fully extended. Brandon squeaked and scrambled across the tile, away from Kensai. Even I took a step away from the vampire.

Then the metallic odor filled my nostrils, followed by the nasty tang of recent death.

No. Please don't let us be too late.

I crossed the foyer, following the scent that had set off Kensai. When I entered the living room, gorge rose in my throat. Blood was splattered over the floor near the remains of a big screen television. The hardwood in the center of the floor had been splintered. Smashed concrete showed through missing or damaged planks. Acrid smoke wisped from the remains of leather couches. A couple of strides brought me to the shattered TV. Sweet honey and sweeter decay coated the scarlet splashes.

This was where Ruby died, but where the hell was her body?

"This is Duncan's." Kensai's words drew me to where he stood next to the smaller stains on a hallway wall leading further into the house. A whiff of distinctive sandalwood confirmed his assessment.

My stomach lurched. Were we too late? I didn't think I could take facing a zombie Duncan. What we'd have to do if Head had already killed my man.

Glass crackled behind me. I whirled in time to catch a glimpse of blank, filmy eyes before Ruby launched herself at me. My back took the brunt of the impact against the wall. Plasterboard cracked and shuddered. Wood framing groaned. White powder filled the air.

Before I could clear gypsum dust from my throat, a slim fist wrapped itself in the folds of my shirt, using it to jerk the rest of my body clear of the dent. My knees smacked hardwood, shooting pain up my thighs. Silver flashed above my head.

The clang of metal interrupted the whole life flashing before my eyes thing. With a shove and some fancy sword work, Kensai drove the dead fairy away from me. He parried her next blow and countered with a thrust to the heart.

Okay, where her heart should have been. A short syllable of Japanese exploded from his lips as he realized the same thing I did.

Zombie Ruby's backhand sent him reeling into the innards of the widescreen. I struggled to my feet when the first pop sounded. Noxious liquid exploded from the blue balloon and across the gory mess of Ruby's chest.

The zombie hesitated for an instant before raising her sword, blank attention fixed on me. Four more balloons impacted. The former fairy seemed to collapse in on her body. She, no, it slumped to the floor. Yellowish fumes wafted from the corpse.

I glanced at Brandon as he lowered the paintball gun. "Thanks."

"*De nada.*" The singer stared at the immobile body, looking a little green. He swallowed hard.

I couldn't blame him. My stomach was trying its best to rebel, too.

"He's outside." Yvonne's harsh whisper froze Kensai as he tried to extract himself from the wires and circuit boards of the ruined television.

"Where?" My voice sounded down right gravely compared to hers.

Her forehead wrinkled in concentration. "The other side of the pool. Near the guest house."

I took a step toward the ruined sliding glass doors when a cold hand on my shoulder halted me. Twisting to glare at Kensai, I mouthed, "Let go."

With a sharp shake of his head, he slipped between me and the doors. *Duncan would flay me if anything happened to you.* Glass crunched under his boots as he eased his way closer.

"Do you have a freakin' death wish?" I hissed. "There's a necromancer out there who doesn't give a shit who's in the way when he tries to kill me."

He ignored me and used his retrieved sword to peer around the tattered curtains. The crackle of more bits made me look. Yvonne stationed herself by the curtains at the other side. Brandon stood behind her, knuckles tight around the paintball gun.

It reminded me of my own gun slung over my shoulder. I pulled it forward, only to have wetness meet my fingers. The plastic barrel was bent, a neat crease in the center I'd bet matched my backbone. The cracked casing had sent a shard through one of the balloons. I shook liquid from my hand. The last thing I needed was for the anti-zombie spell to work on me.

"Are you okay?" Concern laced Yvonne's voice.

I concentrated for a moment. Nope, no dizziness, no tingling in the extremities. The nausea I could attribute to other causes. I nodded.

Unsnapping my hopper, I tossed it to Brandon. He promptly scooped out a handful of balls to replace the ammo he'd used, and dumped the rest in the messenger bag slung across his chest.

Peering over Kensai's shoulder, I shuddered at the scene. Red tinged the pool water. Crimson puddled on the concrete patio.

"Come on out, Ridgeway! I know you're in there!" No mistaking Head's voice, but it had an odd timbre to it, like two soundtracks a split-second out of synch.

Yvonne caught my eye and shook her head.

I stepped around Kensai's outstretched arm. "Stick with the plan. I'll distract him."

Glass snapped and popped underneath the rubber tread of my Nikes. The magick clash had blown out the pool and patio lights, but the moon overhead set everything in sharp relief. A dark figure stood at the edge of the deep end, a pale bundle at his feet.

A deep breath sent reassurance through my soul. Decay didn't mar the familiar sandalwood, but from the sharp metallic aftertaste, Duncan was hurt. Bad. That was why he hadn't answered my call.

"If he dies, you'll have nothing to bargain with, David." My voice should have echoed against the bare walls of the main house. Shadows swallowed the sound. Hell, there wasn't even the faint hum of traffic that normally echoed off the bluffs and canyon walls of Malibu.

"I don't have *anything* because of you, bitch!"

Anger rolled across any guilt lingering over the damage from a two-year-old story. "I'm not the one throwing away a multi-million dollar contract to settle a score."

Harsh laughter filled the air. "Like I give a shit about the money."

"You're right." Déjà vu settled over the bizarre tableau. Why did I attract the supernatural crazies? "From what you did to your supposed best friend, it's obvious you don't give a shit about people either."

"I'm going to take the same pound of flesh you took from me."

I didn't even get the whiff of ozone before the concrete bucked under me. My body shot through the air. Chlorinated water sprayed as I hit the surface with the nastiest belly flop on the face of the planet. Sinking down, my legs contracted in anticipation of pushing off the bottom.

Cold, clammy hands wrapped around my ankles. In the murky water, pale figures surrounded me. I struggled and thrashed, but I couldn't break free. More fingers clutched at my wrists, my clothes. Not the dried up bodies or the squishy, freshly dead of before. These were the bloated corpses of drowning victims.

A silent scream blew the little air left out of my lungs. I'd found the rest of Duke's people.

Chapter 33

Chlorine burned tender nose membranes. My lungs wanted to suck anything to replace the expelled air. Burning need warred with dizziness. Being dead didn't mean I wouldn't pass out from lack of oxygen. Once I was totally helpless, the fairy zombies would rip me apart.

And Head wouldn't have any reason to keep Duncan alive.

A desperate kick freed one leg. The water hampered the zombies as much as it did me. A wild grab missed when I coiled and scissored off the concrete. A couple of them were jerked along for the ride to the surface.

Blessed air met my gaping mouth. The threatening numbness in my limbs faded, and I struck out for the side, my two passengers still trying to claw my left leg apart. Damn, why were all of Head's zombies obsessed with that particular appendage?

I wasn't the world's greatest swimmer, but the nanites made up for my lack of style with raw strength. I grasped the side and heaved my torso out of the water. The fairy zombies clinging to my leg tried to drag me back under, but a hard swing against the edge of the pool knocked them off. Another heave and I rolled onto my back. Wet coughs brought up the water that had managed to seep down my throat.

Slow, mocking claps reached my ears. I leveraged an elbow under me. Head's teeth gleamed under silvery light.

He shook his head. "Stupid bitch."

I swiveled my head. The rest of the fairy zombies waded out of the shallow end, their aim obvious.

My attention jerked back to Head. "You'd kill your own sister?"

Head's eyes widened. I didn't take the bait. He knew Yvonne was in the house, the same way she knew he was out here.

"Stop this now, David," a masculine voice rang out.

Surprise brought me to my knees. Brandon, not Kensai.

The pop singer stood in the ruined doorway, a Rambo-wannabe from his stance and the aim of the paintball gun. Only the death grip on the trigger gave away his anxiety.

"I said, stop it, David." He squeezed off a couple of shots at the nearest zombie. Yellowish fumes encircled the dead fairy before it collapsed to the patio. The rest paused, robots waiting for their next orders.

Except the zombie master was having difficulty processing his ex playing pissed off 'Nam vet. "How c-c—" An audible gulp broke the tension. My attention swung back and forth between the two men. Finally, Head choked out, "What the fuck are you doing with her?" He jabbed a finger in my direction.

"Trying to keep you from doing anything stupider than you've already done." Anger snapped in Brandon's voice.

I didn't dare move. No sense distracting the witch if Brandon could talk him down.

"After what she did—"

"She didn't lock me in her bedroom with a pissed off vampire!" A rush of air, as the singer took a diaphragm-level breath. Roses mixed with the ash and brimstone rolling off him. "Let these folks go. I'll do what I can to help you, David. These people are fair. There's extenuating circumstances—"

"You left me, you bastard!"

If the tears and pain in Head's voice hadn't warned me, the ozone and a deep rumble under the concrete would have. I was on my feet racing for Brandon. *Too late. I'm too late.*

Kensai shot through the door. He shoved the kid into the grass, hard enough Brandon's chin and chest dug a furrow in the pristine yard. With a horrendous crack, concrete yawed open underneath the vampire's feet.

A split-second turned into an eternity. Kensai hovered over the chasm, Wile E. Coyote still running before he realizes nothing's underneath him. A soft, sad smile filled his features. Then he was falling. Earth and stone roared.

I stumbled as the ground flowed under my feet. My knees and hands cracked the concrete when I landed. I looked up. A jagged scar marred the patio where the enforcer had stood.

"Kensai!" No answer. I scrambled for the crack, the opening blurred by tears. I dug and pried the broken chunks, tossing them aside. I reached out, trying to sense where he was, the best place to dig. This couldn't happen. I wouldn't let it.

Something pulled me away from the collapsed hole, something cold and clammy and unyielding. Dead flesh and razor-sharp nails tore at my skin and clothes. Pain stabbed through my abdomen. Screams of rage and pain filled the air, too high-pitched to be Head's.

Obnoxious liquid exploded around me, yellowish fumes filling the air. The ground bucked and twisted under me. I screamed and tore and thrashed at my attackers.

Then warmth gripped my chin, forcing my attention to brilliant blue eyes and flaming red hair. A husky voice murmured, "We've got you, kid. Quit fighting us. You're safe."

No, I wasn't. None of us were with David Head running around and no checks on his power.

Lily pulled the silver fae knife out of my gut. I couldn't stop my scream. After a round of intense pain and a lot of panting, I realized my trio of zombie comedians crouched around me. The fire in my belly subsided enough for me to notice it wasn't lightning illuminating the back yard. I glanced around.

Under the flashing lightshow, Mai crouched next to Brandon

who sat a few feet away. Blood poured down the singer's face from an ugly cut across his hairline. Jake stood over them, his paintball gun sweeping the scene.

Fairy zombies sprawled across the ruined patio. Some obviously shot by Brandon, Jake and the enforcers from the smell, the really gross ones just as obviously dismembered by me.

Near the pool house, energy flared and sizzled between the siblings in a deadly game of magickal dodgeball. Even though she was outmatched in raw power, Yvonne made up for it in accuracy. If David hadn't been holding an unconscious Duncan as a shield, she would have gotten him.

Stan prowled around the other side of the pool toward the dueling pair. My heart lurched into my mouth. He wouldn't do something stupid like start throwing fairy spells in the mix, would he?

But any wishful thinking on my part was quickly nipped. A wild shot by the necromancer didn't hit Yvonne, but the chunk of wood sheared off a nearby tree smacked her in the temple. She collapsed sideways into some charred foliage.

Mai jumped to her feet. "Stan!"

Then I realized the giant tree hadn't lost a chunk, but half the trunk. Three loud pops and the tree was falling. Falling on the half-fae enforcer in its path.

When a tree falls on a half-fairy in a bisexual basketball-playing necromancer's yard, it's pretty fucking loud.

Quiet reigned for a moment before Bill muttered, "Oh, shit." Head turned in my direction. "I hope you got a plan, kid," the comedian added.

Morty and Lily's hands wrapped around mine and pulled me to my feet.

Anger burned cold in my gut now that the knife wounds were healing. "Yeah," I said. "I do." With me being the only supernatural standing between the Normals and a necromancer, I took a page from James Bond. I leapt straight for the bad guy.

Chapter 34

Head's eyes widened and his mouth dropped. I surprised myself, too. My diving launch arced over the pool, and I caught him around the waist in mid-turn as he tried to shift my unconscious boyfriend between us.

The three of us tumbled to the concrete, Head and I wrestling for purchase. Duncan, on the other hand, flopped around like a dead fish.

I winced at that mental image. My distraction let Head plow one of his huge elbows into my cheek. Stars exploded behind my eyeball. Damn, no wonder the other basketball players avoided going mano a mano on rebounds with this guy.

I rolled, not waiting for his follow-up. A wet-sounding crunch came a second later, and Head bellowed.

Crab-crawling, I scooted away from Duncan and Yvonne. Would Mai take the hint and get them out of the line of fire? Oh, hell, was Stan even still alive?

I didn't dare send anything to them telepathically with my lack of control. I needed Head's attention solely on me.

Except I lied to Bill. I didn't really have a plan. I just had to stall long enough for the surviving enforcers and Jake to come up with one.

A wrought-iron patio chair skidded in my direction. Okay, keeping David's focus on me wasn't going to be as much of a problem as I thought with his telekinetic stunts. I flung myself out of the way and onto the cool grass. A chunk of concrete exploded inches away, shrapnel slicing across my face. I rolled to a crouch and grinned at the enraged basketball pro.

"C'mon, Davy. Is that the best you can do? Throw rocks at the zombie?"

"You can't call me that, bitch!" I swear specks of foam flew from his mouth as he stalked toward me.

"Awww, is poor wittle Davy mad?" A flower pot whistled past my head, and I side-stepped further down the sloping yard. "Is poor wittle Davy taking his toys home?" Another chunk of broken concrete flew toward me, and I dodged to the right. Good. My taunts had ignited his rage to such a pitch he wasn't bothering with spells, just telekinetics.

Right now, it was the only point in my favor. My physical strength topped his, but could I take him without killing him? My promises to Yvonne and Brandon clanged in the back of my head.

"Whatsa matter, Davy? Don't like it when someone can fight back?"

He grunted as he launched a folded table umbrella javelin-style. I hopped backwards, and the tip buried into the soft soil a foot from my toes.

"Forgot to bring your mama's corpse to sic on me, Head?"

"Don't you dare talk about her. Don't you fucking dare!" Head stalked after me, fingers flexing like he wanted to squeeze the life, or death, out of me. The whites shown around his dark eyes.

I deliberately lowered my voice. "Y'know, Head, maybe Al Jenkins really is your father. He liked to hurt women, too."

A roar filled with pain and rage and grief echoed through the night. He charged, but I side-stepped, leg outstretched to sweep his out from under him. Not taking any chances, I jumped on his back. He bucked and I went tumbling across the grass.

Three dark shapes raced out of the night, grabbing Head and wrestling him back to the turf. He was no match for the three zombies.

Morty pinned a flailing arm with his knee. "We got him, toots! Do your thing."

I crawled over to David's head and laid a hand on his cheek. The bastard actually tried to bite me. Dammit, it was Sierra Mallory all over again. I closed my eyes, wanting words to convince him to stop this insanity. Words had always been my weapon of choice . . .

. . . and I blinked green spots away from my vision. I sat on a bedspread decorated in stitched basketballs, my hand resting on the cheek of a familiar little boy.

"You're not Yvonne," he accused, scooting away from me. Cobwebs covered him, twining through his dark curls and glowing against his coffee skin. Odd-looking, glowing cobwebs.

"No, I'm not." I glanced around. We were in David's bedroom in the old Nebraska farmhouse. What the hell was going on? How'd I get here? Yvonne was out cold in the yard of his Malibu house. Wasn't she?

Except I knew this wasn't a memory.

I turned my attention back to the six-year-old staring at me through slitted eyes. "She asked me to watch you." It was the best explanation I could come up with.

He eased closer. "What are you?"

"Umm . . ." How the hell was I supposed to answer that?

He peered at my face, an analytical expression on his. "Ya ain't got no wings, so you can't be the tooth fairy." I noticed his missing front teeth. "And your eyes are glowing like a vamp's."

"Look, David, I'm supposed to tuck you in." I reached for the bedspread and stared at my outstretched hand. My skin had a silver sheen under the starlight twinkling through the open window.

"And you don't look like no white woman I've ever seen."

Kids could see through any line of bullshit, so I opted for the truth. "I'm not sure what I am. Someone made me, but I don't think he even knew what he was making." Not for the first time I wondered how much Fred was following Selene and Mallory's orders and how much he experimented on his own when he programmed the nanites that now inhabited my body.

I took a closer look at David. "What do you have all over you?"

He stared at the funky cobwebs a moment before he looked up at me and shrugged. "Dunno."

Then I realized they weren't exactly cobwebs. More like writing. Almost.

The top layer of red looked odd, jerky, reptilian. Like the language a lizard would use, if lizards could use a pen, that is. The middle layer was a deep brilliant green. Not modern writing, but Afro-centric symbols. The bottom layer consisted of a sparkling black pattern. Something so alien that if I studied hard enough, I'd know the secrets of the universe.

I brushed at the fine threads. They dissolved under my touch, turning from their original color to silver before disappearing totally.

"There. Now that you're cleaned up, why don't you lay down? Growing boys need their sleep."

He squirmed under the covers, and I pulled the bedspread to his chin. Earnest eyes stared up at me as I stood. I bit my lip. For a moment, I would have sworn it was the adult David looking at me, no longer filled with hate and bile.

The need for forgiveness tore at my soul. "I'm sorry for hurting you. I was wrong and I shouldn't have taken those pictures of you without your say-so."

A sage nod preceded his words. "S'okay. I'm sorry I got mad at you. Mama says I got a temper and I let it make my decisions."

I bent and kissed his forehead. "Goodnight, David." I rose and turned to leave.

"Am I ever gonna wake up, Miss Sam?"

I looked back at the little boy ensconced in basketballs made of thread. How could I answer when I didn't understand myself? "I hope so, David. I hope so."

Chapter 35

I blinked. The vanilla taste of Twinkies filled my mouth, and the antiseptic smell of a hospital filled my nose.

"Aw, shit. Not again." My head fell forward and landed in a crinkling mass of cellophane.

"Out of my way, boys."

I raise my head to find Bebe elbowing Bill and Morty away from my bedside. A loud belch exploded from my lips.

"Samantha!"

I blinked once more. Mom and Dad hovered at the foot of the bed. I looked around. Mai stood by the door, but her hand wasn't on the butt of her semi-automatic this time.

"What day is it? How's Duncan?"

Bebe shoved the frigid stethoscope down my hospital gown. "Monday morning. Now, shut up."

The damn thing was marginally warmer when she moved it to my back. It didn't stop me from noticing she hadn't answered my question. A ball of ice, far colder than any stethoscope, rolled through the Twinkie mash in my stomach.

"Bebe—" I couldn't say anything more without the ball of ice turning to tears.

She reached for my hand and squeezed. "He's stable. That's the good thing."

Stable? The V-virus healed anything short of beheading or a stake through the heart. What the hell had Head done to Duncan?

I flipped the covers and swung my legs around. "I want to see him."

"Samantha!" Mom screeched.

"Nice to know the color's natural, toots." Morty grinned around the unlit cigar in his mouth.

I flipped the blanket, sheet and my gown back over my lower half. "Anyone who's not a doctor needs to clear the room." I turned to look at Mai when no one moved. "Can I borrow your gun?"

Even Mom barreled through the door. Mai flashed a grin before following my parents and the zombie trio. It was the first time I'd ever seen the woman smile a genuine smile.

The Twinkies curdled in my stomach. Mai had smiled at me even though I'd gotten her grandfather killed last night. If I were Mai, I would have unloaded the full clip into my skull.

Fresh jeans and a clean t-shirt against showered skin improved my mood before I traipsed up to the ICU. I made a quick side trip before heading down to Duncan's room.

Yvonne sat quietly by David's bedside when I entered. Monitors beat a steady rhythm. All of them except for one vital indicator.

I tensed as she rose and rushed toward me. But instead of the attack I half-expected, she embraced me in a hard hug.

She stepped back, holding me at arm's length, and nodded. "Good to see you up. I feared Master Augustine had lied about your true condition to spare my feelings."

The soft beeping filled the silence before I found my voice. "I'm so sorry, Yvonne."

She shrugged. "He's alive." Looking back at the unmoving form in the bed, she still talked even though she kept both hands on me. "Medically, the Normals would write him off as brain dead, but he's not. Deep down, I can still feel him."

When she turned back to me, unshed tears glimmered. "I don't know how you bound him, but it's tight."

Too tight. So fucking tight, the man was essentially in a coma. And I didn't have the slightest clue of exactly what I did or how. "Yvonne—"

She placed warm fingers to my lips. "He's a necromancer. It will fade with time."

Damn it. She wasn't sure any more than Bebe or me. For all intents and purposes, I might as well have killed him.

A soft *whoosh* behind me made me turn. Brandon stood there, a little surprised to see me from his wide eyes. "Hey." His fingers fluttered, then he couldn't seem to meet my gaze. He focused on Yvonne. "The jet's ready. Nurse said they'd be up in a few minutes to take him down to the ambulance."

"Jet?" My attention flicked between the two. "Where're you taking him?"

Yvonne raised her chin. "To a private facility in Miami. Jean-Pierre has made arrangements for his care."

Made sense. Miami was the vampire master's capital. Yvonne could visit her brother as often as she wanted. "Have you come up with a cover story?"

A wry smile tilted the witch's lips. "He was drunk and fell into the pool."

I sighed. It'd be hard to dispute, and knowing the vamps, a second set of medical records supporting the story had been "accidentally" leaked to the tabloids thanks to my former boss.

Former boss. I guess I'd made my decision after all.

I turned to Brandon. "I'm really sorry about—" About what? Ruining his love affair? Destroying his singing career? Sinking him deep in an alien world he wasn't prepared for? I settled with saying, "For everything."

He shuffled his feet. "My bags are already in the car, Yvonne. You want me to take yours down?"

Okay, I didn't expect him to hug me, but I wanted some acknowledgement. "You're leaving Los Angeles? What about your new recording contract?"

Finally, his eyes met mine. "I can fulfill it in Florida." His eyes slitted. "Plan on fucking that up too?"

"Brandon!"

I held up my hand. "It's okay, Yvonne. He's got every right."

He held up his hands. "What am I supposed to say? Thanks for only putting my boyfriend in a coma instead of killing him?"

Guilt sucked on my conscience. I pivoted to leave, but Yvonne didn't release her hold on my arm. The last thing I wanted was to hurt her any more than I had. I stopped.

"For what it's worth, *merci beaucoup, chére.*"

I nodded. "You're welcome. *Bon voyage.*" Her throaty laughter followed me through the door. I could almost have laughed too at my piss-poor French. Almost.

At the end of the hallway, I peeked through the thin window set in the door to the windowless room. Tiffany sat curled in the recliner next to the bed. Black eyeliner and dark purple lipstick decorated her face, a good sign. Her fingers tapped against the pad cradled in her lap to the beat of the EKG. She obviously wasn't concentrating on whatever she had pulled up online.

I followed her gaze to the man lying in the bed next to her. Duncan's skin nearly blended into the sheets. Dark bruises and various cuts marred his chiseled features. My stomach flipped. If his skin still held evidence of his imprisonment, it meant the virus worked on repairing more serious injuries. Blood IV's ran into each arm. I swallowed hard to contain the tears. Bebe had warned me.

Pulling open the door, I edged in as quietly as I could. "How's he doing?" I whispered.

"I have felt better."

The kid and I jumped at the wheezy voice coming from the bed.

My stomach righted itself at the dry clipped humor contained in Duncan's croak.

"Hey." I crossed over to his side. There was a spot of skin relatively intact on his forehead, and I planted a kiss there.

A chuckle rippled into a cough. Tiffany jumped up and her pad crashed to the floor. I gripped the bed rails, unsure of how to help him. He waved Tiffany back before he resumed laughing.

"This isn't funny, Duncan." She glared at him, tiny fists propped on her hips. "You've gone through sixteen pints of blood since they brought you in last night."

The familiar affectionate smile filled his face. "Where's your husband?"

Tiffany's scowl deepened. "They really knocked you on the head. Reverend Mitchell didn't have the chance to finish the ceremony, remember?"

He frowned, and I laid a hand over his fingers. "It's okay. As far as the Normal guests are concerned, the ceremony went off without a hitch, but a freak windstorm blew over a tent and hurt a bunch of people."

Tiffany crossed her arms. "Only because Satan Spawn threatened to stake Caesar with her Manolo Blahniks if the vamps laid any other memory."

I fixed Tiffany with a dirty look. "How many times do I have to tell you? Only I get to call my mom Satan Spawn."

She stuck her tongue out at me.

"Then we call Reverend Mitchell and arrange—"

I squeezed his fingers gently. "Reverend Mitchell got his memories altered too, which is probably a good thing after the way he reacted when you vamped out in front of him."

Another chuckle. "Oh, yes."

I didn't know how much he really remembered and how much he was humoring us. I caught Tiffany's attention and inclined my head toward the door. "Why don't you go get something to eat? I'll stay with him."

Her lips puckered, but before the protest could spew, she gave a sharp nod. "I'll be back."

I toed the standard visitor's chair closer and sat, not daring to let go of his chill fingers. "How are you really feeling?"

"Like I have been run over by a tractor-trailer, then the operator reversed to run me over again." He closed his eyes. When they opened, glowing green eyes pierced me. "If I try to have a real conversation with you, will you flee?"

A lump filled my throat. He was lying in a hospital bed after zombies beat the crap out of him and fairies tortured him, and he still wanted to have *the* talk. I crossed my heart with my free hand. "I promise not to leave until you're finished." I certainly didn't want the lughead to climb out of bed to chase me.

His eyes closed again, making the bruises around them even more pronounced. He said nothing for a very long time.

The pause nagged at me. "Are you okay? Do I need to get Bebe?"

An answering squeeze caressed my fingertips, and his eyes flew open. "No." An undercurrent of fierceness filled his scratchy voice. "I had time to think while Head kept me prisoner. I understand your feelings, however—"

"Yes."

A sigh passed his cracked lips. "Please let me finish—" He blinked as my answer registered, then his eyes narrowed. "What are you affirming?"

I sucked in a deep breath and released it slowly. Yep, the feeling deep in my gut was still there. "Yes, I will move in with you." I held up my hand to forestall him. "But we're not announcing any engagement." I counted to three in English before I added, "Yet."

He nodded, a crazy, happy light in his eyes, even though his face remained its usual stolid countenance. "Agreed."

I couldn't help my own crazy, happy grin in return.

<h1 style="text-align:center">Chapter 36</h1>

A glance at my watch confirmed I was very, very late. Jitters ran along my nerves as I stood across the street from the courthouse, waiting for the light to change. Mom was going to raise holy hell, and it was the last thing Max and Tiffany needed today. Okay, it wasn't just the civil ceremony. I'd been pacing at my apartment all morning in anticipation of a call.

A call I was now receiving from the vibration from my suit pocket. I pulled out the cell phone and punched the button. "Yes?"

"It's a go," Marshall Wagoner's voice warbled over the cell phone. If it wasn't for my super hearing, I wouldn't have been able to hear him over the sax player wailing away behind me. "Loved the video. Absolutely loved it! How soon can they start?"

My face tightened into a wide grin. As the producer of the Vegas Parade of Stars showcase, I knew he'd be interested in my three zombie comedians. A little pride filled me. For the first time in two months, I'd done something without relying on supernatural contacts.

It didn't mean I was stupid though. "Send me the contracts, Marshall. Then we'll talk."

"Gotta ask, honey. Why are you leaving the *Scoop*? Managing comedy acts is a whole different enchilada."

"I needed the change, Marshall. When can I expect the contracts?" I wanted to get my people settled before I dealt with the insanity of packing up my miniscule belongings. Las Vegas was going to be . . . fun. Warmth filled me. A whole new start with Duncan. A whole new career. Maybe it's what I really needed in life. Or death.

"I'm e-mailing them now, sweetheart."

As I flicked the lid shut on the conversation, the white walk figure appeared. Dodging the mass of people parading in the crosswalk, I took two steps outside of the appropriate lines.

The street tilted. My vision blurred. My stomach threatened to heave its contents. *What the fuck?*

Then everything righted again, except . . .

I whirled around, a full three-sixty. The intersection was deserted. No people. No cars. Nothing. The building, the pavement, even the sky had a sepia tone. It felt like I was looking at an old photo of downtown in the library archives.

"What the fuck?" My voice echoed against the concrete. There was no other sound. I looked behind me. The sax player on the corner was gone, too. An empty case lay on the sidewalk. Wind picked up the bills that had been deposited, pushing the greenbacks along the way with an invisible hand. Rod Serling was going to step out of one of those doors any minute. I turned to face the courthouse again.

A man stood in the middle of the intersection. His dark skin contrasted sharply with the white tails he wore. His matching top hat sat at a rakish angle, not even quivering under the onslaught of the hot, dry wind. Dark glasses covered his eyes. Both glove-encased hands gripped the white cane he leaned on.

"I would have a word with you, Samantha Marie Ridgeway." The nasally voice scrapped against my spine.

"I'm sorry. Do I know you?" I took a step forward, trying for the life of me to place him. The man looked like he had tissue shoved up his nose. It would explain his voice.

He tapped his cane on the pavement. "You took something of my father's that was not pledged to you. Return it. Now."

The wind plastered the linen skirt to my legs. "What are you talking about? Who are you?"

Teeth whiter than his suit flashed. "You may call me Baron." The wide smile disappeared. "My father wishes his property back."

Definitely Twilight Zone material. The weird wind pulled strands of my hair out of the neat French braid I'd managed to tame it into this morning. "I've got no idea what you're talking about. I don't know your father."

"Don't play, girl. Return David Jebediah Head to me. Now."

My thoughts tangled as fast as my hair. Was this some fairy trick? "I don't have David. His sister took him to Miami."

The strange man tapped his cane again. "His soul was not yours to take. You have no right to it." Anger laced his words.

What the hell was going on here? My eyes blinked as the wind picked up speed. "Look, I don't have David or his soul. I can't give you what I don't have."

"Fine. If that's the way you want to play, I'll take something of yours in payment." A third tap and he disappeared.

The world tilted again. A car horn blasted in my ear. I jumped. More horns joined in a symphony of noise along with shouting and a few not-so-friendly waves. I raced to the other side of the street. Cars peeled through the intersection, the one with the now-red light. I took a deep breath and looked around me.

Normal. Everything looked totally normal again. People marching on the sidewalks to their various destinations. Cars weaving to avoid buses, pedestrians and other cars. Even Mr. Sax Guy wailed an off-key version of "Moon River."

A fairy illusion. It had to be. They were messing with me because they lost their little gambit. Another glance at the watch said I didn't have time to wonder about my bizarro visitor. But I glanced back at the now busy intersection. A shiver rippled up my spine.

Music blasted through the speakers of the back room at Anthony's. I set the tray on the table, passing out blood, champagne, and in Tiffany's case, sparkling grape juice. Glasses clinked in various salutes. I took a sip of my own flute of bubbly and watched the partiers on the makeshift dance floor. Mom actually looked like she was having fun with John Lannigan boogeying to some retro number until the judge cut in.

I nudged Bebe in the seat next to me. "Think Her Honor is aiming for alpha female."

She grinned back. "Probably. His official mourning period's been over for a year. I think he's enjoying the freedom, but the pressure to mate or abdicate . . ." She shrugged.

Mourning period. The champagne fizz burned its way down. For two minutes, I'd forgotten we'd attended funerals for the last three days. Kensai and Jamal's joint ceremony had been especially tough.

"Master Augustine?" Mai stood next to Caesar. Her staccato delivery drew everyone's attention. Her words rushed out as if she was afraid to stop. "I'd like to volunteer as Duncan's personal daytime guard in Las Vegas."

Caesar was silent for a moment. "May I ask why?"

Mai shot me a look before she answered. "He needs someone experienced with zombies."

Bebe, Max and Tiffany snickered. Duncan tensed next to me, but I had to give Caesar credit for keeping a straight face.

The vampire master turned to my guy. "And your opinion?"

Duncan inclined his head. "The transfer is acceptable."

I had a sneaking suspicion Mai had already approached him.

"We knew we'd have to do some personnel shuffling." Caesar turned to me. "And from what I hear, Sam will need assistance with packing. I've heard horror stories concerning her apartment." He shuddered.

"Hey!" I protested.

Before the pick-on-Sam fun escalated, Alex appeared at Tiffany's elbow. He set a package wrapped in gold with a silver bow in front of her with a flourish. "For you, Mrs. Howell."

Tiffany eyed it suspiciously before looking up at the blond enforcer. "You open it."

He spread his hands in a defensive gesture. "I promise. No tricks. When I cleaned out the photographer's place and erased her memory, I took the rolls she shot before everything went to hell. Got 'em developed for you. Congratulations, sweetheart." As Tiffany's posture eased, he bent and pecked her on the now flaming red cheek.

"Thanks." She ducked her head, trying to rein in the flowing embarrassment. Max reached for the package, only for Tiffany to slap his hand away. "Mine."

She tore open the wrappings and passed around the mini-albums, retaining one for her and Max to view.

Duncan flipped open the one handed to him, and I leaned closer for a look. His arm wrapped around me, cocooning my body against his broad chest.

Tiffany's voice brought me out of my feelings of snuggly contentment. She held up her album to Max, a finger pointing to a specific photo. "This one of your college friends?"

Max shook his head. "I don't even remember this picture getting taken." He shrugged with his good shoulder. "I don't recognize him, but then most of that day is one big blur. I take it he's not one of your friends?"

Duncan reached for the album, and Max pushed it into his waiting grip. Caesar rose to peer over his shoulder, and Bebe pushed closer to me.

My heart froze in my chest. In the glossy four-by-six, a grinning Max stood next to a familiar man in white tails. White teeth gleamed against coffee bean skin. Baron's arm snaked possessively around my brother's shoulders.

Oh, shit.

**Turn the page for a special preview of the
next Bloodlines novel, *Amish, Vamps & Thieves***

Chapter 1

Nerves tingled along the back of Anne Levy's neck as she strode across her brother's hay field under the ripe moon. A deep breath tested the scent in the humid Ohio night air. The spicy apple of a Normal human mixed with the sweet clover and summer maple, confirming the watcher's presence. She glanced to her right. A shadow shifted within the woods bordering the east side of the field.

Her watcher was unimaginative at best, using the same cover as last night. Enforcer training jumped into play despite Anne being home for the first time in decades. A telepathic check found her partner. *Sam? My friend's back.*

The black diamond tickle of Samantha Ridgeway's humor rippled through Anne's mind. *You're sure he's not one of us?*

Yes. Anne let the crimson wash of her irritation filter through the link. Like she couldn't tell the difference between a supernatural and a Normal after sixty years.

Amish or English?

The tips of Anne's fangs pricked her bottom lip as she smiled at Sam's use of the Amish term for an outsider, but her humor was short-lived. She'd already lost everything she cared about in her life. Her home. Her chance for children. Jacob. And Thomas had sacrificed everything he desired to keep the old ways for the sake of their parents. She wouldn't, she couldn't let his sacrifice be in vain.

But if the church elders learned Thomas had contacted her for help, her brother would be shunned. He was in enough trouble for pushing the leadership of the Amish community into hiring an attorney to fight the developers and the state. If the elders found out exactly what she and Sam were . . .

Yo, Anne? You still there?

She shoved away the disconcerting thoughts and drew another deep breath. The various scents were too mixed in the still, thick air to tell if the whiff of plastic came from something the man carried or trash floating down the Killbuck River. *I can't tell from this distance, but he's definitely the same man who observed me from the woods last night while I patrolled.*

The other woman's annoyance swept back in salmon orange wave. *Then maybe you should have questioned him* last *night.*

Based on what? Anne flung the thought back. *He's made no action against me or the livestock.* And there hadn't been an animal attack since she and Sam had arrived in Millersburg. That fact lent credence to Thomas's theory that the culprit behind the livestock mutilations was indeed a supernatural. It also bolstered Sam's opinion they were dealing with a rogue. Anne had learned decades ago not to make assumptions despite the evidence. She needed proof the killings weren't linked to Birkenwald's attempts to force her brother and the other farmers out of their homes.

Sam's mental sigh whispered through her mind. *Doesn't mean he's not a look-out. It's time we had a talk with your friend. I'm at the north fence line of Jacob Miller's property. I'll swing around.*

Anne swallowed her discomfort at the mention of Jacob. No sense giving Sam's tongue any more ammunition. *Are you sure trapping him is a wise course of action? He may be a distraction from the real culprits.*

Oh puh-leease! If a vamp and a zombie can't handle one measly human . . . Sam's mental voice dissolved into peals of laughter. *Besides, the boys would never forgive me if I let you get slimed because the asshole's carrying one of those reaper thingies.*

It's called a scythe. Anne didn't bother to correct her on the other point. Technically, Sam wasn't a zombie, but no one knew what else to call a walking, talking dead person. At least, she hadn't stooped to eating human brains.

Yet.

Anne shoved a lock of hair behind her ear. The short strands irritated her as well, but not nearly as much as Sam's laughter, her poor estimate of Anne's abilities, or the offer of hair accessories earlier. Not that she didn't appreciate Sam's kindness, but the clips weren't—they just weren't . . .

Plain.

The prohibition against adornment stuck to her soul even after all these decades away from Holmes County. Assuming vampires still had souls. She hoped the fact that she still cared about her brother meant she did.

Anne shook her head as she walked, dislodging the hair again. She shouldn't have come home. Crickets chirped in counterpoint to the frogs along the banks, their summer song a reminder she'd never belong here again. Maybe the "boys," as Sam referred to the older vampires of the Augustine Coven, were right. Maybe she *should* join the twenty-first century. But in the sixty-plus years since rogue vampires had forced her into this existence, her faith had brought her comfort—still brought her comfort, even in her darkest times. Wearing her hair and clothes in the old style was part of that comfort as well.

And Jacob had always told her how much he loved her hair. But he wouldn't have loved it quite so much if he knew the monster she'd become.

She suppressed a shudder at the mix of old and new anxieties, and she continued stalking through the clover. She couldn't blame Sam for cutting off her waist-length locks. The zombie had done what was necessary to the ruined tresses. Her hair had become tangled beyond any hope of redemption during her month of captivity at the hands of Sam's creators.

No, she was angry with Master Augustine. She couldn't fault his generosity by giving Sam a place in the coven considering some of the other supernaturals' attitude toward the zombie. But when he charged Sam with the responsibility of being Anne's daytime guard for this trip, neither woman had been fooled about who was supposed to watch whom. Maybe the confrontation with the Normal would cleanse her of the aggravation of having to babysit.

Anne let the mix of irritation and humor slide from her consciousness. From the corner of her eye, she gauged the man's progress as he drifted from tree to tree, matching her pace. He had to be one of the local English boys, his shirt too bright of a blue to be an Amish. Maybe a youth hoping to claim glory or notoriety by discovering what the Millersburg Monster really was. It wouldn't go well if a Normal discovered the perpetrator first and Thomas's suspicion of a supernatural culprit was correct.

No, it would not go well at all.

She sampled the night air again. Her watcher's scent was too rich, too spicy, too heady, for a child. A trickle of warmth seeped through her belly. He was definitely an adult male. Vampire instincts rose, only to be quelled by her will. Her blood need had been well satiated before she and Sam set out tonight, but the desire to hunt her hunter filled her being. Angling her course toward the trees, she closed the distance between them.

Colin Fitzgerald let the night goggles he'd bought at the army surplus store drop from his eyes. The silhouette of the girl headed for the edge of the woods lining the river. For a split second, he would have sworn her eyes glowed, but it had to be a trick of light from the goggles. He shook his head and rolled his shoulders to ease the chaffing of the backpack straps. Keeping to the shelter of the trees, he paralleled her course. A stroll through the woods in the middle of the night was never a bright idea under the best of circumstances. He crossed his fingers he wouldn't break an ankle in a groundhog hole. The damn pests were more of a threat than the wisp of a girl traipsing through Thomas's hay field.

This whole situation was growing weirder by the minute. She couldn't possibly be the person killing and mutilating his clients' livestock. He couldn't believe someone that slight could have the strength to drag a full-grown bull around a pasture.

Not by herself anyway. Even after removing the internal organs.

But she'd been by herself the last couple of nights, just as she was tonight.

Hitching his thumbs under the backpack straps, he dodged around a tree dressed in ivy. Under the full moon, the shadow in the hay field continued toward the fence line separating Thomas Levy's property from the Millers'. Dark clothes cloaked her. A long-sleeved oversized shirt and a calf-length skirt. He didn't have a good look at her lower legs in the foot-high clover, but he'd lay odds she wore plain black stockings and shoes. If it weren't for her uncovered, chin-length locks, she could be any other Amish or Mennonite girl in the area. But something wasn't quite right in her posture as she stalked through the clover. Definitely not one of the demure, humble women he'd come to know since leaving the Philadelphia D.A.'s office and moving to remote, out-of-the-way Millersburg, Ohio.

A quick peek through the goggles showed her continuing on the same course. She might know who was behind the livestock loss. Why else would she be sneaking around his clients' farms this time of night?

Except he couldn't quite call her confident stride sneaking.

He almost wished the girl was a party to one of Matt Jessup's practical jokes. No, not even Matt would sink to that level. He may have a quirky sense of humor—Colin had been the butt of several of the other attorney's stunts—but Matt wasn't vicious. Not like the bastard who was destroying people's livelihoods.

His fingers tightened around the goggles. He knew what it'd cost the Amish farmers to come to him for help. To them, approaching an outsider for aid was unheard of. But an attorney?

The church elders had pitched a fit when they found out Thomas Levy and Jacob Miller had visited Colin's office. An ironic smile twisted his mouth. Well, as much of a fit as an Amish would allow himself. Simon Yoder's face had been beet red, though he never raised his voice, when Colin met with the men of the Millersburg Amish community at Thomas's house. In the end, Simon had been outvoted, the majority agreeing that Colin was best suited to fight Birkenwald Group's attempt to buy out their farms.

At least until Birkenwald decided to play dirty.

Their attempts to pressure state officials into seizing the land through eminent domain was bad enough. Colin swallowed the bile collected at the back of his throat. Torturing the farmers' livestock to death to drive the Amish out constituted raw evil in his book.

He swung the backpack off one shoulder to trade the goggles for a bottle of water.

"What are you doing here?"

He jerked to a halt. A darker shadow separated itself from a maple trunk and glided into a patch of silvery moonlight in front of him. The girl from the hayfield. A sharp gasp escaped his throat. Even though she wore the dark, simple clothing of an Amish, plain was hardly the word he'd use to describe her. Silvery light worshipped her pale face. Dark eyes peered at him through equally dark locks. Elfin features twisted into a frown as she regarded him.

And how had she managed to overtake him? Two seconds ago, she'd been a hundred yards away in the middle of the freakin' clover.

"You're on private property." A challenging step forward, such an assertive move for the slight wisp of a girl. "Who are you and what are you doing here?"

His dry tongue rasped the roof of his mouth. A fairy queen. That's what she reminded him of, the poster of an Unseelie temptress tacked on his nephew Evan's bedroom wall. And that brief memory cracked the wall he'd carefully built over the last year. Maybe he was going insane from guilt if he was imagining fairy queens.

An amused snort silenced the soft rustling of birds and other animals settling in the trees for the night. "If you think I'm a fairy, you really need to get out more."

Oh, shit. I said that aloud? Colin winced. He hadn't made such a fool of himself with a girl since Missy Johnson in sixth grade. Old habits reasserted themselves, and he matched her aggressive body language. "I could ask you the same thing. This is my client's land, and I know for a fact you're not one of his granddaughters."

She blinked, eyes luminous in the moonlight. "You're Thomas's attorney?"

"Yeah. And you haven't answered my question."

Her confused expression melted into one of acid fury. "What are you doing out here? Are you trying to get yourself killed?"

It was his turn to snort in humor. "Last time I checked, I don't moo and I don't chew cud."

"That's no guarantee . . ." Her head tilted, and she—

He shook his own in disbelief. No, she really was sniffing the air like one of Matt's coonhounds.

Her pale face turned back to him. "You need to leave here. Now."

He took a step back, not that he took her warning seriously, but something sent a cold shiver across his skin and raised gooseflesh. It was more than her voice. Her eyes glowed, a warm gold that had nothing to do with moonlight or fairy queens. Human eyes didn't reflect light like that, and there was little light besides the moon. No, not a reflection. Her eyes emitted the glow, a glow growing stronger and brighter.

Colin took another cautious step back. "What are you?"

Hot breath on his neck was the only warning he had before something shoved him face first into dirt and dead leaves. Something heavy landed hard on his back, slamming his temple back into the musty soil. Something that stank the putrid, coppery stink of old blood as well as its own godawful body odor.

Then the smothering weight was gone. High-pitched yips and a higher-pitched battle cry brought his head out of the loam. And into a nightmare.

Air petrified in Colin's lungs. His mind refused to wrap itself around the furry *thing* that clawed and bit at the girl. The beast hunched on its rear limbs, neither totally upright nor on all fours. Colin's eyes refused to focus, as if the shape of the thing declined to stabilize into one form or another.

And the girl wasn't a *girl*. She was the angel of death. Or a demon. This was the dark queen incarnate, dancing and dodging the monster's blows. Her eyes glowed neon yellow under the shade of a massive maple. Fangs extended past lips twisted in a feral snarl. This time Beauty was a beast too, and she charged the furry version.

The two figures tumbled across the branches and decay littering the floor of the woods. Their thrashing threw detritus in the air as each struggled to subdue the other. The thing tossed the girl away. She rolled, coming up in a crouch. When she leapt, the thing landed a solid kick in her gut. The girl slammed headfirst into a trunk, the crack still echoing through the trees when she crumpled into a heap at the roots.

The furry thing limped into the small pool of moonlight. Dark liquid oozed from its left shoulder. It gave Colin a dismissive glance and turned its attention back to the girl, a jagged piece of deadwood clutched in its upraised right claw. There was no mistaking its intention in its awkward steps as it staggered toward the unconscious girl.

Colin fumbled with the backpack lying next to him before he yanked out the flare gun. With a quick prayer, he aimed at the thing and pulled the trigger. A nova burst to life in the clearing, followed by a scream of pain. The nasty odor of burnt fur confirmed he hit his target. From the scuffling against the brush, the thing beat a fast retreat toward the river.

Blinking white spots out of his vision, Colin crawled in the direction of the fallen girl. Guilt dug its way out of the hole where he'd buried it. Once again, his decision made him responsible. *Please let her be okay. Please.* He dropped the flare gun and reached for the dark form. Fingers automatically went to her neck. No pulse. New fear joined old guilt in his intestines. *Dammit! Calm down so you can help her. This is not like Patrick and Evan.*

There! He breathed a sigh at the faint thrum under his touch. The beat was way too slow but steady. He checked for other injuries, trying not to jostle her too much. And trying not to think about the fact they were in the middle of the woods and over two miles from the nearest telephone. He pulled out his cell phone from his jeans pocket, but as expected, the words "No Service" flashed on the screen. Heat surged through his face and hands. He shoved the useless piece of crap back in his pocket.

With tender strokes, he brushed her hair out of the way. Shaking fingers probed her skull, and his heart convulsed at the mushy feeling in the base. Sticky wetness coated his hands. The guilt and fear curdled into a fetid mass.

Something grabbed his shirt collar and yanked him backward, adrenaline overloading his nerves. He twisted to punch at the monster when a feminine voice said, "Just what the fuck are you doing to her?"

Acknowledgements

This book wouldn't be possible without the following people:

Much love to DH for not letting me give up and GK for giving me hugs when I need them.

To Will Graham who still thinks my zombie tabloid reporter is funny.

Many thanks to my critique group, the Panera Pals: Nancy Bowden, Christie Craig, Faye Hughes, Jody Payne and Teri Thackston.

To Nina Cordoba, the best editor that money can't buy (but coffee can).

And a special thank you to Tess St. John, who stepped up to the plate when I needed a proofer. I owe you one, girl!

About the Author

Suzan Harden transitioned from writing information technology manuals for companies and legal articles for a law enforcement magazine to her first love, fantasy and science fiction in all their forms. She's the author of the Millersburg Magick Mysteries, the Soccer Moms of the Apocalypse series, and the Books of Apep series.

Contact Suzan Harden
Facebook: Suzan Harden
Email: suzan@suzanharden.com
Website: www.suzanharden.com

Sign up for Suzan's Mailing List